Pay-off at Ladron

OTHER SAGEBRUSH LARGE PRINT WESTERNS BY
BENNETT FOSTER

Dust of the Trail
Lone Wolf
Rawhide Road

Pay-off
at Ladron

BENNETT FOSTER

J
L P
W
F 754p

20.45

Sagebrush
Large Print Westerns

Library of Congress Cataloging-in-Publication Data

Foster, Bennett,
   Pay-off at Ladron / Bennett Foster
     p.   cm.
   ISBN 1-57490-306-3 (lg. print : hardcover)
   1. Large type books. I. Title

PS3511. O6812 P39 2000
813'.54—dc21   00-059153

Cataloguing in Publication Data is available from
the British Library and the National Library of Australia.

Sagebrush Large Print Westerns are published in the United
States and Canada by Thomas T. Beeler, Publisher, PO Box 659,
Hampton Falls, New Hampshire 03844-0659. ISBN 1-57490-306-3

Published in the United Kingdom, Eire, and the Republic of
South Africa by Isis Publishing Ltd, 7 Centremead, Osney
Mead, Oxford OX2 0ES England. ISBN 0-7531-6366-7

Published in Australia and New Zealand by Bolinda Publishing
Pty Ltd, 17 Mohr Street, Tullamarine, Victoria, Australia, 3043.
ISBN 1-74030-180-3

Manufactured by Sheridan Books in Chelsea, Michigan.

Pay-off
at Ladron

CHAPTER 1

SINGLESHOT COCKED AN EAR FORWARD AND AN EAR back. Jigger, the pack horse, put slack in his lead rope and fell to grazing, and Llano Land looked at the trail. This was the Rincon canyon, he knew. No mistake had been made by the Mexican herder who had drawn the map in the dust and given directions while the sheep blatted and the dogs stood by with lolling tongues. Nor had Llano made a mistake in following those directions. Still there was something wrong. Where the trail entered this little mountain park it had been well defined and heavy. Now, while still well defined, it seemed to Llano that the travel was lighter. Somewhere behind him, men had left the trail, branching out. Llano reined Singleshot around.

Back in the little park, with aspen rustling to his left, he kept his eyes on the ground. There was no branching trail, no mark of travel, but still Land kept his eyes on the earth and spoke to the big horse he straddled.

"Throwing off on us," said Llano. "Some place . . ."

He left the sentence unfinished and swung Singleshot to the left. Among the aspen there were scattered marks of shod hoofs. A horse, crossing a log, had clipped the bark with an iron-shod hoof. Llano nodded and went on.

Beyond the trees the hoof-marks reappeared. Again a trail was beneath Singleshot's feet. The big horse followed it and Llano smiled to himself. Experience had found this trail. The smile changed to a frown as he recalled the experience. Singleshot climbed a rise, protestingly, while Jigger pulled back on the lead rope. Before Land was a little pocket, a cul-de-sac in the hills.

1

This was the Rincon, the thing that gave the canyon its name. There were more aspen, pines interspersed among them, then rock, and then a little cleared park in the Rincon. There was a pole fence thrown across the narrow end of the park and behind the fence stood a cabin, smoke rising lazily from its chimney.

At Llano Land's left a hidden voice said, "Hold it!" coldly, and Singleshot stopped, while Land froze in the saddle. From the cabin a man, a rifle across his arm, emerged and came toward the fence. At the fence he halted, peering at Land.

Land, motionless, said, "Hello, Mat," and waited.

The man at the fence continued his scrutiny for a long minute. Then he let his rifle slide down from his arm until its butt rested on the ground, and returned the greeting: "Hello, Llano."

Land relaxed and Mat McCarthy at the fence said: "It's all right, Shorty." Land heard the click of a hammer lowered and Singleshot moved ahead toward the fence. Mat McCarthy had changed since Land had last seen him. Land remembered a lithe, supple boy who could ride the rough string with any outfit at which he happened to work. Now Mat was heavy, with a belly that threatened momentarily to overflow his belt. Still his eyes were the same, eager and bright and Irish blue, even though his jowls sagged in proportion to his belly.

Mat McCarthy! How long ago had it been? Land counted the years, ten of them. They had gone different ways, these two, since they had left the old Anchor outfit on the Staked Plains. Llano Land and Mat McCarthy, McCarthy taking the wild trail and Land the trail that paralleled it. Manhunter, Llano Land. Hunted man, Mat McCarthy.

"You better light, Llano," said Mat McCarthy. "Long

2

time we don't see each other."

Llano swung down from Singleshot.

"Shorty'll look after yore horses," McCarthy was cordial. "You'll stay the night, of course."

Land nodded. He would stay the night, he knew. McCarthy's cordiality was tight, tense with a little false ring in it. Llano Land knew why that ring was there. He grinned thinly. "You still make sourdough biscuits?" he asked, falling into step with the heavy man.

"Still make 'em," returned McCarthy. "We might have a mess for supper."

The two entered the cabin, McCarthy standing back and making way for Land. There were bunks in the cabin, five men using the bunks, Land estimated. Bunks and a stove and a table. The cabin was none too clean. Land walked over and sat down on a bunk.

"So here you are," said Mat McCarthy. "I been kind of expectin' you, Llano."

Llano Land shook his head. "Not me," he answered, "You've been expecting somebody, but not me."

"Well, mebbe not you exactly," drawled McCarthy.

Land felt for papers and tobacco. The cigarette formed in his fingers and he looked over at McCarthy. "It's cattle with you, isn't it, Mat?" he drawled. "Leastwise I never heard of you dealing in horses or money."

McCarthy's blue eyes were narrow, slitted things. "I speculate in cattle some," he said, consideration in his voice. "Why, Llano?"

Land lit his smoke, let twin streamers trickle from his nostrils. "Because," he said, "I'm looking for horses. For horses and for Jack Ames."

McCarthy let that sink in. His voice was still cautious when he spoke. "Ames been foolin' with horses?" he

3

asked.

Land nodded. "Raising them," he explained. "Not speculating in 'em."

"Oh," said McCarthy, and now his eyes were wide once more and there was no restraint in his joviality.

Land nodded. "Jack left the Anchor two years after you and I quit," he said. "His mother is living at Carpenter. I just came from there."

McCarthy stirred on the bunk. "Yes?" he encouraged.

"Jack's been missing." Land considered his cigarette. "You see, Mat," he threw off his habitual restraint, "I hit it, finally. I staked a man in Cripple Creek. We made it."

McCarthy started up from the bunk. "That's . . ." he began.

Land stifled the congratulations. "We didn't make much," he said. "My share was fifteen thousand. I thought it was enough. I quit and was going to buy a little outfit. Then I found Mrs. Ames in Carpenter." There was silence for a moment and Land drawled meditatively, "Remember the meals she used to cook for us?"

McCarthy nodded. His blue eyes were looking back through the years. "She used to patch my clothes for me," he said, "an' darn my socks."

"An' Jack . . ." Land let it drop there.

"Jack would give a man the shirt off his back," said McCarthy gruffly. "Well, Llano?"

"Well . . ." Land took his time. "Jack had started over to the Ladrones with seven head of horses, thoroughbreds of his own raising. That was a month ago an' he hasn't been back, or written."

McCarthy's checks creased, as his jaw set firm. "Mother Ames know who he sold 'em to?" he asked.

4

Llano Land shook his head. "No," he answered. "She didn't know."

"An' yo're lookin' for Jack?" McCarthy let his voice trail off.

"For Jack an' the horses."

"You might find the horses," said McCarthy, after a moment.

"I thought of that, too," said Land, quietly, "but I didn't tell Mother Ames."

Both men were silent. They knew Jack Ames. There was one thing only that could keep Jack Ames silent for a month.

"Look," said McCarthy heavily, "when you come ridin' in here I thought mebbe you'd been hired. You see," he hesitated, "we kind of deal in cattle here. There's a good market for fat Colorado cattle in Texas, an' sometimes we can turn a Texas steer to advantage in Colorado. I thought mebbe . . . I knowed that you'd been workin' for stock associations an' peace officerin' an' such . . . Well, you got a reputation, Llano."

"I'm looking for Jack Ames," said Llano quietly.

McCarthy considered. "Well, now," he said at length, "I got some connections, Llano. I'll make inquiries around. If the boys know that yo're all through there ain't a reason why they wouldn't help you, that I can think of."

"I'm through," said Land, heavily. "Except for this one job, I'm done. My God, Mat! Do you think I liked it?"

McCarthy pursed his lips. "You followed it a long time," he said.

"Can you stop a thing you've started?" demanded Land hotly. "Would you be here today if you could stop?"

The sudden flare of temper surprised McCarthy. His eyes narrowed as he looked at Land again. "No," he admitted, "mebbe not, Llano. Mebbe you an' me could of taken different roads after we left the Anchor."

The cabin door opened abruptly and three men came in. One was short and curly haired, evidently the "Shorty" to whom McCarthy had spoken, the man who had stopped Llano on the trail. The other two were big, blond men surprisingly alike in appearance. Llano knew them by reputation. They were the Savoy twins. Llano found himself sizing up the three, noting how they stood, how they wore their weapons, little facts about them. He was annoyed. That was a habit that he would have to break himself of. McCarthy made introductions.

"This is Shorty Hamarick, Llano," he said, "an' them two with him are Arch an' Virgil Savoy. I don't know which is which an' I reckon it don't make no difference. This is Llano Land, boys. You heard of him," McCarthy's eyes wrinkled at the corners and a broad smile widened his lips. "Just to make it easier," he concluded, "I reckon I better say that Llano's quit business. He's over here on a private matter."

Hamarick's shoulders slumped and the two big twins walked over to a bunk and sat down, side by side. "There's another boy that stays here," said McCarthy, looking at Llano. "He's away on business right now."

Llano nodded. He wondered what Colorado or Texas herd might be under observation at the moment.

"There's steak for supper," said Hamarick, his voice friendly. "I reckon I'll get at the cookin'." Briskly he rolled up his sleeves and took a flour sack from where it hung on the wall. Llano got up from the bunk.

"I'll walk out an' look after my horses," he said. "That Singleshot horse is kind of proddy sometimes."

6

McCarthy arose to accompany his guest and the two went out.

Hamarick, briskly tucking a flour sack around his waist, looked at the Savoy twins. One lounged lazily on a bunk, the other squatted against a wall and methodically rolled a cigarette.

"Land?" said Shorty Hamarick. "Who is Llano Land, Arch?"

The Savoy twin on the bunk grunted. "You ain't been in this country long, Shorty," he said. "You don't know Llano Land?"

Hamarick, prodding the fire, shrugged. "He ain't known in Montana," he answered.

"I thought he'd be knowed wherever there was cow-thieves," drawled the Savoy by the wall. "Llano Land. Shucks, Shorty, Llano Land is . . . Tell him, Arch."

Arch Savoy stirred on the bunk, "Llano Land," he said meditatively, "used to punch cows with Mat down on the Staked Plains. That's where he got his name. Somebody asked him one time what his name was an' he said, 'Just plain Land.' *Llano* is 'plain' in Mexican, an' he's been Llano ever since."

"An' what does that make him?" asked Shorty, putting a steak into his hot pan.

"*That*," replied Arch Savoy, "don't make him nothin'. But the things that happened to him made him. He had a brother in the Rangers. Some fella shot his brother an' got away. Llano followed that man for two years an' killed him up in the Indian Territory. Walked in where this man was with a bunch of his friends an' took him right there. Gave him his chance an' beat him to it."

"An' then?" Shorty Hamarick, interested, turned from the stove.

"An' then he got a start peace officerin' an' such,"

7

drawled Arch Savoy. "He held down Tascosa for a year when Tascosa was tough. He worked for the stock association in Texas. He worked a season for Wells Fargo, startin' as a shotgun messenger and windin' up by takin' care of the trouble over two divisions. When the railroad got into Colorado he went to work for them. He was their troubleshooter until they hired him to be marshal in Central City durin' the silver rush. I don't reckon there's been a day for ten years when Llano Land could lay down an' sleep knowin' that he wasn't in danger, an' I don't reckon there's been a day in them ten years when he wasn't lookin' for somebody."

Impressed, Shorty grunted again. "I *thought* he looked pretty forked when he come ridin' in here," he said. "You don't reckon he's in here buttin' into our business, do you?"

The Savoys exchanged a flashing look. "Not Llano Land," said Virgil Savoy. "You heard McCarthy say that Land wasn't on business. That's good enough for me. I've heard of Land an' I know McCarthy. Nope. Land ain't here on our account."

"Well . . ." Shorty Hamarick spoke doubtfully, "you . . ."

"Go on an' fry the steak, Shorty," drawled Arch Savoy. "Don't worry about Land. If he'd been lookin' for us you'd of been layin' out in the aspens an' me an' Virge an' Mat would either be runnin' to beat hell or makin' a fight of it. Land ain't here on business. Not at all."

Hamarick turned to the stove again and Virge Savoy straightened from his squat by the wall. "Speed an' nerve," said Virge Savoy. "Llano Land's got 'em both. He ain't so damn' big, but he's got what it takes to get along."

8

Hamarick laughed and spoke above the sound of the frying steak. "Would you be so rampagiously for him if he was here on business?" questioned Hamarick. "Would you, Virge?"

"I might hate a man's guts an' still like the looks of his nerve," answered Virge Savoy. The door opened and Llano and Mat McCarthy entered the cabin.

It was a good supper that they ate that night. McCarthy made sourdough biscuits, at which confection he was a master hand. Hamarick fried potatoes and steak and made coffee and there were stewed dried peaches for dessert.

When the meal was finished and cigarettes had been rolled, Llano spoke again of his mission.

"I'm looking for Jack Ames, boys," said Llano. "He came over here with a string of horses, and he hasn't been heard from for over a month." With that introduction he told what he knew concerning Ames, describing the man, and, more important, describing the horses. "There was a red roan in the bunch," said Llano. "A mare. Then there were two bay geldings and a chestnut, a black mare, an' two claybank horses. Jack branded a little JA connected on the left side of the neck, up under the mane, and he put the same thing on the inside of the near flank."

The men shook their heads. They had, they said, seen nothing of such horses nor had they seen a man that answered Ames' description. "That ain't sayin' we won't see 'em, though, volunteered Hamarick. "We hold cattle in this country sometimes, an' we don't always use the same place. One way an' another we get around. We'll let you know, Land."

"I'd take it kindly," said Llano. "I'm going to Ladron from here. I'll go in tomorrow. Maybe you could get

9

word to me there if you run across something." He knew that these men must have connections in the town. How else could they get their supplies? McCarthy nodded his agreement to Llano's suggestion.

"Ladron's a good place," he said. "We could get word to you there all right. An' I been thinkin', Llano: If Jack was goin' to sell those horses over this way the Duro Grant people would be the most likely folks to buy. They got some English down there that sure like a blooded horse. Time or two me an' the boys been tempted to go into the horse business." Hamarick laughed at that and the Savoy boys grinned. Llano smiled thinly. He knew just how these men would go into the horse business.

The Savoys washed the dishes after the meal and when that chore was done and kindling had been split for the morning fire, the men sat about the little cabin, smoking, talking a little, content with their momentary peace and security.

One of the Savoys pulled a guitar from beneath a bunk and after tuning it, began to strum. He played for a while then laid the instrument aside. McCarthy reached out a big hand, took the guitar and passed it over to Llano.

"Here," he commanded, "you used to play some, Llano. Sing, too. Take a whirl at it."

Llano, a smile on his lips, took the guitar. He checked the tuning, played a few chords and then with fingers flashing, swept into "Hell Among the Yearlings," his foot patting time. A fandango followed the jig, and then gradually the tempo of the music slowed. Llano Land forgot the others in the room. He began to hum, his voice a soft baritone, barely carrying over the tones that came from the strings. First it was *La Noche Blanca*

10

Esta, then *Pena*, and then, harking back to the days of the long ago he sang *The Red River Valley*. As he finished the old song his fingers swept across the strings in a swell of harmony and he looked up. The cabin was silent as death itself. Only the echoes from the last chord lingered.

For a moment the silence held and then Mat McCarthy rose to his feet.

"Damn you, Llano," he said, "that takes me . . . Hell! I don't care if I never steal another cow." He stalked to the door, opened it and walked out. Llano too, arose and went out of the door, and on a bunk, one big Savoy looked at the other.

"A fella with a reputation like he's got," said Virge Savoy, "an' he can play an' sing like that! Hell, Arch, I think . . ."

"Damn it," said Arch Savoy, "I think so too. Mebbe we can find this Jack Ames for him. Mebbe."

CHAPTER 2

IT WAS ARCH SAVOY THAT COOKED BREAKFAST THE next morning. Mat McCarthy's little group of outlaws worked with a smooth precision and lack of friction that might have been envied by other and more honest outfits. Llano thought of that as, leading Jigger, he rode Singleshot out over the trail that Mat McCarthy had shown him. In a way Llano envied McCarthy and his riders. They were untroubled by ethics, by conscience, unworried about anything except the mechanics of living. They thought in terms of cattle, distance, and the submerged markets through which they operated. There was something childlike about the outlaws. Indeed

11

Llano had noted that childlike quality in most of the men who followed the trail with the wild bunch. For the most part they were unmoral, not immoral. There were, of course, the vicious ones, the men who, like rabid dogs, struck at all they met. For those men Llano had no compunction, but for the others, the men who through high spirits, circumstances, or from the fact that convention galled them, had struck out into the untamed trail, Llano felt a certain sympathy, a certain kinship. Of course it was his job to tame those men, to subdue them. That was his work. Llano shook his head. It had been his work. No more.

The morning was fresh and cool. Later in the day it would be hot but the New Mexico sky was clear and clean and the wind was sweet. Topping the rise of the last ridge Singleshot stopped of his own accord and Llano looked down at the country below.

There was a canyon below him which widened gradually until it met another, larger, canyon. The big canyon was the Ladron. A stream, Ladron Creek, ran through it, and there were cottonwoods and willows along the stream. A road crossed the creek and went on down the canyon, now paralleling the water, now crossing it. This, thought Llano, would be the road to Marthastown, the gold camp that rested at the head of Comanche Creek fifty miles west and north. As though to confirm that thought, four high-wheeled wagons, each drawn by six teams of mules, crawled into view below. The drivers sat astride the nigh-wheel mule of each string, controlling their animals by a single long rein that, coupled with a jockey stick, served as a communication with the leaders. As Llano watched, the first wagon rounded a sharp curve, the mules stepping over the chain that connected them with the wagon and pulling hard into their collars.

When the supply wagons had disappeared Llano rode on down toward the main canyon. Dropping from the ridge he lost sight of the stream, the walls of the canyon he followed rising sharp about him. The trail leveled off and the canyon widened, and Llano rode out into the broad Ladron.

Singleshot made for the stream intent on water, and Llano let him go. Circling a motte of cottonwood he reached the creek and as his horse splashed into the shallows and dropped his head to drink Llano found himself suddenly with company. Across the stream, sitting a big bay horse, was another rider, a still-faced, gray-haired man. For a moment the two looked at each other, their eyes saying nothing. Then the man on the bay horse nodded and smiled faintly. Llano returned that smile.

"Nice mornin'," said the gray-haired man.

"Fine," agreed Llano.

The bay horse finishing his drinking, lifted his head and the gray-haired man urged him forward. Splashing, the bay crossed the stream. Singleshot, too, had finished his drink and his lead-colored head with the sharp black-tipped ears pricked forward, followed the progress of the other horse. The gray-haired man halted his mount, waiting courteously. Llano, turning a little, faced him.

"I take it that you are travelin'," said the gray-haired man, looking at the pack on Jigger.

"To Ladron," agreed Llano.

"I am headed there myse'f," announced the stranger. "Would you mind my company?"

Somehow Llano liked the courtesy of the question. Somehow he liked the man who asked it. "I'd be glad

13

for company," he said.

The two rode away from the stream side by side. The gray-haired man was tall, and thin as Llano was thin, with a trim slimness that bespoke muscles pared down until only usefulness remained. His stirrups were longer than Llano's, and his head was above Llano's, although the bay horse and the lead-colored Singleshot were of identical height. The gray-haired man's eyes were light blue, and there was a trim, gray mustache shading his mouth. That mouth curved pleasantly as its owner smiled but the eyes, like Llano's gray eyes, were watchful.

"How are things in Marthastown?" asked the gray-haired man.

"Booming, I've heard," answered Llano. This was a cunning question, he thought. The stranger was probing for information.

"They tell me that the new dredge is really doin' the work," agreed the gray-haired man placidly. Silence followed that statement. Llano lifted his stirrups as Singleshot splashed across a ford in the creek. Jigger, the buckskin, suddenly sullen, pulled back on his lead rope and, mechanically, Llano leaned a little forward as Singleshot pulled.

"Gold," said the gray-haired man whimsically. "Funny what a man will do for gold, ain't it?"

"Sometimes," assented Llano.

"It's helped Ladron, the gold strike has," said the gray-haired man. "Ladron is gettin' to be quite a supply point."

"Lots of freighting," Llano answered and then, throwing out a false lead, "Any chance of a man tying up with a freight outfit?"

"That would depend," said the gray-haired man.

14

Singleshot tossed his head up sharply. Jigger came up on the rope, no longer pulling back. A red roan horse broke from the tree screen of the creek and running full out came toward the two riders. On the running horse a girl on a side saddle leaned back as she pulled against an iron mouth. The red roan was bolting.

Mechanically Llano let Jigger's rope free from his saddle horn. He could feel Singleshot bunch under him. Then, apparently without volition from the rider, the big lead-colored horse was in full stride, sweeping forward, circling to come against the roan and parallel the runaway's course. That was how Singleshot came by his name. He looked like a big slug of lead, such as might come from the barrel of a Sharp's buffalo gun, and he traveled like that same leaden slug. Llano found himself alongside the red roan, found himself leaning forward, his left hand wrapping his reins about his saddle horn. Then his hands went out, settled above those straining hands on the roan's bridle reins, fastened there. "Shot!" said Llano sharply.

Singleshot broke his great racing stride. His head came up, fighting against the martingale, tossing, throwing back flecks of foam. Llano, hard set in his saddle, applied the pressure. Gradually the roan's head came up. Gradually the roan broke stride. Gradually they slowed. From full run to lope, from lope to canter, to trot, to walk. Singleshot stopped, still tossing his head. Holding the roan's reins Llano slid from his saddle.

The girl was breathing hard. Her face was flushed from exertion, her cheeks red with the rich color, and her lower lip was caught between small white teeth. Her eyes were blue, big with fear at the moment, and the wind had whipped away her hat and tumbled her hair

15

until it hung, rich and glossy about her shoulders. The sun caught a tinge of red in her hair, making a glowing nimbus for her face. Llano stood at the roan mare's head, holding the bridle reins, his right hand reaching up to the mare's neck, almost hidden by the roan's mane.

The girl let go a long breath, caught another and let it go. Almost she was sobbing.

"Easy," said Llano. "It's all right now."

"She bolted," said the girl. "We were crossing the creek and she took fright at something. I couldn't check her."

Llano looked past the mare. Other riders were converging upon them. From behind came the gray-haired man, leading Jigger. From the creek came two riders, their horses full out and running. One of these rode a flat English saddle. The other was set heavily on his horse, deep in a stock saddle. The two riders slid their horses to a stop and the man in the flat saddle threw himself from his horse and ran to the girl.

"Are you all right, Gwynn?" he panted. "Are you all right, dear?"

Llano could see the same tinge of red in the speaker's hair, the same high color in his cheeks as in the hair and cheeks of the girl. His eyes strayed past the speaker and caught the glance of the man in the stock saddle. Cold black eyes the man had, and his face was smooth olive. Now he dismounted, coming toward the roan horse. Llano's hand, on the roan's neck, moved softly, stroking the sweating skin, soothing the mare. Suddenly the motion of that hand stopped. Llano's finger encountered roughness, a scar that lifted the satin of the roan hide. His finger traced that scar.

"I'm all right now, Donald," said the girl on the roan. "This gentleman," she looked at Llano, "caught Betty

16

and stopped her, but for a minute . . ."

"The brute should be killed," said the man with the black eyes.

The fair-skinned man turned to Llano. "I am indebted to you," he said courteously. "My sister . . ."

"Why," said Llano, "I was lucky to be where I was." He had taken his hand from the mare's neck and stood now, holding the reins. Singleshot, his business done, was cropping grass.

"I think," the girl on the horse said impulsively, "that you saved my life."

The fair-haired man was holding out his hand. "I'm Donald Rae," he announced. "I don't know what I can say or do, Mister . . ?"

"Land," informed Llano. "There's no need to thank me. I'm glad that I could help out."

The dark-skinned man broke in smoothly. "Hadn't you better take Gwynn to the house, Donald?" he asked. "I'm sure that she is upset."

The girl leaned forward again. Her eyes were bright. "If you will come to Ladron House perhaps I can thank you properly, Mr. Land," she said.

Llano was embarrassed. All this fuss about a runaway horse. "I'm glad that I could help out," he repeated awkwardly.

"You must come to Ladron House, Mr. Land," Donald Rae seconded his sister's invitation. "We are indebted to you. We . . ."

"I'm sure that you can leave the thanks to me, Donald," the dark-skinned man broke in again. "I know that Gwynn needs to get back. She may have been hurt. You must take her in."

Donald Rae looked from Llano to the speaker and then back to his sister. His fresh, open face was anxious.

17

"We'll go," he agreed. "Come, Gwynn. We will see you at Ladron House, Mr. Land."

Rae mounted. Riding forward he took the reins that Llano held up to him. The girl smiled down at Llano. Her smile was tremulous. "You'll come, won't you?" she asked. "I can't thank you properly now. I'm upset. I . . ."

Llano bowed slightly and said nothing. Donald Rae turned his horse, pulling on the reins of the red roan mare. The girl looked back still with that trembling smile on her lips. Llano lifted his hat. His eyes followed the riders. The dark-skinned man spoke at Llano's side.

"You've been thanked enough, Land," said the dark-skinned man, brusquely. "Here." His hand met Llano's. Something warm and round remained in Llano's palm. The dark-skinned man mounted his horse, wheeled the animal and loped off after the man and girl. Llano looked at his palm. There, bright and gleaming, was a double eagle, a twenty-dollar gold piece.

From beside Llano the gray-haired rider commented: "I wouldn't go to Ladron House if I was you, Land. That was Arthur Cameron, the Duro Grant manager. He's paid you off."

Very slowly Llano put the gold piece in his pocket. He looked at the gray-haired man. "I reckon," he drawled, "that you're right."

Singleshot stood and let Llano walk up to him. Llano mounted, rode over and took Jigger's lead rope from the gray-haired rider. He met the gray-haired man's eyes, nodded a little and his thin lips were hard in a sardonic smile. "No," said Llano Land, "I won't go to Ladron House to be thanked."

"Land," mused the gray-haired man. "You wouldn't be *Llano* Land by any chance, would you?"

18

"Not by chance," agreed Llano. "I'm Llano Land, right enough."

"Well, then," the gray-haired man was smiling a little, "I'm Dale Fallien, Llano Land, an' we might as well ride on to Ladron."

Llano nodded. Singleshot moved ahead and Jigger followed. Dale Fallien swung his horse up alongside Singleshot. Llano was looking at the cottonwoods ahead, the cottonwoods through which Cameron and the Raes had disappeared. The gold piece was hot in his pocket.

"Twenty dollars," drawled Fallien. "Kind of a cheap price to put on the girl he's goin to marry, you'd think."

Llano said nothing. He was wondering why a girl like Gwynn Rae would be riding a red roan mare. A red roan mare with a little JA brand under the mane on the left side of the neck.

Fallien's horse took up a trot, and automatically keeping pace Singleshot and Jigger also trotted. Jack Ames' horses, thought Llano Land. Jack Ames' horses, and a girl like that!

The canyon, widening further, debouched into a flat. To the right, set among trees, was a great, square building flanked by smaller buildings that were set about like pigs lining the belly of a sleeping sow.

Fallien waved a hand. "Ladron House," he announced.

Llano nodded.

The two rode on, past the house and its surrounding buildings, and now other buildings appeared. This was Ladron. The horses entered the town, their feet sending up little puffs of dust from the gray dust of the street.

There were squat adobes on either side of the street, geraniums blooming in a riot of color in the windows of

19

the houses. A man, dark-skinned, black-haired, squatted in the shadow by a house, a corn-husk cigarette between his fingers, and from an open door came a shrill voice calling in Spanish for *"Maria . . . ven aca, Maria!"*

Llano reined in Singleshot as a child, dark-haired and black-eyed, trotted across the street toward that calling voice. Somnolence sat upon the town and Llano smiled faintly. He had encountered a thousand such scenes in Sonora and in Chihuahua and along the border. To all appearances Ladron might have come from Mexico and been set down intact amid the hills.

Dale Fallien gestured again. "There," he said, "is the Saint George Hotel. You might stop there."

Something was amusing Fallien. His voice was quiet but that hint of amusement was unmistakable. Llano Land shook himself free of his thoughts. The horses had stopped in front of a two-story building which bore the sign, "Saint George Hotel, 1875," above the shaded porch. Llano looked at that sign.

"Just ten years to collect bedbugs," grinned Llano Land and the amusement in his voice answered that in the voice of his companion. "Yes, I reckon I could stop here. I've got twenty dollars."

There was a hitch rail before the Saint George and to it Fallien and Llano fastened their horses. Fallien, gravely considering his companion, nodded as though he had made a decision. "I believe I'll go on to town," he stated. "I may see you later, Mr. Land."

Llano said nothing, simply nodded. He had not decided about Dale Fallien. Fallien had known him as Llano Land. There were only two classes of men who would pounce upon that name as had Fallien. To which did Fallien belong, outlaw or peace officer? Llano didn't know. Fallien swung off down the street, his long legs stiff in the stride of the man who has spent his days on horseback. Llano, ducking under the hitch rail, crossed the shade of the porch, opened the door and was in the lobby of the Saint George.

The lobby was deserted. Llano rang the little bell on the desk but the action brought no response. The bell sounded emptily and Llano rang it again. Still there was no answer. Voices murmured behind a door across the lobby and going to the door Llano stood undecided. Presently he rested his hand on the door knob, turned it gently and the door opened slightly. Llano could see that the door led to a barroom and he was about to open it wider and step in when words arrested him. Two men were talking in the barroom.

"I tell you, Nathan, I got to have a room!" The voice was deep, gruff and strained. "I got to. I got to get Engra to bed an' get the doctor for her. She can't go no further!"

The voice that answered was higher, shrill with worry, almost plaintive. "My Lord, Will, I can't do it! You don't know what it means. You don't know the pressure that's on me, the way it is!"

Llano let the door sag open. He could see the men now, one short, fat, shirt-sleeved, perspiring; the other, big, lean, rawboned and dressed in bib overalls and blue shirt. The big man wore brogans and there was a straw hat pushed back on his head. Farmer, thought Llano. It was written all over the big man.

The fat Nathan, plainly the hotel proprietor, had his hand on the big man's arm, pleading with him. The big man shook off that hand.

"Pressure!" he growled. "You talk to me about pressure! Think I don't know what it is? First it was Kent Null tryin' to buy my place an' not offerin' half

21

enough. Then fences cut an' cattle in the crop an' Denver Capes comin' over a-sayin' that Grant cattle was bloatin' on my clover an' I had to keep my fences up! Then Dick Wadell comin' out, talkin' about the law an' sayin' that my place was on the Grant! By God, I knew where my homestead was! I saw the map when I filed. Then, last night the house burnin' an' now you won't give me a room for my wife. Mebbe I ain't got the money to pay for it. Mebbe yo're ascairt of the Grant. But I'm goin' to get Engra to bed an' get the doctor! Hear that?"

The last words followed a hollow cough, and for the first time Llano saw the woman. She slumped in a chair, half facing the door, her head lowered. She had stifled the cough in a handkerchief that bore telltale stains. There was no mistaking that cough or the stains. The woman was in the last stages of consumption and the big man was plainly almost at the breaking point. Llano Land hesitated then stepped back a little from the door.

Nathan's mean voice whined: "I can't, Loman. They'd . . . you know what they'd do . . ."

Loman, the big man, moved impulsively. His great hands settled on the back of Nathan's neck and he shook the smaller man as a terrier might shake a rat. "By God!" swore Loman, "you'll give me a room or I'll choke it out of you! I'll . . ."

The outside door of the barroom opened and there was another man in the room, a tall gaunt man dressed in funereal black. His nose was a beak jutting from beneath gleaming black eyes, fanatical eyes, and his voice boomed, deep and ringing: "Brother! Brother!"

Loman seemed to slump. His hands relaxed their grip and the fire went out of his voice and his eyes. "All right, Preacher," said Loman.

22

The man in black faced Nathan. His arm encircled Loman's shoulders and he seemed to steady the big man. There was accusation in the minister's ringing voice. "And you would turn him away at a time like this! Nathan, you will account to the Lord for this day!"

Nathan was looking at the bar. He did not lift his eyes to face that accusation. For a moment the tableau held and then the man in black spoke again.

"Bring your wife, Will. I have a place for you."

Loman, like a man in a trance, walked across to the chair, picked up the frail woman in his arms, and carrying her, went to the door and out. For a moment the man in black stood surveying the barroom. His gleaming black eyes passed over the door in which stood Llano Land, went on and settled upon fat Nathan beside the bar. The deep voice spoke once more:

"And the greatest of these is Charity!" rang the voice. Then the man in black was gone, following those others. By the bar Nathan straightened cautiously, shook himself, and then turned and encountered the bleak gray eyes of Llano Land.

"Maybe," drawled Llano Land, contempt in his voice, "you could give me a room. I can pay for it, you know."

CHAPTER 3

FED, HIS HORSES ATTENDED TO, AND HIMSELF BATHED and refreshed, Llano Land lounged on the porch of the Saint George Hotel and watched the world of Ladron go past. With his boots cocked up on the porch railing and his body cradled in a rawhide-bottomed chair that was more hammock than chair, he smoked and thought. There was more than one thing to think about. First

23

there was Mat McCarthy and his little bunch of rustlers. McCarthy was using a part of the Duro Grant in which to hold stolen cattle. Evidently McCarthy had been doing that for some time. That fact predicated another: Someone on the Duro Grant was complacent. Someone on the Duro Grant, someone in authority, was blinking an eye at McCarthy's activities. That was not Llano's business, but it was an item to be considered. Next, that girl, Gwynn Rae at Ladron House, was riding one of Jack Ames' horses. Llano wondered how she had come by that horse. Probably bought it from Jack Ames. He could not understand a girl like that getting the horse in any other manner. If she had bought the horse, then Jack Ames had money. Horses could be more easily traced than money. Llano frowned at the idea. If Ames had sold the horses it was going to be mighty difficult to find out what had became of him. It was Llano's intention to find each man or woman who had purchased from Ames, and tracing that tortuous course eventually learn the fate of his friend. It would be a long, tough job.

Another thought came to Llano as he sat there. The scene he had witnessed in the bar of the hotel convinced him of the fact that the Duro Grant was a hard outfit. Big outfits sometimes preyed on smaller ranches, Llano knew. Still the things that the big farmer, Loman, had outlined to Nathan, were more than a little out of line. Customary procedure possibly, but out of line nevertheless. This, however, was of secondary consideration. The thing of paramount importance to Llano Land was the whereabouts of Jack Ames and the horses. Llano grinned a little. Perhaps he would not go to Ladron House to be thanked by Gwynn Rae, but certainly he would ask Gwynn Rae where she had acquired the red

24

roan mare. The thought gave him pleasure, not because of what he must ask but because he would see the girl again. Llano admitted to himself that he wanted to see that girl again.

Leige Nathan came out of the door of the Saint George, stopped, and tentatively broached a conversation. "Hot, ain't it?" said Nathan.

Llano fixed the man with a cold eye. He knew just how to deal with men of Nathan's stripe. "Come here," he commanded.

Nathan came over and stood uneasily before Llano. He was not just sure what was coming but whatever it was would be unpleasant he felt certain. Llano had made no attempt to hide his contempt for Nathan.

"Who are that girl and her brother up at Ladron House?" asked Llano.

Nathan let go a sigh of relief. He had expected something else.

"They're English folks," he said hurriedly. "Come over here from England."

"Yes?" Llano was still questioning.

"Yeah. The Duro Grant was sold to an English company about two years ago," Nathan continued. "This Donald Rae an' his sister come here when the place was sold. He's supposed to be in charge." Nathan ventured a derisive grin.

Llano checked it. "Supposed to be?" he prompted.

"Well," the hotel man was apologetic, "Cameron really runs the Grant. Cameron an' Kent Null."

"An' who is Kent Null?"

"He's the Grant's lawyer. He was here before Cameron come."

"Well?" Again Llano primed the pump.

Nathan chuckled. A mean man, he loved to see others

in trouble. "The English company got stuck," he said. "They bought a pig in a poke. They thought that there was boats runnin' up an' down Ladron Creek an' a railroad right at the town. Now they're tryin' to sell out."

"And Null's doing the selling?"

"I guess so. Him an' Cameron. They say that Cameron sold a big outfit in California for some folks there an' that's why he's here. He's a good business man, all right."

"Seems to be," agreed Llano, remembering the twenty-dollar gold piece.

"He's goin' to marry that Rae girl." Nathan was in full stride now and had forgotten the antipathy he had toward this cold-eyed questioner. "Mebbe he won't sell the Grant when he does that. Her father's a knight or somethin' in England an' he owns most of the stock in the English company that bought from the Miraflores heirs."

"Hmmmm," Llano murmured thoughtfully.

"Yeah. Cameron's smart. He ain't as smart as Null, though. It ain't generally known, but Null's the man that sold the Grant to the English people in the first place."

"An' now he wants to sell it again," commented Llano. "Why are these Grant people cracking down on the little outfits?"

The question came like a whiplash. Nathan, realizing suddenly that he had talked freely, perhaps too freely, drew back into his shell. "Are they crackin' down?" he asked innocently.

"Don't pull that!" Llano's voice was a contemptuous drawl. "I heard you this morning, remember."

Nathan shrugged. "Anybody cracks down on folks that steal their land," he said defensively. "The Grant is

26

just lookin' after their own interests."

"And you are helping them. One thing more: Who was that preacher that came in?"

"That's James Gunther." Nathan felt free to talk again. "He rides a circuit out of here. Goes over to Marthastown an' on to Bridger. He's a damn' nuisance. Talks to the Mexicans an' tells 'em that the Grant is makin' slaves of 'em. Tries to hold revival meetin's at Marthastown. He's gettin' in bad. There's a bunch of religious folks that think he's the real stuff, but if he don't keep his mouth shut he'll go out of here with a coat of tar an' feathers. Why last week he butted in on a dance an' . . . ."

"Yes," Llano dismissed the man, "a fella' like that might be a nuisance all right. Did you grain my horses like I told you?"

Nathan recognized the dismissal. "I'll go see the barn boy," he said. "I told him to look after them but I'll go see."

"So do," grunted Llano and leaned back in his chair again. So Gwynn Rae was the daughter of an English knight. . . .

Nathan left the porch and Llano, relaxed, stared up at the big house on the hill. Ladron House. He wondered what Gwynn Rae was doing at that moment. Was she . . . ? Llano brought himself up short. What business did he have thinking about a girl like Gwynn Rae?

As he rolled a cigarette and lit it Dale Fallien came up along the board sidewalk, stepped onto the porch, and walking over seated himself beside Llano. The older man pushed back his hat, brought a short pipe from his pocket and, having stuffed it and lit it, looked over at his companion.

"Tryin' to figure out what you'll do with that twenty

27

dollars?" he asked.

"I've got it spent," Llano answered placidly. Why did this tall gray-haired man rub the raw spot that the twenty-dollar gold piece had created? Twice he had made caustic comment. Llano wondered. Dale Fallien fitted into a pattern somewhere. Perhaps he fitted into the pattern in Llano's mind.

"Llano Land," mused Fallien. "You worked for the Wells Fargo people some, didn't you?"

"Some," agreed Llano.

"An' for the city council in Tascosa, an' for the stock association in Texas?"

"You overlooked being a Ranger for four years and that I pretty near got myself killed the time Red River Tom was hung in Watrous." Llano was mildly amused.

"I knew about that," agreed Fallien. His light blue eyes were fixed on Llano. "Wherever you go it seems like there's trouble. Is there goin' to be trouble here?"

This was a point blank question. Why did Fallien ask it? Certainly if Fallien did not fit into the pattern in Llano's mind Llano must fit into some sequence in Fallien's brain.

"I couldn't say," Land answered quietly. "You want to remember that if there's been trouble wherever I've been, it was there before I came and was gone when I left."

"I see," said Fallien.

"You *may* see," Llano corrected placidly. Just as well to give this inquisitive gentleman something to think about.

Fallien's brows wrinkled with thought. "There's trouble here all right," he said softly. "The question is, how were you hired to settle it?"

"The question is, have I been hired?" Llano let the

thought drop into the troubled pool of Fallien's brain.

Fallien sighed. "I suppose that is the question," he agreed.

Still Llano liked this man. Coolness and competence were written large upon him. The questions had been prying, true, but there had been no hesitancy in Fallien as he displayed his thoughts. Llano threw away his cigarette butt. Maybe he would answer some questions.

"Now," Llano drawled, "suppose you were me and had made a little strike. Enough to start up a small outfit. What would you do?"

"What I'm doin' now," answered Fallien surprisingly. "I'm too old to change. Yo're too old to change yore ways, Llano Land."

Anger formed in Llano's mind. "I'm not," he said sharply.

Fallien shrugged. "Why are you here then?" he asked.

"I'm here . . ." Llano let it drop. He would not answer the questions. "Who, besides the Grant people have money, enough to buy thoroughbred horses?" he asked suddenly.

"You got horses to sell?"

"I might have."

Fallien stared away, his eyes blank. "There's Pat Greybull at Marthastown," he said. "I've heard that he came here from Kentucky an' that he likes a thoroughbred."

"Why," returned Llano heartily, "there's maybe a market for me. There's gold at Marthastown and surely there's a market for horses."

He stood up abruptly and looked down at his companion. "Wouldn't it be funny if I was selling horses?" he suggested, and with that, clumped away across the porch, entered the Saint George and went to his room.

In his room Llano Land settled on his bed. His mind was a turmoil. Too many things to think about. Too many questions. Llano stretched out on the bed and relaxed his muscles while his mind raced.

It was almost four o'clock when Llano left his room. The porch of the hotel was deserted as he strolled across it and turning east walked down toward the center of town. Ladron was active. There were freight wagons lining a warehouse on a side street and at a stage station men were getting down from a coach that had just arrived. Rough men these, booted and overalled, miners for the most part. The stage passengers dispersed and Llano walked on a little further then entered a building on his immediate left. The little half-shutter doors swung behind him and he walked across toward the long walnut bar. This was the Exchange Saloon.

At the moment the Exchange was not heavily patronized. There was only one bartender on duty behind the bar but the length of that counter and the array of glasses told of much greater custom. Two men lounged against the bar, eyeing Llano curiously as he approached. At a faro layout a man looked up, lowered his eyes and then looked again as Llano came closer. Llano, glancing down at the faro dealer nodded a greeting.

"Hello, Flaco," he said.

The dealer flushed, his dull-hued skin reddening. His eyes were troubled but he returned the salutation. "Hello, Land."

Llano smiled a little. He knew why the man was troubled. Flaco had run a wheel in Trinity and had been one of many to whom Llano had issued distinct orders. It had been, "Get out and don't come back!" in Trinity and Llano knew that the man was recalling that occasion.

Llano, too, had recollections. Flaco had had a partner in Trinity, a woman. Llano remembered the girl, a vivid, dark creature with fire in her. He nodded again to Flaco and went on to the bar. The two men who stood there turned their faces away as he stopped before the counter and ordered his drink from the bartender. One of those two wore a star; the other was a rider, a cowman, Llano judged, not a puncher. The man's clothing was flamboyant and more costly than the average rider could afford to wear.

The bartender returned to the two and Llano, taking his drink, put the glass back on the bar and laid a fifty-cent piece beside it. He had intended engaging the bartender in conversation but that apparently was impossible. Now he strolled toward the door, nodding once more to Flaco, and went out. He had scarcely gone before the man with the star was at Flaco's side asking questions. When Flaco answered, the starwearer spoke to his companion and hurried out of the saloon, making for Ladron House on the hill.

Llano went on down the street. At a hitch rail in front of another saloon there were horses. Examining them Llano saw McClellan saddles on two with blue blankets, each carrying the letters, U.S., below the saddles. These were army horses. Llano strolled on, finally stopping beside a striped barber pole. He hesitated a moment and then went into the shop. Barbers, like bartenders, were often founts of information.

"Hair cut and a shave," said Llano, climbing into a chair.

The barber spread an apron across Llano's chest, fastened a towel about his neck and stumped over to his shelf for scissors and comb. Llano noted that the man had only one leg. The other was a wooden peg from the knee down.

31

The barber worked silently. When the expected loquaciousness failed to materialize, Llano asked questions of his own.

"Know where a man could get a few good horses around here?" he queried. He had hoped that Jack Ames might have stopped here at this shop. If so the barber would remember and be might mention the fact.

The barber said, "No," curtly, and then: "Want some taken off the top?"

"You're the doctor," drawled Llano. "There was a fella' selling horses through here around a month ago, wasn't there?"

"I didn't hear of it," said the barber, and his shears snipped.

"I thought maybe there was," Llano's voice was mild.

The barber softened a trifle. "Not that I know of," he said. "You might get some horses from Cameron at the Grant. Maybe he's got some for sale."

"I'm looking for thoroughbreds," Llano suggested.

The barber stepped back to survey his work. "I ain't seen any," he announced.

"Who's the local law here?" asked Llano.

"Fella' named Wadell, Dick Wadell."

"Good man?"

"It depends on what you want him to be good for." The barber was answering no questions. It was like blasting information out of a rock to get it here, Llano decided.

"There's a big man that wears a fancy vest," Land said, eyeing himself in the mirror as the barber turned the chair. "Seems to team around with Wadell. Who's he?"

"Denver Capes. Grant cowboss." The barber had finished with the hair and now was laying the chair back

32

preparatory to shaving his customer. Llano let himself relax.

"I saw some cavalry horses in town," he remarked as he settled himself.

"There's a troop at Bridger," said the barber. "Once in a while some of 'em come over. The Government's been keepin' a troop there since the Pueblos got jumpy. Is that towel too hot?"

Llano said that the towel was all right and spoke no more. The barber was certainly not talkative. Far different from the usual run of barbers.

When his shave was finished and he had paid the peg-legged man, Llano went out on the street again. It was now about six o'clock and supper time. He headed back toward the hotel. When he entered the lobby Nathan was waiting for him.

"There's a message for you," said Nathan importantly. "Cameron wants to see you up at Ladron House."

"Is supper ready?" asked Llano.

"But Mr. Cameron . . ." began Nathan.

"Cameron can come and see me," said Llano, and turned toward the dining room.

"There's a note for you, too," blurted Nathan. "Here." He held out an envelope, small and of heavy paper.

Llano accepted the note and ripped open the flap. The envelope contained a note, the letters round and smooth. Gwynn Rae hoped that Mr. Land had not forgotten that he was to see her at Ladron House. Could he come that evening? Llano refolded the note and placed it thoughtfully in his shirt pocket.

"I'll go up after I've eaten," Llano decided to himself.

When he had finished his meal Llano went to his room, washed his hands and brushed his clothes again.

33

His toilet made, he walked through the lobby, nodding to Fallien who sat there, and leaving the hotel walked up the hill toward Ladron House in which lights were already beginning to appear.

His knock on the door of the big house was answered by a white-haired native who inquired his business.

"I'm Llano Land," was the reply. "Miss Rae is expecting me."

The servant stepped aside and invited Llano to enter. Inside the great hall the man motioned to a seat, asked Llano to wait, and hurried away. Llano sat down and looked at his surroundings.

The place was magnificent. Heavy rugs were on the polished oak of the floor and ancient Navajos of marvelous weave and design hung from the walls. The furniture was heavy, dark with age and gleaming with wax. There were silver candelabra on the table and hand-wrought silver brackets supported candles on the wall. Llano held his hat in his hands and waited. Presently he heard voices and looking up saw Gwynn Rae and a man in uniform descending the stairs. The girl was laughing up at the man.

At the foot of the stairs, she turned smiling toward Llano, and with a word to her companion, hurried across the room, the man in uniform following her. Llano took the hand which the girl held out to him.

"I thought that you weren't coming," said Gwynn Rae, reproachfully. "I expected you this afternoon. Wayne, this is the man that saved my life this morning. Lieutenant Metcalf, Mr. Land."

Llano, releasing the girl's hand, took that of the officer. Llano liked this youngster. There was strength in his grip and his face was pleasant, his brown eyes frank.

34

"We all owe you our thanks, Mr. Land," said Metcalf. "Life would be unbearable here without Gwynn."

"But you don't come here from Bridger often enough to make it more bearable, Lieutenant," laughed Gwynn Rae. "Mr. Land, this is the first time in a month that Lieutenant Metcalf has ridden over."

The officer flushed, "Duty . . ." he began.

"Ah. . . . Good evening, Mr. Land," said a suave voice. Land turned. Arthur Cameron, his hand outstretched, was walking toward him.

Llano could do nothing else but take the proffered hand. The girl and the officer stood by while Cameron gave his greeting and excuse.

"I asked Mr. Land to come and see me," said Cameron. "A matter of business. You will excuse us?"

The girl made a little grimace. "It was I who invited you," she said to Llano, reproachfully. "I'll excuse you if I must, Arthur, but you must bring Mr. Land back. I haven't thanked him properly for this morning." She turned away, her hand tucked under the officer's arm, and Cameron, his hand on Llano's shoulder, said:

"Now, Mr. Land."

Llano allowed himself to be led away.

It was an office to which Cameron took Llano Land. There was another man there, a gray-haired, red, hawk-faced little man whom Cameron introduced as Kent Null. The Grant manager motioned to a chair and going to a cupboard produced a bottle and glasses.

"A drink, Mr. Land?" he asked.

"It's a little soon after supper," replied Llano, "No thanks."

Cameron set the glasses and the bottle on the desk and seated himself behind it.

"I wanted to talk to you, Land," he began.

35

"Yes," agreed Llano.

Null poured a drink. "Just a minute, Arthur," he said to Cameron. "Did you speak to Metcalf?"

"Not yet," replied Cameron, and then, turning to Llano:

"Lieutenant Metcalf commands a troop of cavalry stationed at Bridger. He . . ."

Null interrupted again. "Then I'll talk to him before he leaves," he said. "I'll bid you good night, Mr. Land. Arthur, I'll see you . . ."

"Wait while I talk to Land," requested Cameron.

Null settled back into his chair again.

Cameron leaned forward over the desk. "I didn't know you this morning, Land," he began. "Since then I've learned a good deal about you. I know your business."

Llano nodded.

"You have a reputation," Cameron continued. "Now I suppose that you have come over here because you heard of the trouble we have been having?"

"Have you had trouble?" questioned Land, innocently.

Cameron waved that aside. "You know that we have been having trouble," he said brusquely. "Since the establishment of the Grant boundary we have been having trouble. There are nesters on our land and they've got to be removed."

"So?" Llano drawled the question.

"Yes. Now I'll make you a proposition. You have a reputation and I suppose you live up to it. I want these men off the Grant. I have men who can remove them but . . ."

"Now wait," drawled Llano. "You're going to tell me something I don't want to hear and that you don't want

36

to tell me. I'm over here on a private matter. I want to ask you just one thing: Where . . .?"

Cameron's lips narrowed and his eyebrows drew down into a straight, black line. "I'm not interested in your private affairs," he interrupted.

"But I am," affirmed Llano, and got up from his chair. "I'm not interested in anything else right now."

"Now wait a minute, Land." Cameron, too, arose from his chair. "I want to make you a proposition. I'd like to have you with us but if you won't listen . . ." He let the words trail off.

"If I won't listen?" prompted Llano.

"A man's either got to be with me or against me!" snapped Cameron.

"No neutrals?" Llano appeared mildly surprised.

"No! Either you take what I'm going to offer you or get out of Ladron!" Cameron's voice was flat.

"You lay it right on the line, don't you?" drawled Llano. Methodically he felt in his trousers pocket. His hand came out holding a gold piece and he spun it on the desk top.

Llano Land was angry all the way through. Neither his voice nor his impassive face indicated his rage. His eyes simply had become a washed out gray, blank, watchful, and agate hard. His voice, when he spoke, was as hard as his eyes.

"You made a threat and gave an order, Cameron," he grated. "There's some money of yours. Pick it up! You say there are no neutrals. That's all right with me."

Cameron's face was flushed red. There was madness in his eyes. His hand rested on the edge of the desk. There was an open drawer under that hand and a gun in the open drawer. Llano watched Cameron's face. The eyes would tell him when Cameron's hand started

37

down. Llano's own hand rested just at his belt. A Smith and Wesson in a leather holster nestled there beneath his waist band.

"By God, Land . . ." began Cameron.

Kent Null's voice quiet, even a little amused, stopped the angry man. "Pick up the gold piece and sit down, Arthur," said Null quietly. "You damned fool! He'll kill you if you don't!"

Slowly Arthur Cameron relaxed. Slowly he picked up the gold piece and settled back into his chair. Null's foot, reaching out, pushed the open drawer closed. Now Llano Land looked at the lawyer. There was unwilling respect in Llano's eyes.

"I'm sorry, Mr. Land," said Kent Null. "My friend is a little impetuous. I understand that he made a mistake this morning. You won't join us?"

The answer was in Llano's eyes.

Null smiled thinly. "I'm sorry," he said again. "Good night, Mr. Land. I'll stay with friend Arthur while you show yourself out."

Llano stepped back. His groping hand found the door knob and turned it. He let himself out of the office and closed the door.

CHAPTER 4

LLANO LAND WALKED ALMOST BLINDLY ACROSS THE great hall. Rage, anger, the cold desire for killing that holds a man when he sees a rattlesnake, was almost choking him. He made for the door and as he reached it a silvery voice calling his name, penetrated the anger.

"Mr. Land."

Llano stopped. Gwynn Rae was coming across the

room toward him, and behind her strode Metcalf.

"You aren't going?" questioned the girl. "Now that you have finished your business, haven't you time to stay? I wrote you a note . . ."

It was because of that note that Llano had come. Cameron might have gone to hell before Llano would have answered his summons, but Llano had not been able to forego a sight of this girl. The note had brought him, had subjected him to Cameron's offer. Llano's voice was hoarse as he interrupted.

"I'm going," he said harshly.

Gwynn Rae drew back. Her face suffused with color and her eyes flashed. "You are rude," she said, her voice betraying her anger.

Llano did not answer that accusation. He moved brusquely forward toward the door. Metcalf stopped him.

"Land," snapped the officer, "you can apologize to Miss Rae for your actions. You . . ."

Llano turned, confronting Metcalf. Here was someone he could face, here was an object for his raging anger.

"And you'll make me, soldier?" taunted Llano.

Gwynn Rae had recovered herself. Centuries of command were bred into the girl, centuries of composure and of cool courage.

"Mr. Land saved my life, Wayne," she said. "Perhaps that gives him a right to act so. I owe you my thanks, Mr. Land. You have them and now you may go."

This was dismissal. As though doused by a bucket of water Llano cooled. He opened his mouth to speak, to make some sort of apology for his actions but the words did not come. Metcalf, stepping past him, opened the door and silently Llano went through that door and into the night.

As he walked away from Ladron House a bitter, reckless feeling possessed Llano Land. He had made a fool of himself but there was no recalling his acts or his words. He was a fool. Berating himself he passed the Saint George, passed the dark adobes where peaceful natives slept, and then, at his elbow, there was light and life and noise. Llano turned and entered the Exchange Saloon.

The place afforded a far different spectacle than it had had that afternoon. There was a line of men along the bar, now, and men at the tables. The faro layout was patronized, and a woman sat on the high stool that served for the lookout's seat. Llano knew her. She was Rose Juell. Dark-haired, olive-skinned, her lips a cruel scarlet slash across her face, her black eyes sultry, the girl sat watching the game that Flaco dealt. She was dressed in black satin, the gown cut daringly low, exposing perfect throat and shoulders and hinting at the soft curves of her breasts. At sight of her, Llano's mind was jerked back to realities.

Rose Juell's face was as impressive as that of the man, Flaco, and her eyes were on the players and the layout. Llano stood looking at her for a long minute. He knew the fierce anger that could flame in the woman. As though drawn by his scrutiny, Rose Juell glanced up and her eyes met Llano's. Her face did not change expression but for a moment something flamed in her eyes before she lowered them again to the game. Llano, after that interchange of glances walked on across to the bar and stood there, waiting for a bartender to come to serve him.

As he stood, back to the room, there was a movement beside him and turning Llano encountered the eyes of

Dale Fallien. "And so you went to Ladron House?" questioned the gray-haired man. "I'm surprised that you left so early."

The evident amusement in the voice of the older man lashed the anger that seethed in Llano. Still he kept his voice level.

"I doubt that you are much surprised," he returned. "Still," and now the anger receded a trifle, "I managed to get Cameron to take back the wages he'd given me."

Fallien's eyebrows shot up in a question and now the humor of his meeting with Cameron struck Llano. Amusement supplanted the anger. "It was kind of a jolt to Cameron, too," he observed. "Fact is, if it hadn't been for a man named Null I doubt that we'd have come to terms."

"So Null was there?" Fallien's voice was whimsical. "Quite a fella', Kent Null."

"Considerable," agreed Llano. "You know, Fallien, when we were talking this evening you said that I was too old to change my ways?"

Fallien nodded. "I asked if there's to be trouble, too, you remember?" he agreed.

"I can't say about the trouble," answered Llano Land, "but as far as changing my ways is concerned, you're mistaken. I've changed them."

"Yes?" surprise showed in Fallien's voice.

"I sure have," and there was a reckless tinge in Llano Land's voice. "I'm working for nothing at a job that I know nothing about. That's a change, isn't it?"

Fallien's face was grave. He had caught that reckless tone. "Land . . ." he began.

"And just to prove I've changed 'em, I'm buying a drink," continued Llano. "You with the bald bead! Quit fooling around up there and come here!"

41

He had lifted his voice with the last words and the bald-headed bartender further up the bar raised his head. He had been bent forward talking to Wadell, the deputy sheriff of Ladron, and to Wadell's companion, Denver Capes, the Grant cowboss.

"Come here," ordered Llano imperiously. "Quit wasting your time with the dead beats and bring a bottle!"

Fallien touched Llano's arm. "Land . . ." he began again, anxiety in his voice.

Llano interrupted. "You'll drink with me, Fallien," he stated, and he made no attempt to lower his voice, "an' if those shorthorns have any objection to me taking their pet barfly you can stand by an' see 'em curried!"

Fallien shrugged. "So somebody stepped on yore pet corn," he said, low-voiced. "Just like a kid, Land. You got yore feelin's hurt an' now you want to take it out on somebody."

The words cut like a knife through Llano's mind. He was acting like a kid and he was taking out his anger on strangers. Foolish, but he had gone too far. If Capes and Wadell chose to resent his words he could only back them up.

But apparently there was no resentment in Capes and Wadell. The bartender came, carrying a bottle and glasses, and set them before Llano and Fallien. "Yes, sir, Mr. Land," said the bartender.

Llano looked at Fallien. "Will you take a drink with a damn' fool?" he asked apologetically.

Fallien smiled faintly and lifted the bottle. He knew that Llano had returned to sanity. "It must have been pretty bad," mused Fallien. "I'll take a drink, Land."

The two poured modest drinks, swallowed them and put their glasses down on the bar. Fallien had retired into his mind. Something was going on behind his blank, blue eyes.

The bald bartender returned. "There's a lady wants to speak to you, Mr. Land," he said. Llano turned. Across the room Rose Juell had left the lookout's seat at the faro game. "She's in a booth at the end of the room," said the bartender.

Llano looked at Fallien. Fallien nodded. "I'll wait for you," he said, answering Llano's look.

Rose Juell was sitting in the booth. She did not look up as Llano stood in the entrance but continued to stare down at the table. Llano stepped in, seated himself opposite the girl and spoke to the bartender who had accompanied him. "Whatever the lady wants to drink," ordered Land.

"Wine," Rose Juell's voice was low and husky. The bartender hurried away and Llano sat with his hands on the table, waiting for the girl to speak again.

But it was not until the bartender had brought the wine and glasses and had again departed that Rose Juell spoke. She sat toying with her glass, turning it between her fingers and watching the light flash from its red contents. Llano, impatient, said, "Well, Rose?"

"I heard you out there," the girl said then. "Don't you know that Capes and Wadell are bad, Llano?"

"I spoke out of turn," confessed Llano.

"Do you know what this place is?" demanded Rose Juell.

"It's Ladron," answered Llano. "A shipping point for the mines in Marthastown an' a pretty good town in its own right."

"It's a hell hole," flamed the girl. "Why are you here, Llano?"

"Why should I tell you?" parried Llano.

43

"Are you here to work with Wadell and Capes?" The girl was insistent. "Did Cameron hire you?"

"I haven't a cent of Cameron's money," Llano answered honestly.

"Cameron!" Rose Juell spat the word. Now she lifted her eyes from the glass and looked full at Llano. There was hatred in those eyes, hatred and something else.

"Where did you go after you left Trinity, Rose?" Llano asked.

"What do you care?" returned the girl. "You ran me out of Trinity. I went to Greenwall with Flaco." Defiance in her voice now, defiance and, perhaps, apology.

"With Flaco?" echoed Llano.

Rose Juell shrugged. "He was the best there was, Llano," she said. "And he had money enough to get us out of town."

"I was sorry about Trinity, Rose," Llano looked at his own glass. "I hadn't a choice."

"You thought that you hadn't a choice!" Again the girl looked at Llano, a long searching look. Then rich color flushed her checks and, her eyes were wide while the scarlet lips parted slightly. "I . . . Well, drop it Llano. I'm all right as long as I work here. . . . If Cameron . . ."

"So!" said Llano Land, suddenly realizing why Rose Juell had spat that word, "Cameron!" "Flaco is a weak sister, Rose. Maybe I can do something about Cameron."

"Why should you bother yourself about Cameron?" asked the girl, her eyes on Llano's face. Was there something appealing, something soft, in those eyes?

Llano spoke swiftly. "I think you've got this wrong, Rose," he said. "You think I'm here because . . ." He

44

stopped. Why did Rose Juell think he was here? Llano didn't know.

"I'm looking for horses," he began again. "Seven thoroughbreds. They belonged to Jack Ames. He branded a little JA on the neck. There was a red roan mare and . . ."

Rose Juell moved her hand impatiently and Llano stopped abruptly. "What would I know about horses?" she asked. "Why do you talk about horses to me? I'm here, Llano. Here in the middle of this thing. You are here. I . . ."

Llano stared at his glass. "You . . ." he began.

"Take me out of here, Llano." Rose Juell leaned forward. There was pleading in her voice, pleading and invitation. "Take me out of this. Get your horses and we'll ride. You can't win this game."

"Game?" Llano parried. "What game, Rose?"

The girl shifted nervously. "Are you a fool, Llano Land?" she asked. "Don't you know what you are up against here? You sit there and ask me what game. Don't you see what I'm offering you, Llano? Isn't it enough?"

Llano looked at that dark, tense face, into the wells that were Rose Juell's dark eyes. Indeed he saw what was offered and, for a moment, he was tempted.

Then another face came between Llano Land and Rose Juell, the face of a girl with blue eyes and flowing, red-gold hair, Gwynn Rae's face.

"And what about Flaco?" questioned Llano Land harshly. "Did you offer him the same thing to get him to take you out of Trinity?"

For a moment Rose stared at him, incredulity written on her face, then her hand lashed out and struck hard against Llano's check. The girl was on her feet, all her

45

softness gone, only flaming anger remained.

"Damn you, Llano Land," she flared, her voice low, "I hate you! I . . ." She turned and was gone.

Deliberately Llano raised his hand to his cheek, then lowering it he lifted his glass and drained it of wine.

When he reached the bar Fallien was standing just as Llano had left him. There was still the faint expression of amusement on the tall man's face and for a moment Llano thought that Fallien must know what had happened in the booth.

Fallien lifted his eyebrows as Llano came up and Llano, nodding said: "Let's go, Fallien. That is, if you're through here." Fallien nodded agreement and Llano drew money from his pocket to pay for the drinks. While he waited for his change there was a commotion at the door. Fallien grunted like a man hit low. Turning, Llano saw the cause of the activity. In the doorway was a man in bib overalls, hatless and disheveled. Llano recognized the man. It was Will Loman, the man who had been at the Saint George. His eyes were those of a maniac. Fascinated, Llano followed the direction of those insane eyes. The crowd sensing that something was coming, had drawn slightly apart and Llano could see Kent Null, immaculate and cool, standing at the bar. There was an open lane between Kent Null and Loman in the doorway.

Beside Llano, Dale Fallien was motionless. Llano, shifting his gaze, saw Dick Wadell further down the bar and at a table Denver Capes, the Grant cowboss, had risen and was standing, staring at the new arrival.

Loman's voice croaked from the doorway. "Engra's dead!"

A hush followed those two words. Men stood with glasses poised, half lifted. At the faro layout Flaco held his hand above the case and did not move it.

A big teamster sighed heavily and, as though that sigh were a signal, Loman lurched forward, his voice rumbling as he moved.

"You killed her, Null! You drove us off our place. You stole it an' it killed Engra. God damn your black soul! I'll kill you, Null. I'll kill you with my hands!"

Kent Null still stood at the bar. He had not moved. His face had gone a little pale but there was no tremor in his body, no movement that might betray fear of the great, bear-like man who came toward him, big, gnarled hands half open and outstretched. A woman screamed—Rose Juell, Llano knew—and then heavy in the silence of the room came two thundering shots. Loman stopped his lurching progress. Surprise supplanted the mask of insane hatred on his face, and he half turned.

"Why . . ." he said querulously, almost as a child might speak when commanded to cease some pleasant occupation. Then the big knees buckled. Loman's overalls bagged as he settled into them, sliding down an invisible wall to slump on the floor. He moved once on the floor, a little, pawing movement of the hands, and then was still. Bedlam took the place of the quiet in the Exchange. And then, through that bedlam came Kent Null's voice, cool, his words concise.

"Thank you, Wadell. You did your duty."

Llano turned a little. Clear of the bar Dick Wadell was standing, a smoking gun in his hand, and at the poker table Denver Capes was holstering a weapon and moving clear of his chair. Close to Llano the bald-headed bartender spoke to someone.

"You run an' get Mulligan, Chuck. Tell him to bring his shutter."

Wadell and Capes cleared a space around the body of

47

Loman, forcing back the men who crowded about. It was Wadell who made the announcement, a certain smug satisfaction in his voice when he spoke.

"I got him with both shots. One in the chest an' the other through the belly. Guess the second shot hit his pump."

Llano Land, accustomed to scenes of violence, stayed by the bar. Fallien was at his side and Fallien's eyes were bright and blue. The swinging doors of the Exchange were forced open and men made a path to the body. Llano, looking over shoulders and past craning necks, could see the peg-legged barber carrying a long shutter in his hands. The barber laid the shutter on the floor and spoke casually.

"Somebody get hold of his feet an' we'll take him out." Wadell spoke with a swagger. "You look after him, Mulligan. I'll take care of yore bill."

Mulligan, the barber, answered curtly. "Somebody'll have to! Joe, get hold of the end of that shutter."

The shutter was lifted and Llano could see the movement and hear the thump of the peg leg as the body was removed. Llano turned, looking at Dale Fallien. "I reckon," he said gently, "that we can go, Fallien. There's nothing to keep us here."

Fallien nodded and moved, his shoulders forcing a way through the crowd. Outside, once they had made their way through the men who had crowded the Exchange's door at the sound of the shots, the two walked toward the Saint George Hotel. They stopped on the porch of the Saint George, and, held by some mutual thought, looked back down the street toward the center of town.

"Poor devil!" said Dale Fallien softly. "Poor devil!"

Llano Land was silent. He had shifted his gaze from

the town and now stood looking at Ladron House. Even as he looked a light in the upper story was extinguished.

"I don't know," said Llano Land. "Maybe he was poor. Maybe not."

CHAPTER 5

IT TOOK LLANO LAND A LONG TIME TO GO TO SLEEP. The bed was good enough and the room was cool but Ladron passed back and forth outside the Saint George and the things that happened and were happening in Ladron passed back and forth in Llano's mind. It would be a long time before he forgot the look of madness in Will Loman's face as he entered the Exchange, and it would be just as long a time before he forgot Kent Null's coolness. Kent Null, decided Llano, might be a considerable man, regardless of his affiliations and his crookedness. For Null was crooked. Llano had no doubt about that.

And Will Loman, dead on the floor of the Exchange Saloon. Loman was a happy man. His troubles were over, that was sure. He had loved and been loved by a woman. She was gone and Will Loman had gone to join her. Llano rolled in the bed. In the morning he would go to Mulligan's shop and make arrangements for the funerals. Wadell would not bury the man he had killed, nor would Will Loman and his wife find their last resting place in a potter's field. And so, restless and tossing, Llano Land slept at last.

In the morning Llano was up betimes. He did not wait for the Saint George's dining room to open but went out of the hotel and down toward the town. Mulligan's shop was closed and Llano was forced to wait. He ate breakfast at a little restaurant where teamsters were also satisfying their hunger, and while he ate he was forced to hear again and yet again a recounting of the scene he had witnessed in the Exchange. But it was more than that he heard. There was a grim undercurrent in the talk among these rough men. Pity for Loman was expressed and one outspoken youngster slapped his high boot with his coiled whip and said what he thought of Wadell.

"If you ask me," said the teamster, "Wadell's no better than a damn' murderer. The Grant has got a bunch of bad ones an' Wadell leads 'em. What's Capes but a killer, an' that tinhorn Flaco an' his pardner, Huerta? They all come from the same tree. Someday somebody's goin' to take that outfit out an' hang 'em an' when they do they might as well take Cameron an' Null an' his Nibs with 'em."

An older driver spoke to the young fellow, chiding him, and the boy burst forth again. "What do I care? I ain't tied to this job. Rae's supposed to be the big boss, ain't he? Well then, why does he stand for Cameron an' the rest?"

Another, a weather-beaten, quiet man, interposed a word. Llano recognized him as the man who had driven the stage in to town the day before. The others listened to the stage man with some respect.

"Rae's too busy ridin' an' doin' what he calls huntin', to pay attention to the Grant," said the stage driver bitterly. "His Nibs is high an' mighty an' he leaves the dirty work to Cameron. I'm like Dan, here. I think that sooner or later we're goin' to have to do somethin'. Wait 'til one of you boys has his pardner shot off the seat beside him, like I had mine, an' see how you feel!"

Llano pricked up his ears. Here was fresh information. He had heard nothing of a stage robbery.

When had it happened? he wondered.

The talk lapsed and Llano paid his bill and went out. As he emerged from the restaurant he saw Mulligan unlocking his shop, and went across the street to the man. Mulligan turned as Llano came up.

"About Loman and his wife," Llano said awkwardly, "I want to pay for their funerals. I don't want Wadell to spend a dime and I don't want 'em buried in the potter's field."

Mulligan's hard face softened imperceptibly. "Wanted to pay for 'em, did you?" he rasped. "Well, they're all paid for."

"They are?" Llano was surprised. Then: "If Wadell paid you, hand it back to him. If you don't want to, give the money to me an' I'll hand it back."

Mulligan smiled. "It wasn't Wadell," he said. "I'd give it back to him myself if it was. Nope. It was another party."

"An' not anyone from Ladron House?" insisted Llano. "I . . ."

"An' it didn't come from Ladron House," interrupted Mulligan. "I was asked not to say a thing about it, an' I won't."

Balked, Llano asked another question. "When's the funeral?"

"This afternoon," said Mulligan. "Now I got to get busy. I got Loman laid out but I got to shave him an' dress him."

"If you need anything . . ." began Llano.

"I don't need a thing," answered Mulligan. "Hell! Think I ain't never done this before? The woman had me stumped at first. Seemed like everybody was ascairt to have anythin' to do with the Lomans, but Rose Juell is goin' to dress her an' fix her hair, so I got that 'tended to."

51

Llano stood there for a little time looking at the barber. Mulligan's last words had set Llano to thinking. Rose Juell! She was going to dress Engra Loman. Put clothing on that pitiful body for the last time. For the last time comb the thin hair and then cross the worn hands over the flat breasts.

"The undertakin' business," said Mulligan, breaking into Llano's thought, "is pickin' up. Two last month an' now these two."

"Two?" asked Llano, instantly alert.

"Two," said Mulligan. "There was the shotgun messenger off the stage, an' a cowboy that was found here in town."

Llano's question was sharp. "A cowboy?" he asked.

"Some fella' that nobody seemed to know." Mulligan seemed to be in a talkative mood. "Fella' about yore size with yella hair an' a birthmark on his chin. Found him layin' out in an alley without a cent on him or a thing to tell who he was. I fixed him up an' Gunther buried him."

"A birthmark?" Llano asked slowly.

"Right on his chin," agreed Mulligan. "A little red wedge."

"Nothin' else to show who he was?" asked Llano, keeping his voice even.

"Not much," answered Mulligan. "He'd had his left leg broke below the knee. Some bastard had slid a knife into him an' emptied his pockets. Didn't leave a thing."

Jack Ames! Jack Ames with yellow hair and a wedge shaped birthmark and a left leg broken below the knee. Llano remembered when Jack had broken that leg, riding a bad one. Jack Ames was dead, and here, standing before Llano was the man who had buried him.

"What did Wadell do about that?" asked Llano, not

52

realizing that his voice was harsh.

Mulligan looked questioningly at the man before him. "Why, not much," he answered. "He brought him in to me an' he made some inquiries around. The fella' had been showin' a big roll around town the night before an' that's all he learned."

"And they took him for his roll," said Llano, slowly. "Thanks, Mulligan." He turned then, and walked up the street. Mulligan, after a momentary pause, went into the barbershop.

Llano went on to the Saint George. He stumped into a chair on the porch. There he stared moodily out across the street. He had known that Jack Ames was dead and still he could not reconcile himself to the confirmation of that knowledge. Ames, dead and buried in a potter's field, and Llano Land alive and here. There was nothing that Llano could do for Jack Ames, but there was something that he could do for Llano Land. He could stay here in Ladron. A cautious inquiry here, a careful checking on who had bought the horses and when, a word overheard, men watched and weighed, and sometime Llano Land would know who had killed Jack Ames. Then he would know what to do.

Dale Fallien mounted the steps to the porch, seated himself and looked sharply at Llano. Llano continued to stare out across the street. Fallien rolled a cigarette, and respecting his companion's mood, maintained the silence. Presently Leige Nathan came out and looked at his two guests.

"Dinner's ready," said Nathan.

Fallien arose and Llano got up slowly from his chair. The two ate their dinner together and when they were finished Fallien asked:

"You goin' to the funeral?"

Llano nodded.

"So am I," returned Fallien. "I'll meet you on the porch in about half an hour." With that he left and Llano went to his room. There he made a careful toilet, cleaning his boots, brushing his hat and clothing, donning a clean shirt and a black string tie. So clothed he sat down, for it was not yet time to meet Fallien.

Minutes passed and then realizing that it was time to go, Llano rose from his chair and walked through the corridor to the lobby. Fallien was outside on the porch, and nodding to Nathan, Llano went on through the lobby and joined the tall man. They walked down the street together, wordless, their boot heels sounding sharply on the boards of the sidewalk. Presently Llano spoke.

"I don't know why, Fallien," he said. "I don't know you nor your business, but here I am with you. When I step in to take a drink, you're there, when I eat a meal you're there, when I walk down the street, there you are. Why, Fallien?"

"Ladron's a small place, Land," commented Fallien.

"But that doesn't explain it," Llano answered. "Are you crowding me?"

"I might ask you the same," Fallien replied tonelessly. "I find you wherever I go. Are you crowding me, Land?"

Llano stopped. Fallien likewise halted and the two looked at each other. Suddenly Llano shook his head. "I'm a fool," he said. "Forget it. I'm just jumpy."

"Why," said Fallien, "I might be jumpy, too. We'll both forget it." Again they resumed their walk.

As they neared the center of the little town they began to encounter more and more people. There were wagons tied to hitch rails, wagons with women in them. Men

54

stood in the shade of porch awnings, little groups of grim faced fellows, sun hardened and toughened by the desert. Strange faces these, faces of men that did not belong in Ladron, and Fallien striding beside Llano muttered to himself.

"What's that?" queried Llano.

"I don't like it," muttered Fallien.

"You don't like what?" Llano was blunt.

"I don't like that crowd in town," Fallien answered. "If the Grant men are wise they'll keep out of sight."

"Why?" asked Llano.

"Look at this crowd," replied Fallien. "Can't you feel it, Land?"

They were passing a little group of men as Fallien spoke and Llano looked at the hard, harsh faces.

"Pretty salty," he said, low voiced. "You reckon . . . ?"

"They're in town for Loman's funeral," Fallien explained. "If John Kinney or Park Frazier was in town I'd say that it might be somethin' else. Kinney's in jail in Bridger an' Frazier's out of town so . . ."

"Who are they?" interrupted Llano.

Fallien glanced at his companion. "You've been here a day," he said brusquely. "Didn't Cameron tell you about Kinney? Didn't he mention Frazier?"

"Cameron," Llano said slowly, "tried to hire me to jump nesters off their claims. Cameron says that there are nesters on Grant land. We talked about that and that was all."

For a moment there was disbelief in Fallien's eyes. Then those eyes were masked with blankness again. "The new Grant boundary has just been confirmed by the territorial legislature," he said slowly. "I reckon there are nesters on Grant land."

"And . . . ?" prompted Llano.

"There's Grant an' Anti-Grant here, Land," continued Fallien when they had gone a few steps. "John Kinney an' Park Frazier are the men that lead the Anti-Grant. An' that's why I'd say there'd be trouble if they were here."

"You know a lot about it," said Llano dryly.

"It's my business . . ." began Fallien. Then checking suddenly, "I know somethin' about it, Land."

Llano looked quizzically at his companion. Fallien had said, "It's my business . . ." and stopped. If he had completed the sentence he would have said, "It's my business to know about such things." Was there a star under Fallien's shirt? Was there the little gold shield of a deputy U. S. Marshal fastened in some hidden spot on his clothing? Or was Dale Fallien, like Llano Land, a professional trouble shooter, a man seeking employment? Was he a spy, or what was he?

"Here's the church," announced Fallien. "Shall we go in?"

"Might as well," agreed Llano.

Gwynn Rae did not sleep well. She had remained with Wayne Metcalf for half an hour after Llano Land's departure and then had excused herself. Arthur Cameron and her brother had come in and joined them and she left the three men deep in a discussion of horse breeding.

In her room when she had undressed, she had sat for a long time beside her dressing table. Llano's actions and words had puzzled her and had hurt her. She had reacted instinctively and now she was wondering what had caused it all. As she sat beside her dressing table she was stirred from her thoughts by two dull, booming

56

explosions. For a while longer she sat, waiting, listening to hear if those shots were repeated and then, finally, when there was no more sound, she had extinguished her lamp and gone to bed.

She lay beneath her coverlet, her mind busy. Something had been done, something had been said to Llano Land that had caused that fierce outburst. She had questioned Metcalf concerning her rescuer and Metcalf, knowing something of Llano, had answered her questions. Now the brown, lean face of the man with anger blazing from his eyes, came between the girl and sleep. Llano Land! Some of his exploits, some of his adventures, Metcalf had told her, and seeing the man himself had intrigued her fancy and made the tales more true. What had happened that had lighted that fierce fire? The girl could not guess.

When she slept her slumber was troubled and when she wakened the next morning Llano Land was still in her thoughts.

At breakfast that morning her brother was silent and the talk was between Cameron and Metcalf. These tried to arouse Donald Rae's interest, bringing up both horses and hunting, subjects upon which Rae generally was eloquent, but this day he did not respond. When he did break his silence it was to ask a question.

"Where is Kent?" he asked, looking at Cameron.

Cameron shook his head slightly and made answer. "Kent has gone out of town for a day or two," he said. "Capes is with him."

Donald Rae disregarded that headshake. "Is that on account of what happened last night?" he persisted.

Cameron looked annoyed and Metcalf seemed worried. "Kent had business in Bridger," said Cameron. "There are papers to sign at the courthouse. He has

57

gone to attend to that."

Rae appeared satisfied with the explanation and asked no more questions. Talk lapsed about the breakfast table.

All during the morning Gwynn Rae busied herself with duties about Ladron House. She had assumed the ordering of the household since her advent, acting as chatelain of the castle, and she took a pride in the management of the great house.

At noon, when luncheon was served, she joined Metcalf in the hall and they stood waiting for Cameron and her brother. Gwynn Rae looked up at the soldierly young fellow in uniform that stood beside her. Metcalf's face was calm but there were firm lines about the eyes, and the mouth was tight lipped and strong. Gwynn knew that this man loved her. He rode from Bridger, a distance of sixty-five miles, coming as often as he could for a few hours with her. A gentleman, Wayne Metcalf, with generations of breeding behind him. His eyes were kind as he looked down at the girl.

"What happened in Ladron last night, Wayne?" demanded Gwynn. "Why was Arthur so upset this morning?"

Wayne Metcalf spoke honestly. "There was a man killed in town last night," he said, evenly. "A man named Loman. Dick Wadell was forced to shoot him to prevent his killing Kent."

"But . . ." began Gwynn.

"Loman's wife had died," continued Metcalf. "It seemed that he blamed Null for that. The man must have been insane with grief. He attacked Kent in a saloon and Wadell was forced to shoot to save Kent's life."

"But Arthur . . ." persisted Gwynn. "Why should that

58

affect him? He asked . . ."

Cameron and Donald Rae, entering the room at the moment, cut short the question.

"Lunch?" said Cameron. "My dear, you can't imagine how pleasant it is to have this place managed so well, particularly by so charming a manager."

Donald Rae put his hand beneath his sister's arm and they walked to the dining room together.

When the meal was finished Metcalf drew Gwynn aside. He must leave the next morning, he said, and now while he was here, would Gwynn be kind to him? Would she ride with him that afternoon? The girl could hardly refuse and leaving Metcalf, went to her room to change to her riding habit. When she reappeared the officer was waiting in the hall and the saddled horses were before the door. Metcalf helped the girl to mount, cradling her foot for a brief instant in his locked hands, then when he had mounted his big cavalry charger the two cantered away from Ladron House.

Their ride led them far afield. At times they rode slowly, side by side, and Gwynn Rae listened while Metcalf in his slow, southern drawl, spoke of his home in Virginia, and of his mother and sisters there. The girl knew what the young officer was leading to and the knowledge thrilled her. Still, when his voice lowered further and he began to speak of himself, she would not let him continue. The red roan mare was faster than the charger. The girl laughed tauntingly. They must race. Metcalf, wisely falling in with her spirit, forbore saying the thing that was uppermost in his heart and accepted the challenge gaily.

So they rode, and when the sun lowered a little, returned to Ladron, choosing another route than the one that they had followed on the ride out. So it was that approaching the town they topped a hill and riding down its side, saw a group of people gathered together. Both realized too late that they had come to the graveyard.

Metcalf tried to turn aside and circle the cemetery but Gwynn would not be dissuaded. She was suddenly contrite. Why should she have enjoyed herself in the company of this man who loved her, when here on the hillside there was sorrow and heartbreak and suffering?

"We must go down, Wayne," she insisted gently, "After all, it is the least we can do," and so, perforce, Wayne Metcalf rode beside the girl down the hill until they reached the outskirts of the crowd.

Llano Land and Dale Fallien came out of the church with their hats in their hands. They stepped aside from the door and waited until the rest of those people who had listened to James Gunther emerged. Women in calico, carrying their sunbonnets; children in clothing that had been cut down for them from worn out garments of their elders; hard, brown-faced men. The congregation that had listened to the funeral services of Will and Engra Loman, filed out and stood in the church yard.

When the pine boxes containing the bodies had been carried from the door and put in the bed of a wagon, Mulligan mounted to the driver's seat and starting the team began a last slow journey up the little hill above the church. On foot, the dust streaming up as they walked, the people followed, and suddenly Llano Land found that he was not alone with Dale Fallien, but that Rose Juell walked between them. Rose placed her hand on Llano's arm and silently fell in step with him.

The journey was short. Atop the hill, not three

hundred yards from the church, there were two open graves. Into these, one at a time, Mulligan and three others lowered the pine boxes that some native carpenter had made, and when they stepped back, Gunther came forward.

"There is nothing more to say," said James Gunther, standing at the heads of the graves, and his voice rang deep with the words. "I commend the souls of these two, man and wife, to God, and their memories to the hearts of their friends. Earth to earth . . ." and clods rattled down upon the wooden boxes . . . "ashes to ashes . . . dust to dust . . . Let us pray."

Heads were bowed and there was silence. Then Gunther lifted his head and turned, and Mulligan, spitting upon his hands, seized a shovel and again earth rattled down on the hollow pine. About Llano Land and Rose Juell and Dale Fallien, men and women stirred and turned, and low voices that had been stilled by Gunther's eloquence, began to hum once more. Llano put his hand beneath Rose's arm and with Fallien on the other side, they started to walk down the hill, following the slowly moving crowd.

It was then, not fifty feet from the graves, that Gwynn Rae swung the roan mare into their path and stopped them. Llano stepped forward, his face uplifted and his eyes eager.

"I . . ." Gwynn Rae began. "Mr. Land . . ."

But the thing she had been about to say was never finished. Rose Juell, after one glance at the face of the man beside her, wrenched her arm from Llano's grasp and stood at Gwynn Rae's stirrup. The rage that possessed her showed in the hard, resentful face which she turned to the younger girl.

"You!" flared Rose Juell. "You had the nerve to come

61

here. You dared to come after what you've done! It was you and your kind that killed Engra Loman. You and your brother and Kent Null and Arthur Cameron that drove Will Loman crazy. Oh, it might have been Wadell that did the shooting and killed Will, but it was you and the rest like you that made him lose his place. You took the roof off his wife's head. That killed her! She was already dying of consumption, but that made no difference to you. She hadn't a place to stay! She hadn't . . ."

"Rose!" Llano pleaded softly, "Rose, be still. You don't know what you're saying. You . . ."

"I won't be still!" flamed the girl. "She asked for this when she came here. She can take it. You," she turned on Gwynn, "can sit there on your horse and listen to what I tell you." Her eyes were on Gwynn's and under their flame Gwynn turned her head away. Metcalf reached out his hand, intending to take the roan mare's bridle and turn the horse, but Rose Juell, not to be stilled, read the final indictment that was in her bitter mind.

"Dick Wadell shot Loman," she shrilled. "At least he was honest about it. He shot him. He didn't sit by and let someone else do the dirty business while he took the profit. Wadell's a murderer but he's better than you!"

What more she might have said cannot be told for Metcalf at last caught the roan's bridle and swung the mare, and James Gunther coming up, his face sorrowful but his eyes glowing and bitter, laid his hands on Rose Juell's shoulders and swung her toward him. Sobs shook Rose Juell as Gunther held her, while on the red roan mare, Gwynn Rae, the proud English girl, sat, her head bowed, her body huddled into her broadcloth riding habit.

Llano Land watched Metcalf lead Gwynn's mare away. He watched James Gunther shepherd Rose Juell toward the church, and then he felt a hand on his shoulder. Dale Fallien's voice drawled words in his ear.

"I reckon it had to happen," said Fallien, "but . . . My God . . . !"

What more he might have said Llano did not know for at that moment Mulligan, his work finished, came up and stopped beside them. The barber's square face was impassive.

"The job's done," he announced.

Fallien put a hand in his pocket, pulled out money and handed a gold piece to the barber. "Thanks, Mulligan," he said.

Here was the answer to a riddle Llano had asked himself. An answer that proposed a new riddle. Dale Fallien had paid for the funerals of the Lomans. Dale Fallien had paid for them, but why? Out of regard for the man and his wife, or had Fallien, as had Llano himself, been filled with the determination that these two should go out of the world without a debt to the Duro Grant?

CHAPTER 6

THE TWO MEN, FALLIEN AND LAND, WALKED BACK toward the center of town. There were still wagons on the streets, other wagons and an occasional horseman riding in from the direction of the church. There were, too, little groups of men standing here and there. Some of the faces were familiar to Llano, some he had seen during his short sojourn in Ladron. It was plain that the town was dividing, separating into two parts, each

63

faction choosing a location, each faction waiting for the other to make a move.

"I don't like it," said Fallien, striding along beside Llano. "It looks bad, Land."

Llano made no reply for a moment. They walked on and presently Llano drawled: "There won't be anything."

"An' why not?" demanded Fallien sharply.

"Because," drawled Llano, "there's nobody to start it. If Null was to show up or if Wadell was to stick his head out, the whole thing might blow up, but Null an' Wadell are too wise for that."

"Mebbe you're right," agreed Fallien.

"I am right," Llano assured. "Wait an' you'll see. There! What did I tell you?"

One of the little groups on a corner had broken up. Three of the men who had stood there walked over to a wagon and, untying the team, climbed into the seat and the bed, backed the team away from the rack and started down the street. Another went into a store and emerged followed by a woman and a tow-headed boy. They also sought a wagon, backed it out, and began a slow progress toward the edge of town. Fallien seemed easier as he looked at Llano.

Llano shrugged. "There isn't a man in the bunch," he remarked casually. "There's maybe some part-men that would follow a leader, but there isn't a man."

"You talk like you were sorry," snapped Fallien. "You sound like you wish there'd be trouble."

"Maybe I do," returned Llano. "So long, Fallien."

He left the tall man staring after him and went on up the street toward the Saint George.

Llano had decided to move. It was past four o'clock but he wanted to shake the dust of Ladron's streets from him, wanted to get away. This thing, this trouble, was sucking like quicksand at his feet. He could feet it drawing him in and down. And it was not his trouble, not his business. Despite the strength of the feelings that welled in his mind when he thought of Engra and Will Loman, despite the pain that arose, sharp and yet somehow sweet when he thought of Gwynn Rae, Llano Land would not let himself be immersed. He was, in the final analysis, an onlooker, a spectator. His business was not with the Duro Grant, nor yet with the troubles of those who dwelt upon the Grant property. His business, and he forced himself to recall the fact, was to investigate the death of Jack Ames. And that was all; not Gwynn Rae, not Kent Null, not Arthur Cameron nor Flaco nor Rose Juell, but Jack Ames and Ames' murderer. Llano turned in at the door of the Saint George, and called for Nathan. When the hotel proprietor came Llano spoke shortly.

"I'm pulling out for Marthastown," he said. "I want my gray horse. You keep the other one here 'til I get back."

Nathan expostulated. It was late, said Nathan, and Marthastown was fifty miles away. The road was bad and there had been robberies on the road.

"I want that gray horse," answered Llano, "and I want him now."

So Nathan, his argument checked, went out of the lobby, and Llano Land went to his room. In his room he packed his saddlebags and carrying them, walked out into the lobby again. At the hitch rail Singleshot stood on three legs and fought flies, while in the lobby Nathan came forward with a bill.

Llano paid the bill and carrying the saddle bags walked out to his horse. When he had put the leather pouches behind his saddle he fastened them there, and when he had made sure that the cinch was tight, he swung up. Straddling the leather and turning Singleshot away from the hotel, Llano rode west, up the little hill past Ladron House. In front of Ladron House stood three cavalry horses, and two men, both in uniform, eyed Llano as he passed. One of these men bore the stripes of a sergeant and the other was without mark of rank. Llano nodded to them and went on.

Singleshot was a pacing horse. There are those who believe that a pacer can never make a cowhorse but even they cannot refute the fact that a pace covers ground. Singleshot, between daylight and dark, could put a hundred miles behind, and now, fresh and strong from his long rest the big, lead-colored gelding fairly ate up distance.

Still Llano did not urge the horse. He knew that somewhere between Ladron and Marthastown there would be a place to stop. The very nature of the country demanded that there be such a resting place, for at the head of Ladron Canyon the roads must branch, one toward Marthastown and the other toward Bridger. That would be the site for a stopping place and Ladron Canyon was not over twenty-five miles long. So Llano rode easily, letting Singleshot choose his gait and his path along the wagon road, while Llano, riding, watched the country.

His mind was busy as he rode. Llano had played a fool, or so he told himself, when he had refused Cameron's offer of employment. Given the knowledge that he now had concerning Jack Ames' death, he might have acted differently. The red roan mare that Gwynn Rae rode was an Ames horse. Llano would have given a good deal to know how the girl had come to own that

66

horse. But, by his actions, he had definitely cut himself off from any chance of obtaining that knowledge. He couldn't go to Cameron and ask how the Grant had come into possession of the mare. Not now he couldn't.

There was a chance that he might strike a lead in Marthastown. Discreet inquiries in the mining camp might unearth information. So Llano thought as Singleshot paced along. At least the trip would take him out of Ladron, and at the moment Llano wanted to be away.

He passed the mouth of the little canyon that led up to the pass to the Rincon. For a moment he was tempted to turn aside and go to McCarthy's. He could tell McCarthy what he had learned concerning Jack Ames' death and perhaps McCarthy could help him. Then Llano put the idea aside. He did not want to see McCarthy. He wanted to see no one, talk to no one, until his mind was more at rest.

Beyond the little canyon Llano came upon a wagon train, six wagons, each with four teams of mules, traveling toward Ladron. He passed the train, nodding to the drivers on their horses, and to the roustabouts who sat upon the wagons, and continued on his way. The sun had slipped behind the brown top of the big mountain at the head of the canyon. There were shadows, deep and dark, on the road. To Llano's left a creek came down. Singleshot, unchecked, watered at the creek and then went on.

Now the shadows merged and another creek ran into the canyon from the left. Climbing a long hill, Singleshot stopped at the top to breathe. The hills spread out to right and left, and before Llano lay a valley, bathed in the dusk. In the valley, the lights of a house glowed dimly. The lead-colored gelding swelled his ribs and sighed, swelled and sighed again and then under the urge of a nudging heel, went on down the slope.

As he climbed the hill Llano had left Ladron Creek. Now he encountered it again, three little forks coming together to make the main stream. He crossed two of these and riding up a little slope was at a building with corrals and a barn behind it. A man hurried from the barn and as Llano dismounted a plump gray-haired little woman appeared on the porch of the house.

"Can I stop the night?" asked Llano.

"This is a hotel," answered the woman on the porch. "Come in."

Llano removed his saddle bags, gave terse orders to the native who held Singleshot's reins, and climbed the steps to the porch. The little woman held the door open and Llano walked into the light.

Signing his name on the register Llano asked concerning supper and was informed that it would be ready as soon as he wished it. He was forced to smile at the gray-haired woman who spoke so quickly. "I just want to wash," he said.

"You can wash in your room," announced the woman. "You come this way, Mr. Land."

Llano followed her as, lamp in hand, she went down a corridor. She opened a door, put the lamp on a table and showed him where there were a washbasin and towel. "I'm Mrs. Stamps," she announced as she returned to the door. "Mostly them I know call me Gra'maw. You wash an' clean up an' supper'll be ready for you." With that she was gone, leaving Llano chuckling. He could readily understand why Mrs. Stamps was known as "Gra'maw." She must mother the whole community.

As soon as he had removed the dust of travel, Llano returned to the lobby. There a man sat reading, his back to Llano as he entered. The reader turned as Llano approached and nodded pleasantly. Llano, startled, returned the nod. The man was Kent Null.

"Headed for Marthastown, Mr. Land?" queried Null, folding the paper he held and putting it into an inner pocket.

"I'll go there in the morning," replied Llano. "Are you riding over?"

"Yes," Null nodded his agreement. "Tomorrow. I have business there for the Grant."

Llano made no reply to that and Gra'maw Stamps appeared in a door to the right and informed Llano that supper was ready.

While he ate the meal Llano pondered on Null's presence. He wondered if there was someone with Null and what Null might be doing in Marthastown. Finally when the meal was finished, he arose from the table and returned to the lobby. Null was still there and with him was black-haired Dick Wadell. Llano would have passed them by, going on to the porch, but Null stopped him.

"You know Mr. Wadell, Mr. Land?" he asked and when neither spoke: "Let me make you acquainted then."

Wadell held out his hand and perforce Llano took it. He dropped Wadell's hand after a perfunctory pressure and started on toward the porch. Again Null stopped him.

"We would be glad if you would ride with us to Marthastown tomorrow, Mr. Land."

"If we start at the same time," Llano agreed cautiously, mentally making up his mind that the start would not be simultaneous.

"Your time will be ours," Null said graciously. "Will

you have a cigar, Mr. Land?"

"Thanks," said Llano shortly. "I don't use 'em," and turning again he made his way to the porch.

Sitting on the steps he rolled a cigarette and having lit it, smoked reflectively for a while. He had thrown that cigarette away and was rolling another when Null came out alone and stood above him.

"Pretty night," said Null.

"Nice," agreed Llano. He lit his cigarette. Null seated himself on the step beside him.

"That's quite a horse you ride," commented Null, looking at his companion.

"Pretty fair," answered Llano.

"Fast," said Null. "Ever race him?"

"No." Llano puffed his smoke.

"Cameron said you came up on that mare of Gwynn's as though she were standing still." Null's voice was cheerful. Apparently he chose to disregard Llano's ungraciousness. "I told Arthur that the mare was too spirited for Gwynn."

"That roan mare is a good horse," Llano offered. He had turned toward Null now and was looking intently at the lawyer. If Null wanted to talk horses perhaps Llano could find out how the Grant had come by the roan. "Was she bred around here?" Llano continued.

Null, sitting in the light that came from the door, shook his head. "Arthur bought her from a miner," he said. "Someone from Marthastown. This man went broke in Ladron and sold his horse. The Grant bought her."

"I see," said Llano. "Good horses in Marthastown?"

"Some," Null answered. "Are you interested in horses, Mr. Land?"

"Some horses," Llano answered Null's query. "I like thoroughbreds."

"Thoroughbreds?" Null got up and his cigar tip glowed red, then died away.

Llano waited. Let Null make the conversation, let Null do the leading. Out on the road, hoofs pounded. There was a splashing in the fords of the little creeks. A rider, his horse running, appeared in the light that came from a window, going past the house toward the barn. Llano moved on the steps and Null, above him, was tense. Inside the house there was movement and Mrs. Stamps' voice, high and sharp. Llano got up from the steps.

As he moved toward the door he heard sounds again, the muffled thudding of hoofs on the road. Null was beside him, had passed, and was opening the screen door of the house. Llano poised a moment, listening. The screen slammed and again Mrs. Stamps' voice came, more shrill than before. What was this? Llano didn't know.

As he laid his hand on the screen to open it horses again splashed in the ford, many horses now, and coming rapidly. As a voice hailed out of the night Llano relinquished his hold on the door handle and stepped back. Men were riding up, stopping their horses before the porch, dismounting. Llano, turning, could see some of them in the light from the door. They made an odd sight: gunny sacking had been used to mask men and horses. The men were covered, some with robes and bandanas tied about their heads, others with sharp pointed hoods that ran down into capes. There was one masked in a sheet. The horses likewise were disguised, only their ears and eyes showing through holes in their masking.

The screen door opened and Mrs. Stamps came out on the porch.

71

"What do you want?" she demanded.

The man in the sheet answered that question. "We want Kent Null an' Dick Wadell," he said hoarsely. "We know they're here an' we want 'em."

"They ain't here . . ." began Gra'maw Stamps, fury and fright in her voice. "They ain't . . ."

"Don't lie," said the white-sheeted man sternly. "We know they're here. Bring 'em out if you don't want the place burnt!"

Gra'maw Stamps moved swiftly. She reached inside the door and when her hand reappeared it clutched a shotgun. The white-sheeted man who had climbed the steps of the porch, moved as swiftly as the woman. He wrenched the shotgun from her hands before she could lift it, and held the weapon away. In the shadows Llano could not but admire this old woman. She was protecting her guests and her property.

"Trot out Null an' Wadell," commanded the sheeted man. "Bring 'em out."

"What do you want with Null," demanded the woman. "What . . ."

"We're goin' to take him out an' hang him to the nearest cottonwood," came the answer. "You know about Engra an' Will Loman? You heard what he done to them?"

Gra'maw Stamps collected herself. "This is my place!" she announced. "It's a public house. I treat you all alike. Grant men an' Anti-Grant men. You know that. You know that I'll feed anybody that stops whether they got money or not. Like enough I've fed some of you. You go away! You ain't goin' to take anybody from my house an' . . ."

There was an interruption. Kent stepped through the doorway and stood in the light, his face calm and impassive. He made an impressive figure there, for all his light body and scant height. Calmly he confronted the men on the porch and in front of it and his voice was composed as he spoke.

"What do these men want, Mrs. Stamps?"

"They come for you an' Dick Wadell," answered Gra'maw Stamps. "They say they're goin' to take you out an' hang you. I been tellin' them . . ."

"Wadell is gone," said Null. "Word of your . . . ah . . . arrival preceded you and Mr. Wadell has ridden away. As for me I am here but I do not know what I've done to warrant your hanging me."

"You know what you done, Null," growled the man in the white sheet. "You killed Will Loman an' his wife. Took their place away from 'em. We ain't goin' to waste time on you, Null. Are we, boys?"

There was perhaps a little uncertainty lying behind the fierceness of those last words. Perhaps there was a request for confirmation, for help. If so, that confirmation came. There was a concerted movement among the half dozen men on the porch and in front of the house, a surging forward. Null stood stolid, not moving. Mrs. Stamps gave a little scream and reached out toward the white-sheeted man.

From the darkness beyond the porch Llano Land spoke coldly, three words: "Hold it, there!"

Llano had stepped away from the door when the horses came up, fading into the shadows. With Null's advent and the concentration of attention upon the Grant lawyer he had slipped over the porch rail and now he stood to the left and behind the men in front of and on the porch. His was the position of command and he held it.

The words caused consternation among the hooded

figures. Some turned and two started down the steps. Llano stopped that.

There was utter finality in his voice as he spoke.

"I'll kill the man that moves," said Llano Land.

The group on the porch froze. There was a slight relaxing of Kent Null's shoulders and his voice was easier when he said:

"Thank you, Mr. Land."

Llano could have cursed the man. He had hoped to remain unidentified. Forced to take a hand in these proceedings he had hoped that his part would never be known. Now, by his words, Kent Null had identified him and, more than that, definitely tied him up with the Duro Grant. Null must have seen that, for he spoke again, making assurance doubly certain.

"That is Llano Land, gentlemen. Perhaps you have heard of him. If not, may I say that he is the man that brought law to Trinity and that he is considered a dead shot. What do you intend to do to these men, Mr. Land?"

Llano's voice was hoarse with anger. Null had betrayed his identity and now there was nothing to do but go on. "Line up!" he commanded. "Move easy. I'm Llano Land, right enough, and I mean what I say."

There was a little movement on the porch. Disguised men, afraid of that cold-voiced man in the dark, shifted position until they formed a straggling line. Null spoke again.

"Shall I strip off the masks?" he asked.

"Let the masks alone!" ordered Llano harshly. "Gra'maw, you go down behind 'em. Take their guns. Get your shotgun. Stay behind 'em now!"

Mrs. Stamps was of the pioneer breed. She had been prepared to defend her guests; now she obeyed Llano's

74

orders. Down the line she went, careful to keep behind the men and in the clear. Some wore their weapons belted over their disguising robes; others did not, but from each man she took a heavy pistol, and at the end of the line she stopped.

"I got 'em all," said Gra'maw Stamps.

"It's easy," said Llano Land, out in the darkness, "to come riding in and run it over a woman an' man that isn't armed. It's plenty easy, when you got yourselves covered so nobody can know you. There isn't a man amongst the bunch. You're a bunch of whipped pups. Now you fork your horses and don't come back! Get out of here an' keep riding!"

For an instant the men on the porch stood still. Then the man in the sheet moved toward the steps, and the others, breaking line, followed him. They went down the steps and not stopping, went to their horses. The white-sheeted man swung up. He wheeled his mount toward Llano Land.

"Land!" he said bitterly. "We'll remember you, Land. So the Grant has hired another killer, has it? Well, we won't forget. We'll . . ."

"Shut up!" Llano snapped contemptuously. "Ride your horse out of here and thank God I'll let you. Get!"

As he spoke he stepped into the light. There was the blue steel of a weapon glinting in his hand and his face was hard and stern. More than the weapon, his face enforced the command. The man in the white sheet wheeling his horse, moved out, and one by one the others followed him. When they were gone Llano holstered the Smith & Wesson in the leather at his waist band and walked toward the steps.

"Thank you, Mr. Land," said Kent Null courteously. "I am indebted to you."

"You're indebted to Mrs. Stamps," said Llano. "It was her I acted for. As far as I'm concerned, Null, they could take you out and hang you high as heaven and I wouldn't move, but when an old lady takes the play I'll step in."

"I see," Kent Null said slowly. "I see."

"It's good you do," answered Llano. "Let's go inside, Gra'maw."

"But they'll be back," began Gra'maw Stamps. "Some of 'em will have rifles on their saddles an' they'll get some more men an' . . ."

"They won't be back," Llano said contemptuously. "Not that breed. They'll ride a long ways and in the morning they'll have a tall tale to tell about what they should have done and the bunch of men that jumped 'em. I'm going to bed, Gra'maw. There won't be trouble tonight."

He pushed past the little old woman and the small man who stood beside her, and went to the door. At the door he stopped and looked at Kent Null.

"I don't like you, Null," said Llano deliberately, "but I'll hand you this: You've got guts and you're smart. Good night, Gra'maw."

The screen door slammed and Llano Land was gone.

"Well . . ." said Gra'maw Stamps, after a moment's pause. "Well, I do declare. Hadn't you better get your horse an' ride to Ladron, Mr. Null? Ain't you afraid they'll be back?"

Kent Null was standing, staring at the door. He spoke absently to Gra'maw Stamps. "They won't be back tonight, Mrs. Stamps," he said, musingly. "No, he is right about that: they won't come back. But I'm not so sure that he is right about the rest. I'm not so sure that I am as clever as I thought."

76

CHAPTER 7

FLACO WAS A SHORT, SQUAT MAN. HE HAD NO OTHER name than Flaco, no name that he answered to. In Trinity he had been accepted by the gambling fraternity but that acceptance had come by accident. He was not of the top flight by nature, and nature had had her way with him. A sleeve hold-out, drink, a stuffed box, and in a final pinch a double-barreled derringer, were his stock in trade. And when the cards went wrong, a knife or a piece of pipe in an alley served in lieu of skill and cold nerve.

Flaco had brought Rose Juell from Trinity. For a time, in Greenwall, they had been together. Then Ladron had beckoned and they had answered, and now, in Ladron, Flaco had lost Rose. The girl worked now for the Exchange Saloon. She was paid a weekly wage and given a percentage on the drinks she sold and on the money that came in over Flaco's faro table. Independent, she had shortly rid herself of Flaco, he having served his purpose. Now, having had the girl, Flaco was athirst to possess her again. Too dull-witted to know that such possession was impossible, he strove to regain the thing that he had lost. His want had grown into a consuming passion until all that Flaco could think of was the dark haired woman.

Of course he had lucid intervals, times when his thoughts of Rose were submerged by other knavery, and during those periods Flaco was a good hand and an adjunct to Dick Wadell who carried out Cameron's orders. Flaco did those things that were too far down the scale for Wadell to do.

Flaco's partner was a native named Huerta. Huerta

was tall where Flaco was short, and thin where Flaco was heavy set. Aside from that the difference between them was that Flaco was afraid and Huerta smoked marijuana and feared nothing. The two stayed together, engaging in whatever form of profitable villainy they could find.

On the night of Loman's funeral, Flaco, accompanied by Huerta, went to the door of the long adobe house where Rose Juell stayed. Having freed herself from the man, Rose now held herself aloof, speaking to Flaco only when she was at the Exchange. Selecting her door from the others that opened on the street, Flaco knocked.

Rose answered. "Who is it?"

"Flaco," answered the squat man. "Let me in, Rose."

Rose Juell was too tired to argue. She was, she believed, perfectly competent to handle Flaco. She knew that Flaco feared Cameron and she had more than an idea that Cameron desired her. Besides she carried a knife in her garter, a slim, vicious weapon, and she knew that she was smarter than the man outside. To avoid disturbance Rose opened the door.

Flaco, with Huerta following him, sidled into the little room and looked around. Like many another of her kind, Rose Juell was intensely religious, although she subscribed to no particular church or creed. A cross hung in a corner of the room and on the wall there were two prints, both gaudy, both highly colored, and both culled from some magazine issued for use in a Sunday School. There was a bed in the room, a table, two chairs and a little dresser. Aside from that, one corner was curtained off to make a wardrobe.

"I wanted to talk to you, Rose," Flaco remarked, seating himself, while Huerta squatted down against the wall.

78

"Go ahead," said the girl listlessly. There were circles under her dark eyes and her face showed tired lines.

"You talked to Land last night," continued Flaco. "Why is he over here, Rose?"

"He didn't tell me," Rose Juell lied, and looked at her questioner from beneath lowered lids.

Flaco disregarded that. "Is he goin' to work the same thing he did in Trinity?" he demanded.

Rose shrugged. "I don't know," she answered listlessly.

"Is he goin' to work for Cameron?" Flaco pushed his questions.

Rose shook her head. "He didn't tell me what he was going to do," she said impatiently. "If you want to know about Llano Land why don't you ask him?"

"You could find out," said Flaco cunningly. "You could . . . Look here, Rose, Land's sweet on you an' you know it."

"He's not!" The girl refuted Flaco's statement. "He . . ."

"But yo're sweet on him," persisted Flaco. "You could get him to tell you what he's here for."

"How?" Rose lifted her eyes to the gambler.

Flaco grunted. "There's ways," he said evilly. "You know how, Rose."

"You'd better get out of here!" The girl spat the words at the man. "Who do you think you are, Flaco? If Cameron found you bothering me, he'd . . ."

Flaco shrugged. "Cameron is goin' to want to know what you been foolin' around that preacher for," he suggested. "Cameron ain't goin' to like that. You can't stall Cameron off like you stalled me, Rose."

Rose Juell got up from the chair beside the table. "James Gunther is too good a man for you to touch with

79

your dirty tongue," she said bitterly. "I know that you don't like him and that Cameron don't like him. That's because you're afraid of him. He can see through you and he can see through Cameron. He knows what you are trying to do. If James Gunther ever says the word you and Cameron and all of your dirty bunch will be on the road to hell, and I hope that you burn there!"

Flaco came out of his chair as though he had come in sudden contact with a hot coal. "Damn you!" he berated, "I was good enough for you to go with out of Trinity, an' now you try to spit on me. You think Cameron's sweet on you an' that he'll help you. Cameron knows what you are. He'll take you an' use you an' throw you out. You been honeyin' around that preacher. You think he can help you. You called Land over to a booth last night. I suppose you told him you'd . . ."

The gambler stopped before the fierceness in Rose Juell's eyes.

"Damn it, Rose," he mumbled, "you ought to do somethin' for me. After all, I helped you out when you needed help. You could find out what Land's doin' over here, couldn't you? By God, I got to know. I . . ."

A fire of anger was burning fiercely in Rose Juell. Her eyes flamed and under their heat Flaco retreated. "I'll tell you what Llano Land is here for," grated the girl. "He's here to look for a man named Jack Ames and for some horses Ames had. If you know . . ." The girl stopped. Flaco had suddenly turned a dirty gray. His eyes were big with fright.

"You do know!" Rose Juell made accusation. "You know about Ames. Was he that yellow haired cowboy that . . ?" She read her answer in Flaco's eyes. Her hand went to her mouth, stifling the scream that formed in her throat.

"Damn you, Rose!" snarled Flaco. "You . . !"

"You killed him!" The girl's words were a whisper, her voice hoarse. "That's where you got that money. That's . . ." The girl was pale. The anger had gone from her eyes and fear took its place. She had guessed too much and guessed correctly. Flaco's face told her that. Beside the wall, Huerta, a marijuana cigarette between his lips, stirred uneasily, and Flaco took a step forward.

"Now, Rose," said Flaco smoothly.

"What are you going to do?" The girl's voice lifted. "What . . . ? My God, Flaco!"

Flaco was edging forward. "I'm goin' to teach you not to talk," he purred. "I'm goin' to take yore pretty throat and squeeze it 'til you can't talk. You'll tell Land I killed Ames, will you? You'll . . ."

"I didn't tell him anything," said Rose hoarsely. "I didn't . . . Flaco . . !"

Flaco went on, apparently not heeding the interruption. "You'll tell Land that I took Ames' money? I don't think you'll ever tell him anythin'!"

The man sprang suddenly, his short, thick arms reaching out for Rose. Rose Juell screamed. As Flaco leaped she shoved the table toward him, checking him momentarily, and as he recoiled from the table she flung herself at the door, clawed it open and, still screaming, fled down Ladron's street.

Flaco, bouncing back from the table, tripped over Huerta and sprawled on the floor. He gathered himself, came up from the floor and, flinging a curse at Huerta, threw himself through the door. Rose was already some twenty yards away, running, heading toward the main street of the little town. Flaco jerked the derringer from his waist pocket, raised it and then, some sanity returning to him, lowered the gun again. He stepped

81

back through the door, reached down a hand and jerked Huerta to his feet.

"You damned fool!" raged Flaco. "Why didn't you stop her? Why didn't you help me? Do you know what she'll do now? She'll find Land and if she hasn't already told him she'll tell him now."

"What?" said Huerta stupidly.

Flaco cursed again and shoved Huerta. The taller man reeled against the wall, struggled and regained his equilibrium. Flaco was already going out through the door and as a dog follows his master, Huerta followed the gambler.

Rose Juell ran until she reached the corner and turned into the main thoroughfare of Ladron. She knew that Flaco would follow her and she knew that if Flaco caught her he would kill her. The girl had been distraught and hysterical when she had talked to the squat gambler. Earlier in the day, she had dressed the body of Engra Loman, a trying enough experience. She had attended the funeral and had heard James Gunther speak. Then she had met Gwynn Rae and had thrown an accusation at that proud woman's face. Gunther had pacified Rose, had talked to her soothingly, speaking of peace and forgiveness, and Rose Juell, still perturbed, had at last gone to her room. Now this had happened, this thing that had unleashed all the evil in Flaco. Rose Juell knew that the gambler meant to kill her, would kill her. Terror stricken she sought refuge and the only haven that occurred to her was Llano Land.

Llano Land would protect her. Llano Land, when she told him that Flaco and the man Huerta had ambushed Jack Ames, killed him and taken his money, would act, act at once. Llano Land would kill Flaco, Rose Juell was sure, and because in Flaco's death lay her only safety,

82

Rose Juell fled toward Llano Land. Not that she reasoned these things, not that she coldly calculated upon Flaco's death. No, the girl turned instinctively toward Llano Land because he was strong and straight and a haven, and because she loved him.

She slowed her gait on the main street, hurrying but not running. Past curious men, past stores, past the Exchange Saloon, she made her way toward the Saint George Hotel, and in the lobby of the Saint George she asked Nathan for Llano Land.

Nathan grunted. Llano Land, he said, was gone. Llano Land, Nathan implied, was a damned fool. He would be back, Nathan believed, because he had left a horse. When Llano would return Nathan did not know.

Rose Juell looked about her uncertainly. "I'd like a room," she said. "I want to stay here until Mr. Land comes."

Nathan shook his head. "This is a respectable house," said Nathan virtuously. "You can't have a room. An' I'll tell Land when he comes back that he can't have you comin' here. He can keep his women out of the Saint George."

Rose Juell turned, seemed to slump. The fire, the life, went out of the girl and only fear remained. For an instant she stood, poised there in the lighted lobby of the Saint George. Then, with her head lowered, making no retort to the smug Nathan, she went out of the door. Llano Land was gone and with him Rose Juell's last hope was gone.

On the walk in front of the hotel she stood for a few moments, trying to collect her thoughts, trying to think of some way out. Somewhere near were Flaco and Huerta, and Rose Juell knew that she must have a refuge from them. And there, standing in front of the Saint

83

George, she caught at and grasped an idea, a feeble straw that might float her to safety. There was one man in Ladron to whom she could go, one man that was a tower of strength. If she could reach the house of James Gunther she believed that she would be safe. So, gathering her skirts in her hand, she set out, fearful of the shadows, frightened by the men she passed who leered at her. Rose Juell, who had never before known fear, now sought the safety James Gunther might afford her. Down the street she went, and near the end of the street, near the little church that stood isolated as though to avoid the contamination of the town, she came to an adobe building, stopped, and knocked on the door.

There was a pause then and Rose Juell knocked again, a frightened tattoo of trembling knuckles. Then the door swung open and James Gunther stood in the light. In his left hand was a leather bound book, a Bible, and in his right, held firmly and cocked, was a heavy Colt. The light streamed out past him and struck Rose Juell's face, reflected the terror in her eyes. She held out a hand and Gunther, laying the pistol aside, stretched out his own strong right hand and caught that extended by the girl.

"Come," said James Gunther in his deep, strong, kindly voice. "Come. And whatever it is, it need frighten you no more."

Rose Juell caught her breath in a choked sob and allowed herself to be led into the house.

In the Exchange Saloon, Flaco, with Huerta moving behind him like a somnambulist, sought Denver Capes. He caught the eye of the tawny-haired Capes, nodded toward a booth and went into it. After a time Capes broke off his talk with the bartender and strolled over. Sliding into a seat in the booth Capes looked at Flaco.

"Well," he growled, "what do you want, Flaco?"

Flaco scarcely knew how to begin. The expedition during which he and Huerta had killed Jack Ames had been strictly a private affair and Capes knew nothing of it save only that Flaco had suddenly come into possession of money. Flaco shrugged, looked at Huerta for help, and receiving none from that source, turned again to Capes.

"I been havin' some trouble with Rose," he began awkwardly. "Looks like she's quit me."

Capes laughed scornfully. "She never was with you," he jeered. "Still, that'll be good news to Cameron."

Flaco disregarded the jibe. "I was tryin' to find out what that damn' Land is doin' over here," he continued. "Rose got him off in a booth last night an' I thought mebbe she'd found out somethin', so I asked her."

"An' she told you to go to hell," surmised Capes. "What do you care what Land's doin'? He'll be took care of."

"I found out what he was doin'," said Flaco. "He's over here lookin' for a man. There . . ."

"Lookin' for a man?" Capes lifted his eyebrows.

"Yeah," said Flaco. "A fellow named Ames. He had a bunch of horses. He sold 'em in Marthastown . . ." Flaco stopped. He had said a little too much.

"Sold 'em in Marthastown, did he?" Capes cocked up his eyebrows again. "An' then what happened?"

There was no use stalling. Flaco had to go on. "Me an' Huerta rustled his roll," he completed sullenly.

Capes thought for a moment. "Ames," he mused. "He wouldn't be that fella that Dick found out in an alley about a month ago, would he? The fella that had a knife hole in his back?"

Flaco shrugged. "I . . ." he began.

"You killed him an' took his roll," Capes stated flatly. "It looks like Land might make a find of you, Flaco."

"Well?" said Flaco defiantly. "What about it? Is that any worse than stoppin' the stage, killin' the messenger an' takin' the pay load?"

A slow color flooded Capes' face. "It seems to me," he drawled, "that you know just a little too damn' much, Flaco. Mebbe you been around here too long."

Flaco held up his hand. "Now, Denver," he placated, "I ain't never talked. I ain't never said a word. Land's lookin' for Ames but you know he worked for Wells Fargo once. You know . . ."

"Well?" snarled Capes.

"Well," Flaco set his feeble inventive powers to work, "he's still workin' for 'em. This Ames business is just a stall. The express on the stage is all Wells Fargo, ain't it? Wouldn't the Wells Fargo like to know what happened to that shipment? Pat Greybull has been raisin' hell, you know. Now here comes Llano Land . . ." Flaco let the words trail off. Cunningly he stopped in time.

Denver Capes' face darkened. "So Land's lookin' for the men that took the gold shipment," he mused. "When Dick gets back we'll see if Land can't find 'em."

Flaco breathed a sigh of relief. Llano Land's destiny, he felt, was now assured and in competent hands. Capes turned to Flaco again and there was a cruel smile on his face.

"Now, Flaco," he chided, "about that cash. You wouldn't go an' freeze two good friends like Dick an' me out of that deal, would you? How much did you get? I reckon we'll just split, fifty-fifty."

CHAPTER 8

LLANO LAND DID NOT SEE KENT NULL IN THE morning. Despite his assurance to Mrs. Stamps and to the lawyer, Llano was far from confident when he left them. He went to the room that Mrs. Stamps had assigned him, but he did not undress. He sat down on the bed and waited. After a time he stretched out but still stayed awake, listening. He wondered who had brought the word of the night riders to Null and Wadell, and he wondered why Wadell had fled without the lawyer.

After midnight, when nothing more happened, Llano slept, to awaken at intervals, and finally when morning broke, he arose and went to the kitchen. Mrs. Stamps, looking much as though she had spent a sleepless night, had coffee on the stove and was making biscuits when Llano entered the room. She greeted him cheerfully, told him that there was a washbasin outside, and when he returned to the kitchen, his face shining and his hair combed, she poured him a cup of coffee and made him sit down at the kitchen table.

Llano sat there drinking his coffee and Gra'maw rolled out the biscuit dough and cut it, filling the greased pans. As she worked she talked and Llano learned a number of things concerning the Duro Grant. Gra'maw Stamps was grateful to Llano for his intervention. She thanked him for that and when Llano waved the thanks aside, she divulged information.

The Duro Grant, so said Mrs. Stamps, was spreading out. A boundary had recently been confirmed and now the Grant claimed land that had been held for a long time by small ranchmen and farmers. The Grant, or so said Gra'maw, was offering two alternatives to those men who were on Grant land: They could either pay a small rental to the Grant and thus be assured of protection, or they could vacate the property. The ranchmen and farmers themselves were substituting another alternative: They were sitting tight, refusing to pay rent and refusing to move.

"You see," explained Gra'maw, sliding pans into the hot oven, "they know if they pay rent they're admittin' that the Grant owns the land. They won't vacate. I don't blame 'em. All they got is in their little places. They're just stayin' still. The Grant gets deputies an' such out to move 'em an' they get together an' ride like they done last night. I expect I know every boy that was on my porch but I'm glad that you didn't make 'em take off their masks, Mr. Land."

"There was no use to it," said Llano. "I didn't want to know who they were. All I wanted was for 'em to pull out."

Gra'maw Stamps looked cunningly at Llano. "I hung them guns out on the corral fence last night," she announced. "They was all gone this mornin'."

"Mmmm," Llano grunted.

"An' the horses were back," said Mrs. Stamps, triumphantly.

"Were the horses gone?" asked Llano.

"That Dick Wadell," Gra'maw spoke contemptuously. "He was out in the barn when Len . . . when word come in that there was a bunch comin'. Wadell had taken a horse an' run an' he left the corral gate open and the horses got loose. That's why Null couldn't get away. That Dick Wadell is a skunk."

"Hmmm," said Llano again.

Mrs. Stamps sighed. "There's trouble in the country,"

88

she stated. "Even for a peaceful body like me. I've paid my rent to the Grant an' I ain't complainin'. I guess they'll let me stay here as long as I want to. But when they start to shut down the mines . . ."

"What?" demanded Llano.

"The new boundary cuts right square through Marthastown," said Gra'maw. "Of course the Grant will try to grab the land. There's gold on it. They'll try to shut down the mines an' then there *will* be trouble."

Llano let go a long, tenuous whistle. "Trouble!" he echoed.

"Them miners," affirmed Mrs. Stamps, "won't just lie down an' take it. They'll fight. Then the Grant will fight back an' my business will just be ruined."

Llano got up from his chair. "I'll bet you that the biscuits are done," he announced. "If I could have a couple of biscuits an' a little bacon I'd go along, Mrs. Stamps."

Gra'maw bustled to the stove. "I'll fix you a place in just a minute," she announced. "You set right back down an' I'll fix it for you."

When he had eaten breakfast and paid Mrs. Stamps, over her protests, Llano went out to the barn. Singleshot was in the corral and he nickered when he saw Llano. The horse had been fed, the barn boy said, and Llano went into the corral, caught the gelding and saddling, mounted. As he rode off toward the north he waved good-by to Gra'maw Stamps who stood on the porch and flapped a floursack dishtowel at her parting guest.

The road to Marthastown led up a little valley. On either side mountains reared themselves, and a creek, muddied and roiled by the placer operations above, cut through the center of the valley. Llano crossed the creek a time or two and presently came to signs of mining operations. Here the gravel from the bedrock had been gouged up by a dredge and having been washed clean, redeposited in long windrows. After a time Llano came to the dredge itself, a gaunt skeleton with bowels made of boiler plate, that growled and grunted and rumbled as the endless chain of buckets fed the maw. There were men at the dredge, on it and about it, and Llano rode over, quelling Singleshot's apprehension, and accosted the men.

Pat Greybull, so the dredge operators told Llano, was in town. At his office, they shouted, and Llano, thanking them, rode on.

Above the dredge there were other operations. There were long sluices and at these men toiled. A ditch ran water and men threw gravel and earth into the wooden boxes, allowing the water to float away the lighter material and leave only the heavy, gold bearing sand. Llano had no time to stop. He rode on and within a mile Marthastown lay before him.

At one time Marthastown had boasted eight thousand men. In those roaring days the town had had its man for breakfast every morning. Now the production of gold had steadied and the first wild boom was over. Still the town was populous for there were men driving tunnels in the hills, men placering the creek and prospectors drifting in and out. All of these required service and Marthastown had its saloons and gambling halls, its stores and warehouses, its dwellings and its hotel. Llano Land, riding toward the center of the town, saw these things, saw miners off shift loafing along the walks, saw women look from curtained windows and smile, saw merchants in their stores, and eventually arrived at the building that housed Pat Greybull's office. A ragged boy pointed out the place and Llano, dismounting, tied

Singleshot to the hitchrail and went in.

There was a railing inside the room he entered and two men behind the railing. One was a clerk with a green eye-shade. The other was short and gray and red-faced. He turned as Llano entered and, advancing to the railing, looked at his visitor.

"What can I do for you?" asked the short man.

"Mr. Greybull?" inquired Llano.

The short man nodded. Here was a direct, forthright man, Llano saw, a man that would answer yes or no and not equivocate. Llano went directly to his business.

"I'm here looking for a man named Jack Ames," explained Llano Land. "Do you know anything about him?"

"Who are you?" demanded Greybull.

"My name's Land," answered Llano. "Llano Land. I'm a friend of Ames. Ames had some horses . . ."

"I bought a horse from him," interrupted Greybull. "A bay gelding. He had seven horses and he disposed of them here. Sold them all. There are one or two around town now. Some of the men that bought from him are gone."

"How long ago did you buy the horse, Mr. Greybull?" asked Llano. "I'd like . . ."

The door behind Llano opened and Kent Null, with Dick Wadell behind him, entered the office. Null nodded pleasantly to Llano, spoke to him and turned to Greybull. Greybull's face was dark with color and there was an angry glint in his eyes.

"Are you busy, Mr. Greybull?" asked Null pleasantly. "If you are . . ."

"I'll come back," said Llano to Greybull. He nodded to Null and Wadell and turning on his heel left the office.

Strolling down the street Llano looked into the windows and stopped at one of the saloons. He was impatient. Null and Wadell had come in at the wrong time. There were questions that Llano wanted to ask Greybull, questions concerning Jack Ames and the men with whom Ames had associated. Here he might pick up some trace, some clue to the thing he sought. When he came out of the saloon he received a surprise. Across the street, mounted, was one of the Savoy twins and, as Llano stopped at the sight, Shorty Hamarick came out of a butcher shop and walked toward a pack horse that the Savoy held by a lead rope.

The Savoy had seen Llano and he grinned and nodded. Llano, crossing the street, returned the greeting. He halted beside the mounted man and said Hello, including both the Savoy and Hamarick in the salutation. There was meat on the packhorse. Hamarick was unlashing the rope that held the pack in place and Llano could see part of a side of beef.

"Hello, Land," greeted Hamarick, and Savoy, still grinning, said: "How are yuh, Land?"

"I didn't look for you here," said Llano.

Hamarick's smile was broad. "We got beef," he said, "an' they got dust. Always a market for beef in Marthastown."

"I imagine so," agreed Llano. He knew that the beef on the pack was stolen, knew it as well as if he had taken the animal himself. It was none of his business. In a way he and these men were allies. Mat McCarthy had said that he would help Llano and these were Mat's men.

"Where's Mat?" asked Llano.

"Holed up in the cabin," answered the Savoy. "When you comin' out, Land? We been lookin' for you."

"I'll stop in on my way back," announced Llano. "Don't you boys get to town? I kind of thought that I'd buy you a drink in Ladron."

"We been busy," said Hamarick. "They'll take that beef, Arch. We might as well unload."

Arch Savoy started down from his horse and Hamarick began to unlash the pack. He grinned wryly at Llano. "Don't help us," he said, derisively. "This ain't yore kind of beef, Land. Wait 'til it's cooked an' the curse is offen it."

Llano laughed. "You boys eat with me an' we'll see if the curse is off," he grinned. "I'll meet you at the Chink's at dinner time."

Both Savoy and Hamarick laughed, and Hamarick, speaking for them both, agreed. "That joint down the street uses our beef," he said. "We'll meet you there."

Llano looked to where Hamarick was pointing, saw a restaurant sign, and nodding, went on down the street while Arch Savoy casually shouldered a side of beef and carried it into the butcher shop.

Llano Land killed time around Marthastown. He stopped in the stores, in a saloon or two where he took a modest drink, and sat on the steps of one of the stores while he watched a prospector loading two burros preparatory to a trip into the hills. The prospector's wealth of profanity was marvelous and Llano listened to that packing in awe.

While he loafed, Llano watched Greybull's office. Null and Wadell did not come out and presently Llano rose and strolled down the street toward the restaurant for it was almost noon.

Within a few moments of his arrival at the restaurant Hamarick and Savoy rode up, stopped, and tied their horses. When they joined Llano he could tell that both

93

had been drinking for the whiskey was heavy on their breaths.

Hamarick hailed Llano, said that he was ready to eat, and suggested a drink before the meal. Arch Savoy concurred in the suggestion and Llano, falling in beside the two accompanied them to a saloon two doors from the restaurant. The drink that Llano bought called for a round from Shorty Hamarick and that called for a round from Arch Savoy, so in place of one drink there were three taken before the men left the bar and went out on the walk again.

As they emerged from the saloon Kent Null and Dick Wadell rode toward them, coming from the direction of Greybull's office. Hamarick saw the riders and without a word to Savoy or Llano started out into the street. As Wadell and Null came abreast of him the short man threw up his hands and the horses stopped.

"I been wantin' to see you, Null," said Hamarick, loud enough for any who might care to listen, to hear. "When you comin' out? Mat wants to talk to you."

Null's face flushed slightly. He looked at Wadell and then at the short man on the ground. "I don't know what you mean," he said sharply. "Who are you? Who is Mat? I've never seen you before."

"Why, you . . ." began Hamarick, but Dick Wadell, spurring his horse, struck the short man with the beast's shoulder and Shorty Hamarick went down into the dust of the street. Before he could scramble up, Null and Wadell had ridden on, and Arch Savoy, who had run out into the street, seized the small man and spoke sharply to him but in so low a tone that Llano could not hear the words. Savoy brought Hamarick back to the sidewalk and helped the little man brush the dust from his clothing. Neither Hamarick nor Savoy made any

94

explanation of the incident and Llano made no comment although his mind was filled with questions. When Hamarick's clothing had been readjusted the three went into the restaurant. There Savoy and his companion sought the washroom. When the two rejoined Llano both were silent and Hamarick was considerably more sober than he had been.

The trio ate their meal and parted outside the restaurant, Savoy and Hamarick taking their horses and Llano walking on up the street toward Greybull's office. Before they separated Arch Savoy had urged Llano to come to the cabin and Llano had promised an early visit.

In Greybull's office the same eye-shaded clerk greeted Llano and told him that Greybull would be back in a few minutes. Llano waited, watching the door. Presently it opened and the small man came in. His face was flushed and there was anger in his blue eyes. There was a paper in his hand and he came around the railing and straight toward Llano Land.

"You wanted to talk to me, did you?"

"Yes," Llano answered, wondering what was coming.

"Do you know what this is?" snapped Greybull, striking the paper he held in his hand.

Llano shook his head.

"You lie!" Greybull's words were like a whiplash. "You work for the Duro Grant. Null told me about you. You rode in with him. Last night you saved his life. You know what this is as well as I do. It's an injunction issued by a Territorial Court to make me stop operating on Grant property. Your damned deputy, Wadell, just served it. You can take this and go back to Null and Cameron and tell them to go to hell. I won't stop operating! I'll make them eat this thing, hear me? Eat it!"

The stocky little man, temper completely gone, crowded in to Llano, waving the paper, almost striking Llano in the face with it. Llano caught that jerking arm and pulled Greybull down.

"Listen," commanded Llano Land, "I don't work for the Grant or anybody else. If you can make Null eat that injunction it's all right with me, but don't try to feed it to me. When you calm down and get some sense I'll come back and talk to you." He pushed Greybull aside and stalked to the door. At the door he turned and looked back. Greybull, almost insane with rage, was tearing the injunction into shreds and the eye-shadded clerk was coming around the corner of the railing. Llano shrugged and walked on out of the office.

Outside Greybull's office he untied Singleshot from the hitchrail, and mounting, rode down the valley. There was nothing in Marthastown to detain him, nothing further there for him to do. In his mind Llano threw a curse at Kent Null. Null had very thoroughly stopped Llano, had very thoroughly identified Llano with the Duro Grant. From now on Llano was a man without friends. Without friends because he would not throw in with the Grant and because in the eyes of those not of the Grant he was a Grant man. There was one place where Llano would be welcome, one place where he could be what he was and nothing else, and that was in the outlaw cabin of Mat McCarthy. Llano determined to go there. His visit to Marthastown had gained him nothing except the information that Jack Ames had sold his horses there. Jack was dead, killed for the money he had made from his horses. Llano shrugged. He had time, plenty of it. There was no hurry. He must move slowly and very, very surely in his search for the man that had killed his friend.

CHAPTER 9

KENT NULL WAS A SMART MAN AND AN unscrupulous man. His mind worked smoothly in tortuous channels and when he arrived at a conclusion he acted upon it. Null had arrived at two conclusions, one being that Llano Land was dangerous to his plans and to the future activity of the Duro Grant, the other that Mat McCarthy and his men had outlived their usefulness. Having arrived at these conclusions he proceeded to act upon them. When Null reached Ladron, riding back from Marthastown, it was nine o'clock, although he had changed horses at Mrs. Stamps' inn. Wadell, restless and ill at ease, left the lawyer at Ladron House and went on to his own dwelling in the town. Null had said nothing of Wadell's defalcation at the inn. Wadell had run, scared to the marrow, and left Null to face the music. Null was alive through the intervention of Llano Land and Wadell had learned of that from the barn boy at Mrs. Stamps'. But Null had made no comment, had shown no feeling, and Wadell was now more frightened of the little lawyer than he had been of the men who had come to hang them both.

Leaving his horse behind Ladron House to be looked after by a man from the stables, Null went through the rear entrance of the dwelling and directly to Cameron's office. Cameron was there, a bottle and glasses on the table, and his feet comfortably lifted to a chair. He looked up when Null came in, nodded, and gestured toward the bottle and the glasses. Null poured himself a drink, tossed it down and seated himself on Cameron's desk so that his leg trailed over the edge.

"How did Greybull take your little present?" Cameron asked, looking up at Null.

Null swung his leg and smiled in reminiscence. "He didn't like it," he answered. "I've never seen a man quite so angry as Pat Greybull. He swore that he would not quit operating and that we could do what we pleased but that the dredge would continue to run. Greybull, you know, is still in debt for the dredge. He lost a gold shipment that might have put him in the clear and now I understand that the company he bought from is pushing him a little."

Cameron nodded, his dark face intent. "But, you had no trouble?" he asked.

"None at Marthastown," Null answered. "Arthur, that man Land worries me."

Cameron's face darkened. "Why?" he asked bluntly. "I've already decided what to do with Land."

"Kill him, I suppose," said Null. "I'm afraid not, Arthur, I'm in his debt."

Cameron straightened. "In Land's debt?" he asked incredulously. "How?"

"Because he saved my life," returned Null. "Last night Wadell and I stopped at the Stamps' Inn. We had visitors. There were several of the men from the upper country that rode down with the pleasant idea of hanging Wadell and me. Len Connors brought in the word of their coming and Wadell took his horse and ran. He was considerate enough to turn all the horses out of the corral when he left and I was on foot. If Llano Land hadn't stepped in I'd be dangling from a tree."

"And Land stepped in?" Apparently Cameron couldn't believe that.

"He did. Most decisively. Mrs. Stamps and I were on the porch and our visitors had announced their intention,

98

when Land came out of the dark and covered them." Null laughed mirthlessly. "I made sure," he continued, "that they learned his identity. That, somehow, did not please Mr. Land."

"Then your visitors think that Land is with the Grant?" asked Cameron.

"They do," answered Null. "Llano Land has a reputation that we could use, Arthur."

Cameron leaned back in his chair and appeared to be engrossed in the thought. "You are smart, Kent," he said finally. "A clever man."

Null shrugged, "I have thought so," he answered. "Now I'm not so sure. What about Wadell, Arthur?"

"Wadell," returned Cameron, slowly, "is a coward, but he is useful. I still have a little work for Dick Wadell."

"I see," said Null. "Our friend Gunther?"

"Perhaps," Cameron shrugged.

"There are some others that have outlived their usefulness," suggested Null. "Today in Marthastown one of McCarthy's men stepped out into the street and stopped me. He said that McCarthy wanted to talk to you. Wadell knocked him down with his horse and we rode on. Hasn't Mat McCarthy about finished his work, Arthur?"

Cameron nodded slowly. "I think so," he agreed. "McCarthy knows too much, Kent,"

"Then?" said Null.

"Then we can eliminate McCarthy!" There was a quiet savagery in Cameron's words.

Null mused a moment. "I believe," he said slowly, "that the chest which contained the gold shipment is still intact, Arthur. I believe that I could find it. Suppose that that chest were to be found at McCarthy's cabin?

Suppose a posse of Grant men were to make that discovery and that McCarthy and his men were to resist that posse? The chest, of course, would be restored to the Wells Fargo and no doubt Greybull might feel more kindly toward the Grant."

"Just the chest, of course." Cameron caught the suggestion. Null nodded. "That would do very well," he said.

There was silence between the two for a moment and Cameron reached for his glass and the bottle. When he had taken another drink he spoke again.

"Metcalf, the fat-headed fool," drawled Cameron, "has ridden away filled with the idea that Gwynn's property is in danger. If we have trouble at Marthastown we can count on Metcalf stepping in."

Null smiled. "The power of the government," he murmured. "Love is a wonderful thing, Arthur. It could make Wayne Metcalf forget his position and his orders. Still, I suppose that aiding officers of the territory in their duty and keeping the peace might fall under his jurisdiction."

Cameron shrugged. "If not we can't be worried," he said. "At any event Gwynn is seeing a good deal of Metcalf."

"Too much?" Null lifted his eyebrows.

"Too much," said Cameron heavily.

"Then I take it that you do not prosper there," commented Null.

"I can wait," Cameron answered. "After all, when this thing is done and the Grant is cleared, will be time enough for me."

There was silence for a moment as both men mused. Null smiled quizzically. "Do you prosper elsewhere, Arthur?" he asked.

"What do you mean?" snapped Cameron.

"Rose," there was a glint of amusement in Null's eyes. "After all, Arthur, you are paying her to stay at the Exchange Saloon. You freed her from Flaco and she ought to be grateful."

Cameron flushed darkly. "She will be," he promised.

"But as yet she isn't. I see." Null laughed. "Have you thought what effect that might have on the future, Arthur? Suppose that Gwynn's brother, Donald, were to discover your little affair. Suppose . . ?"

"That fool!" snapped Cameron. "Give him a horse and he thinks of nothing else. He should have been a farrier. There's no danger from him!"

Both men laughed and Null helped himself to the liquor. "The whole Grant," he said. "Miles of land. Grazing for sheep and cattle, gold in the hills, coal to mine when the railroads come, and Arthur Cameron the Lord of the Manor."

"And Kent Null with his nest feathered and a finger in every pie," rejoined Cameron quickly. "Don't forget that, Kent."

Null laughed again, a quick, harsh bark of amusement. "You don't trust me, Arthur," he said.

"No," agreed Cameron, "but you can be bought."

Again there was silence between the two, each man immersed in his own thoughts. Then Null spoke. "We have yet to account for two men," he said, "James Gunther and Llano Land."

Cameron looked up quickly. "Gunther, yes," he said. "The man is a power. He talks too much and people listen to him. We have Gunther to account for and I intend to take care of that matter, but what about Llano Land? What can he do?"

"Llano Land," said Null slowly, "can kill you and me

and Wadell and Capes. Llano Land, my friend Arthur, holds our plans at the end of his trigger finger. I am afraid of Llano Land."

"Why then," Cameron said heavily, "we must account for Llano Land, too."

Null laughed ruefully. "You forget," he said, "that he saved my life. A poor thing, Arthur, my life, but somehow I value it."

Silence again. Then Cameron spoke. "But not as much, I hope, as you value some other things, Kent?"

"No," agreed Kent Null, "not so much as I value other things, Arthur." Rising from the desk he nodded to Cameron and turned toward the door. "A night's sleep won't hurt me," he said, and then laughing ruefully, "It was little sleep I got last night. Good night, Arthur."

Cameron answered, "Good night," and Null went out, leaving the manager of the Duro Grant to help himself again to the whiskey and stare reflectively at the doorway through which Null had passed.

Cameron sipped his drink, sipped again, and then, cradling the glass in his hands, spoke half aloud. "So McCarthy knows too much," said Arthur Cameron. And then, after a pause, "But not so much as Kent Null!"

For a time Cameron sat quiet, then getting up, he took his hat from the pair of antlers that hung on the wall, and walked to the door. At the door he paused, lifted a revolver from its holster in his hip pocket, and examining the nickel-plated thirty-eight in the light, restored it to its resting place. His toilet made, he went out.

Leaving Ladron House he strolled toward the still active town. At the cross street below the Exchange Saloon he turned, went a few doors further and then stopped and knocked. A voice from within the building demanded his identity and when he had answered the door swung open and Cameron went in.

Dick Wadell was sitting on a bed at the side of the room Cameron entered, and Denver Capes closed the door and followed Cameron into the room. Cameron pushed out a chair, sat down on it so that he faced Wadell, and Capes walked over and sat down beside his partner.

"So you got back?" said Cameron to Wadell.

Wadell nodded. "Come pretty near not makin' it," he answered. "There was a bunch jumped Null an' me at Gra'maw Stamps' place. We like to not got away."

"I heard about that," commented Cameron dryly. "Null came near not getting away but Dick Wadell looked after his own bacon all right."

Wadell flushed and was about to speak but Cameron forestalled that. "You served that paper," he said. "How did Greybull take it?"

"Pretty hot," said Wadell.

Cameron nodded. "Things are coming to a head now," he announced. "It won't be long. Greybull and the Marthastown men won't take that injunction lying down. They'll fight. Then we'll have the soldiers out and get things settled the way we want them settled. There is only one thing that bothers me now and that is McCarthy. He knows too much."

"Well?" said Wadell.

"What did you do with the Wells Fargo chest?" asked Cameron. "Did you break it up or burn it?"

Wadell shook his head, and Capes, who had been silent, reached under the bed upon which he sat and pulled a heavy, iron bound box out. "There it is," announced Capes.

"I want that chest planted in McCarthy's cabin,"

103

ordered Cameron. "Then I want you to take a bunch out there, Wadell, and search the place. You'll find the chest and McCarthy will have that stage robbery to account for."

"What good will that do?" asked Wadell. "It'll make McCarthy sore an' he'll spill his guts about what he's been doin'. He . . ."

"When you bring McCarthy and his men in they won't be talking," Cameron said significantly. "The chest is to be planted out there so that Greybull won't have so much to think about."

"Oh," grunted Wadell, "that way, huh?"

"That way," agreed Cameron.

"We was just talkin' here, Dick an' me, about Gunther," said Capes. "Rose has quit Flaco an' she's stayin' in Gunther's house. She an' Flaco had it out last night."

"At Gunther's?" Cameron turned to the Grant cowboss.

"Yeah," Capes nodded. "Flaco's scared of Llano Land."

"I'd think he would be," said Cameron dryly. "Flaco has had one experience with Land and that ought to be enough."

"Flaco wants me an' Wadell to take care of Land," announced Capes, his voice matter of fact.

"I see," said Cameron. "Are you going to do it?"

"We thought we might," Capes answered casually.

Cameron thought deeply for a moment. "And Rose Juell is at Gunther's," he said slowly.

"Yeah," Capes flashed a look at Wadell and then faced Cameron. Cameron wet his lips with the tip of his tongue.

"Gunther was out at Spears' place today," Wadell

announced. "He was talkin' out there. Spears was about in the notion of payin' rent to the Grant an' Gunther talked him out of it."

"Yeah," agreed Capes. "I was out there this afternoon. An' all that Ortega bunch at the San Carlos Mesa have been listenin' to Gunther. I had ol' Ramon Ortega talked into comin' with the Grant an' Gunther went out there an' stopped it."

"Gunther talks too much," Cameron said decisively. "Gunther is about through."

"If somethin' happened to Gunther we'd have the whole world to fight," warned Wadell. "These Mexicans think Gunther is just God."

Cameron scowled. He was thinking, studying out a situation.

"Suppose," he began slowly, "that Gunther was killed an' it was blamed on somebody besides the Grant. Then what?"

"Then half the Mexicans that are holdin' out an' some of the others, too, would be with us," said Capes quickly.

"And Rose . . ." Cameron didn't finish the sentence.

"Rose would have to get to somebody that would keep Flaco off her," Capes was blunt. "Flaco's afraid that she's goin' to talk to Land an' mebbe tell him too much."

"Mebbe . . ." began Wadell and stopped.

"Maybe what?" demanded Cameron.

"Mebbe she'd come to you," finished Wadell in a burst of daring.

Cameron didn't speak for some time. When he did speak his words were slow. "If it could be made to look as if Land killed Gunther," he said, "and if the Grant men took Land an' killed him for it there might be some difficulties settled and it might be worth something to the men that arranged it."

Wadell and Capes exchanged a look. "We're goin' to be busy with that McCarthy thing," said Wadell slowly, "but Flaco hates Gunther's guts."

Cameron got up from his chair. "How many men have you now, Capes?" he asked.

"Twenty, more or less," answered Capes, "an' then there's Flaco an' Huerta. Twenty-four countin' them an' Dick an' me."

Cameron nodded. "That ought to be enough," he said. "And then of course," he smiled wryly, "we can depend on the soldiers."

"When do we start?" asked Wadell bluntly.

"Why," again Cameron smiled, "what's the matter with now? Good night!"

He walked to the door, turned and surveyed the two for a moment and then the door closed behind him.

Left alone Dick Wadell and Denver Capes stared at each other.

"I don't like it," Wadell said suddenly. "Here's McCarthy that knows too much an' McCarthy's on his way out. Here's Gunther that talks an' Gunther's leavin'. Where does that put you an' me, Denver?"

Denver Capes shrugged. "I've got mine in the bank at Trinity," he answered. "Someday pretty soon Denver Capes is just goin' to fade out of the picture an' he ain't comin' back."

Wadell nodded. "An' when you go one way I'm goin' the other," he announced. "We ought to collect heavy for this, Denver."

"Don't fret," said Denver Capes. "We will. Now, how we goin' to plant Gunther on Land?"

CHAPTER 10

LLANO LAND WAS A GOOD HOUR BEHIND KENT NULL and Dick Wadell leaving Marthastown. He took the trail south out of the place, passed the sluices and the dredge and within three hours was at the Stamps' inn. Having left Marthastown shortly after one o'clock he still had daylight, and Singleshot, although he had covered country, was not tired, so Llano rode on. He let the big horse take his time, knowing that at the end of the ride there would be feed and rest for the horse and a fresh mount for himself.

Down the Ladron Canyon darkness overtook Llano but he continued his ride, sure that Singleshot would keep the trail, and that Ladron lay at the end of the road. It was late when he sighted the lights of the town and riding down past the dark bulk of Ladron House, came to the Saint George. Turning Singleshot over to the boy at the stable, Llano went into the hotel. There was no one in the lobby of the place and so, taking his room key from a rack behind the desk Llano went to his room, undressed and went to bed.

He awakened early, dressed and went to breakfast. When he had finished the meal and was crossing the lobby Leige Nathan accosted him.

"Rose Juell was in here early last evenin'," said Nathan. "Said she wanted to see you an' when I told her you were gone she asked for a room."

"Did you give it to her?" asked Llano.

Nathan shook his head. "I don't keep that kind of women here," he said virtuously. "You better tell her so. Next time she wants to visit you, make it some place else besides my hotel."

Llano looked at the man with bleak, gray eyes. "Some day, Nathan," he drawled, "I'm going to take time off and educate you. When I get done you'll run a hotel and you'll take people in and be glad to. Did Rose say what she wanted?"

Nathan shook his head and Llano, after a final inspection of the man, went out. At the Exchange where he stopped, the bartender had no word of Rose Juell. She had not been in the night before and Flaco had not attended his game. The bartender didn't know where either of them was, but he was able to tell Llano where Rose lived. Accordingly Llano left the saloon and went on down the street, turned off and presently reached the adobe where Rose had kept her room. There was a tall, gaunt man lounging in front of the place and of him Llano asked concerning Rose.

Huerta shrugged. "No 'sta aqui," he answered Llano's question and where Llano persisted Huerta shrugged again and said, "Quien sabe?"

There was nothing to be gained from this lout, Llano saw, and so he left. Further discreet inquiries failed to disclose Rose Juell's whereabouts and finally Llano gave up the search and went back to the Saint George. There he ordered Jigger saddled and when the buckskin horse with the black cross over his shoulders was brought around Llano mounted.

Jigger was one of the old Spanish strain. Not so reliable as Singleshot, he could, nevertheless, hold his own with the redoubtable gray gelding. Indeed Jigger had points of his own that Singleshot did not possess. Jigger could buck like a released spring and bite like a snapping turtle. More than this he would bite at any time and he was as apt to buck at the end of fifty miles as he was under a cold saddle. Mounting Jigger was like climbing on a keg of dynamite: It might go off, it might not. Llano climbed his horse in the middle of the street and Jigger disappointingly ambled off the way a spotted pup trots off under a wagon.

Llano headed east out of Ladron with the intention of visiting Mat McCarthy. McCarthy's cabin was west and north but Llano had no intention of advertising his purpose.

When Llano cleared Ladron and the town was well bebind, he turned Jigger north and let the horse out. Jigger struck a springy canter and broke from that into a lope, fighting his head to be allowed to run. Llano held him in.

On north he went and then, some three miles from the town he turned back toward the west. There was a canyon entering the Ladrones here and that canyon's divide dropped down into Rincon Canyon.

Llano passed a ranch in the canyon, a small place where a tow-headed boy peered curiously at the strange rider and then ran into the cabin. The young rider worked on up the trail that extended above the ranch, topped the divide and so rode down into the Rincon. Up the Rincon he went, through the small parks and flats and so came to the park bordered by the aspens and turning, went through them. It was noon.

There was no smoke from McCarthy's cabin and no sign of life about the place. The surly Jigger tossed his head and fretted but the gate in the pole fence was down and Llano rode through, not stopping to replace the bars. McCarthy and his men had left them down and Llano would leave them so. Outside the cabin he dismounted and walked toward the door. The door was open. Evidently McCarthy had left in a hurry. Llano grinned a little. There was more than one reason why

McCarthy might leave in a hurry. Llano wondered if he had made his trip in vain, if McCarthy was gone on some foray or if the men who used the cabin were now in Texas or in Colorado, "speculating," as Mat said, in cattle.

There was one step up to the cabin door. A log, its surface hewn to some semblance of flatness, formed that step. Llano set foot upon it. A sound came from inside the cabin, a thud. Perhaps a pack rat moving and disturbing supplies left there. Llano lifted his other foot ready to set it on the doorsill. There was a gasp inside the cabin, a gun roared and hot lead brushed Llano's cheek!

Llano, swinging back, his back against the cabin wall, had a gun in his hand. Jigger, away from the doorway, stood with head high and ears pricked forward. Inside the cabin there was silence.

Was that shot a mistake? Llano did not know. It might be that one of Mat McCarthy's men was inside, perhaps the man that Llano had not met on his first visit to the place. Llano had come unannounced, deceived by the apparent lack of life about the place. Now he must give his identity.

"I am Llano Land," he said evenly, loud enough so that the man inside must hear. "I've come to see Mat."

Silence followed that announcement. In the aspens above the cabin a jay spoke raucously and a chipmunk chattered shrilly, then all was still.

"I'm Llano Land," Llano announced again. "Do you hear me? I've come to see Mat McCarthy."

Still no answer from within. Llano was pinned against the wall. There was one door to the cabin and only one. If he stepped away from his place by the door, Llano exposed himself to fire from a window. There were other windows, other means of exit from the cabin; for Llano there were none. He waited, listening, his eyes intent on Jigger's head. The buckskin stood stock still, ears erect, looking at the cabin. From inside came a little movement, a sound as of something being moved across the floor. Motionless, his eyes on Jigger, Llano waited.

Time ticked past. The jay called again, scolding, cursing this interloper. Within the cabin all was still and Llano, breathing shallowly, listened and watched his horse. Jigger lost his tenseness, the ears were less erect. The black tall swished at a fly. Jigger tossed his head, fighting the insects. Then the ears came forward sharply and the horse looked to the right.

Whirling away from the door Llano Land heard a gun bellow again, the sharp "thunk!" of lead into the logs which a moment before he had pressed against. Then the Smith & Wesson in his own hand kicked back sharply, once and then again, and from the further end of the cabin a man fell forward onto the sod, his hat falling clear to expose his blond hair. For a moment Llano stood poised. Then slowly, gun held ready, he walked forward and looked down.

"Capes," said Llano Land softly. "Denver Capes. And what are you doing here?"

Denver Capes made no answer. There was an account in the bank at Trinity that would never be withdrawn.

When he had stood for a moment looking down at the man he had killed, Llano walked back to the door. He hesitated there fractionally and then went into the cabin. A window, open and with a bench below it, showed how Capes had left the cabin. There were beds neatly made on the bunks, there were dishes, clean and piled on the table. The coffee pot was still warm on the stove when Llano felt it. Out in the center of the room was a

111

box, metal bound and heavy. The stencil on the box read, "Wells Fargo Express Company." Llano opened the box and looked at the empty interior. After that brief inspection he walked out. On the step he stopped and then sat down. His hands produced papers and tobacco. Llano Land rolled a cigarette and glanced at the blond hair of the man at the end of the cabin.

That cigarette was gone and so were two others when the jay in the aspens announced callers. The jay shrieked harshly and Jigger lifted his head from his grazing. Llano stood up, his hand resting on his belt buckle. A horseman came through the grove, Mat McCarthy. After McCarthy came others. Mat McCarthy dismounted, his blue eyes keen and questioning.

"What happened, Llano?" demanded Mat McCarthy.

Llano gestured with his left hand. "I'd come to see you, Mat," he said, his voice low and drawling. "Capes was here when I come in. It seemed like he didn't want me."

Mat McCarthy's blue eyes were wide and round. Behind McCarthy Arch and Virge Savoy were dismounting. Shorty Hamarick still sat his saddle.

"Capes?" said McCarthy incredulously. "What would he be doin' here?"

"I don't know, Mat," said Llano and took his right hand from his belt buckle. "There's an empty Wells Fargo strong-box inside. Mebbe . . ."

But Mat McCarthy, with an oath, had crowded past Llano and was inside the cabin door. The Savoy twins had come forward and Llano stood aside to let them enter. Shorty Hamarick was dismounting.

McCarthy came back out of the cabin. There was anger on his fat face, anger and something else: fear. "Capes!" snarled Mat McCarthy. "He brought that box out! He was tryin' to plant that stage robbery on us. Damn his black heart. Damn him. . . !'"

"Capes?" said Llano Land gently, "or the Duro Grant? Which, Mat?"

McCarthy drew himself together with an effort. He looked at Llano. "The Grant, I reckon," McCarthy answered evenly. "I guess the Grant figures us no use any more."

Llano waited. McCarthy looked at the gray-eyed man a long moment, a hard penetrating look. When he spoke it was to voice thanks. "I'm obliged, Llano," said Mat McCarthy. "You got here about right. An' now we got to get out of here. There'll be a posse along lookin' for this box unless I'm mistaken. Come on, boys!"

"Wait," commanded Llano, "what is this, Mat?"

McCarthy spoke hurriedly. "We moved the corner stone for the Grant, Llano. They paid us to do it an' they let us alone here. Now somebody has decided that we know too much. We got to go. Don't you see, Llano?"

Llano Land nodded. "But what about . . ." he jerked his thumb toward where Capes lay.

McCarthy looked in that direction. "That's so," said Mat McCarthy. "We got to plan this. Arch, you get the horses. Virge, you an' Shorty get inside an' start packin' up. We'll head for the Junta hold-up. I'll be with you in a minute." He turned to Llano.

"An' you killed the Grant cowboss," said McCarthy, smiling thinly. "I reckon you'll come with us, Llano."

There was nothing else for Llano to do. He recognized the correctness of Mat's reasoning and he knew that Mat and his men must be gone from the cabin and gone quickly. Denver Capes had come alone and in advance to plant that Wells Fargo strong box. There would be a posse on Capes' heels, a posse riding not far behind him. Llano joined the feverish activity in the cabin.

Arch Savoy brought in horses from the little trap behind the cabin. Bedding was rolled hurriedly and thrown over horses' backs to be lashed there. Cooking pots and pans, tin plates, cups, knives and forks were tossed hurriedly into a gunny sack. Within ten minutes after the arrival of Mat McCarthy the inside of the little cabin was gutted of its portable contents. Then Virge Savoy, without a word, lifted the body of Denver Capes and carried it into the cabin. Shorty Hamarick, as though working out a prearranged plan, emptied kerosene from a two-gallon lug over the puncheon floor and lighting a match threw it down. A puddle of kerosene caught and blazed, and Mat McCarthy, with a final look at the place, backed out of the door.

"Let's go," ordered McCarthy.

The men mounted. McCarthy led the way, not taking a path through the aspens but riding on west from the cabin, following a little trail that seemed to end in the rock wall of the rincon. Behind Mat came the others and back in the little cabin smoke seeped from the log walls.

At the rincon wall Mat reined in sharply. There were two horses there, one carrying a stock saddle, the other with pack equipment in place. No need to say whose horses these were. Their owner lay in the cabin, flames licking around his inert head. Mat McCarthy dismounted, untied the animals and fastening the lead rope of the pack animal to the tail of the saddle horse, mounted again and went on, leading his charges. Behind McCarthy the others, too, resumed their progress.

There was a narrow cleft in the rock wall of the rincon. It sloped up steeply. McCarthy's horse, scrambling for footing, entered the cleft and climbed.

One by one the other riders and the loaded horses took that trail. Up they went and came out on a bench. A steep slope arose from that bench, loose rock rolled, the horses clattered over stones and paused before each foot was set down. Still they went up that impassable trail, belying it, making it passable, and at the top with the wall of the rincon dropping off below them, they stopped to breathe.

It was there, sheltered by pines, that Mat McCarthy peered back, looking down toward the place from whence they had come.

"Look!" exclaimed Mat McCarthy.

The others obeyed that command.

There below them in the rincon the cabin flamed, a funeral pyre. As they watched a little group of horsemen, a dozen of them, rode through the aspens, halted and then came on toward the cabin at a run. They saw the horsemen slide their horses to stops, saw a man fling himself from the saddle and run to the cabin, saw him recoil from the fierce heat.

And then Mat McCarthy spoke again. "Come on," he ordered. "They found what they was lookin' for, God damn 'em! Come on, boys!"

Again they rode and now McCarthy bent toward the north. Along ridges where bare stone rattled beneath shod hoofs they took their way. Up and up, while the brown slope of Copper mountain towered above them and the pines and aspens gave way to aspens alone and then to the little gnarled cedars that cling to the timberline. Bare rock and grass now, and then they were dropping down and down and down until the pines grew thick once more. Moss was soft beneath the shod feet of the horses. Water splashed and the moss gave way to tall grass and then, beyond the spongy ground, a little trickle of water formed.

Mat McCarthy turned and looking back at Llano grinned until his teeth showed like the teeth of a snarling dog. "Here," said McCarthy, "we stop here."

Back of Llano, Arch Savoy growled. "How will Bill find us?"

McCarthy's look was one of flashing scorn. "Bill will come to the cabin an' on from there," answered Mat. "Bill showed us this place. Remember?"

Arch Savoy nodded and his twin spoke for the first time. "Let the Grant try to find us," said Virge Savoy. "Let 'em try!"

Llano Land looked at the hard set faces about him. "Why," drawled Llano, "the Grant may try, Savoy, but it looks to me like it would be up to you to find the Grant," and under the grim humor of that comment the faces relaxed.

"We'll find the Grant," vowed Shorty Hamarick. "We'll find the Grant, Land, an' when we do they'll know it!"

CHAPTER 11

JAMES GUNTHER SERVED HIS LORD IN TWO CAPACITIES: first, as a minister of the gospel, carrying the Word to the outlying communities about Ladron and to Ladron itself; and second, as a social reformer. In a later day James Gunther would have been an evangelist, in an earlier day, a prophet. A big man, Gunther, and strong, he carried his load with a high head. A part of his duty was to visit Marthastown and this he did, driving out from Ladron weekly. At Marthastown he preached to a few faithful men and women and then went on to Cottonwood and to Daylight, other small mining communities.

116

Besides preaching the gospel James Gunther preached the brotherhood of man and practiced humanity. The night was not too cold or the day too hot to find him in the saddle when he was called. He had fought diphtheria, that dread disease of the outlands; and smallpox, and had set broken bones and christened children and comforted those left behind when a loved one died. James Gunther was worshipped and looked up to and believed in by many, and by a few he was cursed and watched as a dangerous man, a man who thought too much and talked too much.

At noon on the day Llano Land left Ladron enroute for Mat McCarthy's, James Gunther prepared to leave for Marthastown. Rose Juell's presence made his preparations complicated. It had been simple enough when he had only Maria, his Mexican housekeeper, to speak to, but now he felt responsible for this strange, dark, beautiful woman who was troubled and to whom he had given refuge. Rose Juell was frightened, James Gunther knew, and he knew too, that there was something besides fright preying upon her.

She had not confided in him and he had asked for no confidences, content to believe that they would come in time. In a way, Gunther was proud that Rose had come to him. The preacher knew something of her background. Men had told Gunther of the woman, for Rose Juell was not without reputation, and Gunther had listened when they spoke. He knew her for a wild and willful wanton. Her coming to him for refuge was an entering wedge and Gunther, wise in the ways of mankind, wished to do nothing that might turn Rose from him.

When the simple noonday meal had been eaten the minister arose from his table and spoke to Maria. "I am going to Marthastown today," he announced, "I will be back by Saturday."

Maria nodded as one long accustomed to such statements, but Rose Juell sprang up from her chair, her face troubled. "Marthastown!" she exclaimed.

Gunther nodded. "I go each week," he said gently.

"But you can't . . ." began Rose, and then realizing the futility of what she had been about to say, " . . . take me with you!"

Gunther smiled and shook his head. "No," he answered, "I can't do that."

Rose stood beside the table. She knew that Gunther could not take her with him and she was afraid to be left in Ladron alone. If only Llano Land were in Ladron! Llano Land was strong and could protect her!

"Something is troubling you," said Gunther.

Maria had gone out of the room. Rose Juell came around the table. She stopped before him. "You've been kind to me," she said. "And how have I paid you? By bringing my troubles here!"

"That is all the payment I ask," Gunther's smile illuminated his face. "I have not pried, Rose, but if you could tell me . . ."

Rose Juell sat down in a chair beside the table and clasped her hands on the red and white oilcloth cover. "I've got to tell you," she said. "I've got to talk to somebody!"

Gunther sat down.

There was silence between the two for a moment and then Rose spoke. "I love a man," she began, her voice low. "I love him and he doesn't even know that I'm alive. I'd go to hell for him! Do you hear? To hell!"

Gunther's hand reached out and covered the tightly clasped hands of the girl. Under the pressure of that hand Rose Juell regained a measure of her composure. She smiled tremulously at Gunther. "You're good," she said, her voice low. "Good. You understand."

"This man," said Gunther gravely. "What are you to him, Rose?"

"Nothing," answered the girl, "I've had my own way to go ever since I can remember. I've danced and sold drinks on percentage and sung in saloons, and I've dealt faro and banked roulette. I've been . . . I've done a lot of things, James Gunther, but I've never loved a man before. And this man won't look at me!"

"And the man?" insisted Gunther.

"Is Llano Land," said Rose Juell. "And I've told you that he doesn't know I'm alive. The last time I talked to him I told him I hated him!"

Gunther smiled wisely. "I think," he said gently, "that you must wait. If you love Land you will sacrifice for him. Eventually he must know of it."

The words seemed to comfort the girl. She was silent and Gunther spoke again. "Why did you come to me?" he asked.

"Because I was afraid," answered Rose Juell. "I've taken care of myself for a long time but I never was afraid like I am now."

"And you are afraid . . ?" suggested Gunther.

"Of Flaco," completed Rose Juell. "He came to my room. He meant to kill me. I got away and came here."

"You should have gone to the officers," said Gunther.

"To Dick Wadell?" Rose laughed, her voice a little wild. "Don't you know what Dick Wadell is? Why, Flaco and Huerta work for Dick Wadell. They do what he tells them to do."

Again Gunther considered, frowning darkly. Then he arose from the chair beside the table. "I must go," he

119

announced. "I drive to Mrs. Stamps' tonight. I will think of what you have told me, Rose, and when I come back I will know what is best to do. Stay close and do not leave the house. No one will molest you here."

The girl also arose as Gunther did. She studied his strong dark face earnestly. "I'll stay here," she answered. "I'll stay. I know you will figure it out for me. But you won't tell . . . You won't say anything to Llano Land?"

Gunther shook his head. "I will not speak to him," he promised.

Rose was content with that and Gunther, smiling at her turned, and walked from the room. Within a few minutes Rose Juell heard the buckboard bearing the minister pull away from the house.

The buckboard rattled up Ladron's Street and James Gunther looked to right and left, nodding to women and men in doorways, smiling at children playing in the street. Beyond Ladron House he turned the team to the right and so began the ascent of Ladron Canyon, and as the buckboard followed the winding of the canyon road two men saddled horses in Ladron: Flaco, the gambler, and his partner Huerta. Gunther drove his team not rapidly but steadily. The two ponies hitched to the buckboard were gentle. They were a gift of Juan Villareal, the head of the thirty families of Villareals, who, a devout Catholic, liked and respected "Padre Gunther." As he drove, Gunther meditated upon the things that Rose Juell had told him and from those thoughts his mind turned to others, turned to thoughts of the Duro Grant. He saw the Grant stripped of its glamour, stripped to the nasty nakedness of greed and rapacity and cold-bloodedness that was its skeleton. He sighed.

120

He did not note the passing of time or of the winding and twisting of the canyon road. The horses forded the creek without his guidance, climbed the hills, indeed once paused to breathe before they progressed further, and all this James Gunther did not see or note. He had reached the little stream at the head of the canyon, the creek called "Segundo," before he emerged from his preoccupation. He lifted his eyes then only because two men rode down the little trail that ran beside that creek, and hailed him. Then he stopped his team.

He recognized these two men and recognizing them knew for what they had come. There was no question in James Gunther's mind as to their mission and, for a moment, he was afraid. For a moment he thought of escape, of lashing the gentle horses and making the wheels of the buckboard fly. For a moment James Gunther thought of those things and then he resigned them. The bay ponies stopped.

Flaco and Huerta rode up beside the buckboard. There was a grin on Huerta's long, thin face and a cigarette dangled between his lips. For an instant Gunther caught a trace, a faint odor foreign to the clean smell of the pines, foreign even to the smell of burning tobacco.

Flaco did not smile. Flaco was grimly in earnest. Flaco wheeled his horse abreast of the buckboard's seat. "Where is Rose?" demanded Flaco.

All the way up the canyon and over the hills that paralleled it Flaco had been nerving himself for the thing he was to do. He had drunk not once, but many times, from the bottle in his saddle pocket. He had steeled himself, and finally he had hit upon an excuse, a plausible reason for the thing he did. James Gunther had stolen Rose Juell. James Gunther had taken Flaco's

121

woman. James Gunther was to be killed, deserved to die.

"She is safe," answered Gunther, evenly. "What do you wish, my friends?"

"Get out of that buggy!" ground Flaco between his teeth. "Get out!"

Huerta was already on the ground. Gunther hesitated. Life was sweet and there was still work to do. If Flaco dismounted, if Flaco quit his horse, there was a chance for escape. But Flaco seemed to read the mind of the man on the buckboard seat. Flaco, with an oath, jerked out a gun, a heavy Colt, and covered Gunther. "Get out!" he rasped.

Gunther wrapped the lines carefully about the whip socket. He secured them there. He stepped over the wheel and from the wheel to the ground. He faced Flaco and Huerta. Huerta had taken a knife from his waistband. It was the sight of that knife that unnerved Gunther, that shook his stern resolution.

Gunther was a big man, big and strong with a boyhood of hard farm work behind him and a manhood of hard, manual work. His resolution broken, he whirled, turning to Huerta. A big hand struck out and Huerta reeled back.

Now the smile was gone from Huerta's face. He came in snarling, spitting his venom like a Gila monster, and Gunther met him and grappled. A part of Huerta's shirt ripped free and flapped with the struggle, and unnoticed, something fell from the pocket of that flapping shirt. The men reeled back and forth, two strong men at grips, and Gunther the stronger. Then, Flaco, who had slipped from his saddle, struck in with his heavy Colt, beating down, savagely. The bay ponies, frightened, snatched the buckboard away, the wheels spinning on the road, while Gunther staggered back and Huerta, knife raised, leaped in.

The knife was dull silver when it came down. It was darker when Huerta raised it again and plunged it down once more. Up and down! Up and down!

Then Flaco snapped, "*Bastante!*" and caught the descending arm, while, from up the road came a long call:

"Ho! Preacher!"

A horse pounded and Huerta, jerked back to his senses, seized the bridle reins of his horse in his bloody hand and Flaco swung himself into the saddle and the sharp stones rattled along the side of Segundo Creek. The willows waved and a trout in a pool fled away to hide under a rock, then all was still until the long call came again: "Preacher! Preacher!"

James Gunther did not answer.

Dale Fallien, long and tall and tired, with the dust of travel upon him, rode around the bend above Segundo Creek and reined in his horse.

Fallien did not dismount immediately. Fallien's tired eyes had seen death in many forms and now they looked at it again. Gunther lay with his arms reaching out. The back of his coat was slit to ribbons and a little, bright trickle of red ran down over a stone to form a pool.

"Preacher," said Dale Fallien, softly. "Preacher!"

Then he dismounted and holding his horse by one rein bent over the man on the ground. For an instant he was stooped, then he stood erect again and his blue eyes, bright now, were searching the ground and the surroundings. One thing he saw. Fallien took a long step and bending, picked up a tobacco sack, a limp oblong of muslin partly filled. This he put into his pocket.

There was nothing else to see, nothing more, and

123

Fallien, turning, mounted his horse and rode away. When he returned he was driving Gunther's buckboard and his own horse followed behind. Stopping the team, Dale Fallien wrapped the lines around the whipsocket as Gunther had done. As Gunther had done, he climbed over the wheel.

His long arms lifted Gunther and placed him in the bed of the buckboard. For a moment Fallien stood, his eyes photographing every detail of the place. Then he climbed again to the seat and unwrapped the lines. The bay ponies stood, and Fallien, looking back over his shoulder, spoke to James Gunther.

"It's a big country," drawled Dale Fallien, "but not big enough, I reckon."

The bay horses moved, slowly, and the wheels of the buckboard turned monotonously as Dale Fallien drove ahead toward Ladron. Down the long canyon the pines made dark shadows in the setting sun but on the hills above, the aspen leaves, white, caught the last rays of light and threw them back and forth in dancing notes as the wind blew. So James Gunther began his last long trip and his last service to these people that he had adopted.

Dale Fallien drove into Ladron at dark and stopped behind Mulligan's shop. There he knocked on the door and when Mulligan answered Fallien told the barber what had happened. Mulligan said nothing at the moment but helped the tall man carry Gunther into the back room of the shop and lay him on a long table there. Then Mulligan, looking at Fallien, spoke slowly.

"I been expectin' this," said Mulligan. "I reckon it's tore now."

"What do you mean?" asked Fallien.

"I mean," Mulligan answered, "that the whole

124

country will be up over this. Gunther was liked. The Mexicans think he's the Almighty, that's all. What'll they do when they find out?"

Fallien shook his head and Mulligan looked musingly at the dead man on the table. "Him an' me," said Mulligan, reflectively, "was sort of pardners, you might say. I fixed 'em up an' he buried 'em. I don't reckon you'll have to tell the law about this."

"Why?" questioned Fallien looking at the stocky barber.

"Because," Mulligan's voice was harsh, "there ain't much doubt with me that Wadell already knows about it. You can go an' hunt him up if you want to, though."

Fallien scrutinized the barber closely and Mulligan continued to look at Gunther. Then, making up his mind, Fallien nodded curtly and went out, and Mulligan with hands that were gentle for so rough a man, began to take the ribboned coat from the dead man.

CHAPTER 12

SOMEHOW THE NEWS OF JAMES GUNTHER'S DEATH spread over Ladron during the night. It went from mouth to ear, sibilantly. Gwynn Rae, wakening in the morning, found Eliza, her serving woman, red-eyed from weeping, and upon asking the reason for the grief learned that Gunther was dead. Eliza added details, distorted details, true, and when Gwynn Rae went down the stairs to the great hall and met her brother and Arthur Cameron she was in possession of a number of facts and a greater number of fancies. The girl seemed to have no appetite and Donald Rae commented upon the fact, whereupon Gwynn blurted out what she had heard.

125

The men were silent as they received the news and Donald Rae looked questioningly at Cameron.

Cameron nodded. "I had heard of it," he said. "One of the men told me this morning when I was at the stables. Gunther was killed, murdered."

"Is there any information?" asked Rae, and again Cameron nodded.

"A man named Fallien brought Gunther in," he said. "Fallien has been around town for the last two weeks. He is a gambler or a mining speculator, I believe. He was riding in from Bridger when he found the body."

"But do they know who killed him?" asked Rae.

Cameron shrugged slightly. "There is a rumor," he answered, "Llano Land had had some trouble with Gunther. It seems that Land has a woman here in town, Rose. The story is that woman fled to Gunther away from Land and that Land was angry. Wadell has a posse out now looking for Land." Gwynn Rae looked at the speaker and at her brother and then, leaving her meal practically untouched, rose from the table and left the men.

For a while the girl moped about the great house. Then, its somberness oppressing her, she ordered a horse and went to her room to change into a riding habit. Without leaving word for either Donald or Cameron she mounted, and rode away, no immediate destination in mind, simply the idea of leaving Ladron House possessing her.

Well out of Ladron, riding north, she turned the roan mare toward the hills and so by coincidence Gwynn Rae rode up the canyon that Llano Land had traversed, the roan mare taking the same trail that the yellow Jigger had taken.

As she rode the girl was troubled. The fact of James

126

Gunther's death was like a blow, a greater impact following lesser impacts. James Gunther! Gwynn had seen him about Ladron and once had seen him at close quarters. On the day of the funeral, when Will and Engra Loman had been buried, Gunther had come to Rose Juell and led her away. Rose Juell pouring vituperation upon Gwynn, had ceased and gone with Gunther. There had been a magnetic force about the man, a personality that had driven hard from him and impinged upon those he met. Gwynn had felt the force of that personality.

Thinking of Gunther and Rose Juell brought Llano Land to mind. With a start Gwynn realized that she had been thinking of Llano all the time, that it was not Gunther's death nor the flaring words of Rose Juell that obsessed her, but rather that quiet-faced, gray-eyed man who looked at her so steadily. She had never seen a man like him. Gunther might have possessed force, Arthur Cameron, too, was powerful and Kent Null was filled with unforeseen strength. These things the girl knew, but Llano Land was different from these. When Llano Land entered a room, when she thought of Llano Land, exciting possibilities filled her mind. The man was galvanic, he had a faculty of remaining motionless and yet filling those about him with a sense of latent power. What would it be like to be loved by Llano Land? Gwynn shuddered. Was Land a power for good or for evil? She did not know. She knew only that he filled her with a strange dread and yet that she was drawn to him. And thinking of Llano, yet another man was brought to mind: Wayne Metcalf.

Metcalf was gentle. Metcalf had nothing of the dynamic personality of Llano Land. Metcalf was silk where Llano was steel, smooth where Llano was hard

127

and rough, untried whereas Llano Land had lived in the smoke of guns and stood against singing lead, and yet there was an odd resemblance between the two. Somehow, Gwynn could not tell how, those two so dissimilar and yet similar personalities, were bound to meet. Would they clash? Gwynn could not say.

She threw off the thought of Llano Land and her eyes grew dreamy. Wayne Metcalf. She had been hard put to forestall Metcalf. The officer loved her, the girl knew. He was ready to declare that love and yet . . . and yet Gwynn was not ready for that declaration. Frankly the girl analyzed herself. Metcalf was a gentleman, a man of position and of fortune. He was in the Army because that was the career that the Metcalfs followed, not through any necessity. He was attractive, gentle with a strong gentleness. He was all that a girl, even a girl like Gwynn Rae, might desire . . . and yet. . . . There was Llano Land! The roan mare tossed her head and fought the reins. Gwynn Rae looked up, her mind emerging from her meditations. There was a cabin beside the road Gwynn followed. A pole fence surrounded the cabin and over the top of the fence peeped two small tow heads. Gwynn reined the mare to a halt and looked at the cabin, at the straggling fence, and at the tow heads. Beneath the yellow hair, blue eyes showed anxiously, and small, freckled faces were set in earnest lines.

"Hello," said Gwynn, impulsively, and moved the mare closer to the fence.

The taller of the tow heads answered the salutation. "Hello."

Gwynn could see the immature lines of womanhood beneath the blue shirt and tattered overalls of the speaker. The boy, smaller of the two, scuffed a bare toe in the grass beside the fence and smiled. Two front teeth were gone and the gap was startling in that wide-spread grin.

"Could I have a drink of water?" asked Gwynn.

"Get the lady a drink, Johnny," commanded the girl-child, and continued to stare at Gwynn's riding habit and at the girl. The boy, after a moment more of appraisal, scurried away.

"Do you live here?" asked Gwynn.

The small girl nodded solemnly. "Me an' Johnny an' mama," she answered. "Papa used to live here but he's in jail at Bridger." There was a matter of fact tone in her voice as one long accustomed to the statement.

"In jail?" said Gwynn, startled.

"He wouldn't pay rent to the Grant," explained the girl at the fence. "They put him in jail. They said he stole cattle."

The small boy, Johnny, came through the gate and, advancing on Gwynn, tendered a rusty dipper filled with water. Gwynn bent from her sidesaddle to take the dipper. The boy stood in the road, staring up at her.

"What is your father's name?" asked Gwynn, after taking a drink.

"John Kinney. I'm Meg Kinney, an' that's Johnny."

Gwynn sipped again from the dipper, emptied it and tendered it to the boy. He took the handle and stood, still staring up at Gwynn.

"Do you know the lady in the big house in Ladron?" queried the girl at the fence. "She's a lady, mama says. She wears silk dresses and shoes and she has a girl to comb her hair. Do you know her?"

Gwynn looked at the speaker. The small girl was very earnest. "I know her," said Gwynn.

Eagerness showed on the small face. "Does she sleep all day?" questioned Meg. "Does she sleep all day an'

129

dance all night an' does she eat field larks an' bread an' cake?"

For a moment Gwynn Rae wanted to laugh, then the earnestness of that freckled face stopped her. "No, dear," answered Gwynn. "I don't think she does that."

Disappointment registered on the upturned face. "Mama said that she did," said Meg. "She said that the Grant wanted us to pay rent on our land so that the lady could have a new silk dress and her brother a new horse. Mama says that she's a . . ." a pause while Meg searched for the word, ". . . a harpy," she brought out triumphantly.

Gwynn Rae started slightly.

"Are harpies nice?" queried Meg Kinney.

"I'm afraid not, dear," answered Gwynn. "Where is your mother?"

"She's in the field," said the girl. "She has to work in the field since Papa was put in jail."

Gwynn stared again at the cabin, at the pole fence and at the children. She was looking at them with new eyes, eyes that had never seen before. The cabin was dilapidated and needed repairs. The fence showed broken gaps. The children were ragged, shoeless, but clean.

"Is your mother going to pay rent to the Grant?" asked Gwynn Rae, her voice a little harsh.

Meg Kinney shook her head. "She's going to get papa out of jail," she answered with implicit faith. "Mama says that this is our land and that she doesn't have to pay rent for it. She says that the Grant will take it if she does." There was a pause, then, "That's a pretty dress."

Gwynn glanced down at her broadcloth habit. Her face whitened.

The small girl's eyes were wistful. "Bring the dipper

130

an' come in, Johnny," said the girl. "I've got to put supper on for mama."

"What are you going to have for supper?" asked Gwynn, her voice tight.

"Squash," answered the girl. "We've got lots of squash. Would you like some?" politely.

"Not tonight, dear," said Gwynn gently. Her hand fumbled in the small pocket of her habit. There was a coin there. She brought it out and held it toward the boy in the road. "Thank you for the drink," she said. "Here . . ."

"We don't take money for water," announced the girl by the fence. "We . . . Here comes mama!"

Gwynn looked up. A slight figure, covered with blue overalls and a blue shirt, the whole topped by a tattered straw hat, was striding toward the fence.

The woman stopped beside the children and looked at Gwynn Rae. No older than Gwynn her face showed hard, harsh lines and was weathered and worn. Still a certain beauty remained. This woman must have been lovely, would still have been beautiful except for the wear of weather and of fatigue. For a long moment she stood and then she spoke.

"So you have come to frightening the children now?" she said slowly. "The Grant has fallen to that! Come, Johnny. Come away." One arm she placed about Meg's shoulders. Her eyes searched Gwynn.

"But you don't . . ." began Gwynn. Then angrily, "I stopped for a drink of water."

"You've had it!" harsh contempt in the woman's voice, "Now you can go. And you can tell Cameron and the Grant that I won't pay rent and that I'll hold my place in spite of them."

"I want. . ." said Gwynn.

131

"Go!" commanded the woman by the fence, her arms protectingly about her children. "You may put us off and you may keep my husband in jail, but you can't have these!"

Something blinded Gwynn Rae. Tears, hot and scalding, fell upon her cheeks. The red roan mare, impatient, moved, and Gwynn did not check her. So this was what the Duro Grant did? So this was what it meant to have land and cattle. And to talk of rights and "squatters," and "our land"? Gwynn turned the mare and the animal, rested and impatient, moved at a canter down the road. At the fence Margaret Kinney stood, head raised defiantly, her arms about her children, and watched the roan mare and her rider disappear.

Gwynn Rae rode back the way she had come, and if she had been bemused as she rode into the hills she now had even more of which to think. Those children, babies really, and their responsibilities, so gravely shouldered, and that slight, worn woman who had faced her. Gwynn was not angry but she was stirred to her depths.

So this was what it meant to have the Duro Grant, to live in Ladron House, to wear silk next the skin, to play upon a great square rosewood piano? It took things like that broken cabin and that toil-worn woman and the shoeless children to make a world in which Gwynn Rae ate from Spode china and drank from crystal and rested her elbows upon damask while she laughed at a man across the table. It took these things!

The sky darkened as the sun slid down and the mountain tops were gold with purple beneath the gold. The roan mare's hoofs beat a tattoo on the road. Gwynn Rae shook her red-gold head and her eyes were dark with knowledge and with pain.

Dinner was past when she reached Ladron House.

132

Arthur Cameron paced back and forth in the hall and Donald Rae stood with his hands locked behind him staring out of the window. The fingers of his hands twisted in his anxiety. The two men met the girl as she entered.

"Gwynn," began Cameron angrily, "where have you been? What kept you so late? We . . ."

Anger was crystal clear in Gwynn Rae's mind as she looked at Cameron. "I think," said Gwynn Rae, a great lady, "that you have mistaken your place, Mr. Cameron. I am the one to ask questions." And with that she swept past Cameron and to the stairs, her riding skirt trailing. At the stair she stopped.

"Donald," said Gwynn Rae, "can you come to my room? I should like to talk with you."

Surprise showed in Donald Rae's face. He nodded, and with a glance at the glowering Cameron, followed his sister. He was gone for a long time and when he returned below stairs Cameron was still in the hall. Donald Rae's fresh, boyish face was troubled.

"My sister has been talking to me, Arthur," said Donald Rae. "Tomorrow I want to go over the Grant's affairs with you. Things are wrong."

"What is wrong, Donald?" asked Cameron.

Donald shook his head. "I haven't paid enough attention to what is going on," he said. "We ought not to have trouble on the Grant."

Cameron smiled. "There isn't any trouble," he countered. "We have some people on Grant land and we are informing them that they must pay rent to us. For that we give them protection and privileges. Certainly that is only right. Those who refuse to pay rent, we are caring for by legal measures. Gwynn is upset, Donald. Something has happened to upset her."

Donald Rae flushed. "Gwynn . . ." he began, and then stopped. It would not do to inform Cameron concerning his stormy session with his sister. "Just the same I think it is time I took my duties more seriously," he announced lamely. "After all, Arthur, I represent the syndicate and I am responsible to them. My father is a principal stockholder."

Cameron smiled. "I'll be glad to go over things with you," he said smoothly. "There is a matter engaging me now that I would be glad to be advised upon. Since the northern boundary of the Grant has been confirmed we find that Marthastown lies inside the Grant limits. The gold that has been taken from there legally belongs to the Grant. We have notified Greybull and the other miners that they are operating unlawfully. They have cheated the syndicate out of hundreds of thousands of dollars. Now Greybull tells us that he will not cease to operate his dredge and the other miners are also operating. What would you suggest, Donald?"

Donald Rae stared at his questioner. Slow of mind, more interested in horses and dogs than in any other things, he could not quite comprehend what Cameron had told him.

Cameron spoke again. "Of course," he said softly, "we can go ahead and ignore Greybull's acts. We can let them rob the syndicate, your father among others, of what is rightfully theirs. We can withdraw the actions we have begun, to recover what has been stolen and let them continue to steal. If we do that they will think we are afraid, of course, and . . ."

Donald Rae's fist thumped down on the top of the table that was beside him. "No!" he said. "We can't do that! I'm not afraid of . . ."

Cameron interrupted, nodding. "I thought that you

would want to proceed," he said. "I'll be glad to go over things with you tomorrow, Donald, and explain what we have done. Perhaps, after all, you have been a trifle negligent in your duties. I'm glad that Gwynn mentioned the fact."

"Gwynn!" Donald Rae's face was red. "What does a girl know about business? I'll be in your office early, Arthur. Early."

"That will be fine," Cameron smiled. "I'll go to the office now and begin to put things in shape so that we can find them easily. Good night, Donald."

He turned and walked away and Donald Rae, after a moment's hesitation, went to the sideboard and poured himself a drink from the decanter that stood there.

In his office Cameron found Kent Null, lounging in a chair, a glass of whisky and water in his hands. Null looked up inquiringly.

"The girl talked to Rae," said Cameron, answering that look. "He thinks that he is going to take hold of things. I'm to have a talk with him in the morning and go over the Grant affairs."

Kent Null nodded. "And that will be fine," he commented.

"Why?" Cameron frowned.

"Because," said Null, "matters are coming to a head at Marthastown. Now, no matter what happens, Donald will take the responsibility for it. You and I, Arthur, are in the clear so far as the syndicate is concerned."

Cameron's face cleared slowly. "By George, you're right!" said Cameron. "You're right, Kent. No matter what happens Donald will be responsible."

Null laughed. "Donald and Lieutenant Metcalf," he amended. "They'll pull the chestnuts, Arthur. Our fingers won't be burned."

CHAPTER 13

HIGH IN THE HILLS, IN THE HIDDEN SPOT THAT MAT McCarthy called the "Junta," Llano Land helped make camp. Horses were led through the pines that fringed the mountain bog and there, in a little park hidden by the pines and aspens, were hobbled and turned loose. Back in the pines Virge Savoy swung an ax and trees fell. A lean-to went up, cross-thatched with pine boughs. Poles were cut and set and a tarpaulin thrown over them and pegged down to make an open ended A of canvas. A fire twinkled among the trees and the dusk closing in as the sun set behind Copper mountain made the fire a red coal that blinked and winked like the coal in a smoker's pipe.

Llano took a hand in the work and when the activity was done and Hamarick was cooking over the fire, Llano seated himself on a log beside Mat McCarthy.

"An' now what?" asked Llano.

"I was goin' to ask you the same," answered McCarthy. "We're goin' to lay up here. We got connections in Ladron. Word will come out to us after awhile an' then we'll know what's what, but what about you, Llano?"

Llano disregarded that question. "Your connections in Ladron may not be so good," he drawled. "When I first found you, Mat, I knew that the Grant was letting you stay where you were. I didn't know why. You told me that you and your boys moved the Grant boundary marker. Was that why they let you alone?"

McCarthy finished stuffing his pipe, lit it and puffed twice. "That was why," he said quietly.

"And when you moved the marker you knew what it

136

meant," insisted Llano. "You knew what you were doing. You knew the sort of hell you'd let loose on the Grant."

McCarthy shrugged. "Look, Llano," he drawled, "I'm a cow thief. I'm fat old Mat McCarthy, a damn' rustler. The two Savoys will be hung if ever they go back to Kansas. Hamarick's on the wanted list in Montana. Do you think we stopped to figger things out when it was put up to us to move that rock?"

Llano was silent for a moment. "You got another man," he suggested.

Again McCarthy's fat shoulders lifted. "A wild kid," he said. "Bill Westfall. He lived in this country. He threw in with us."

Llano returned to the attack. "You threw in with the Grant," he accused. "You . . ."

There was anger in McCarthy's voice as he interrupted. "I told you we didn't figger," he snapped. "We had a hideout. We had a place to hold cattle. We were let alone. Capes an' Null propositioned us to move that rock an' offered us shelter for what we were doin'. We didn't think. Who'd think ahead in a business like ours?"

Llano grunted. "But you're thinking ahead now," he commented dryly.

"Yo're damn right I am," the anger in McCarthy flared out. "We didn't think of the killin' an' trouble we'd let loose when we moved that rock or we wouldn't of done it. Now, by God, the Grant has turned on us. The Grant can look out. They rode in to the cabin today ready to kill us like we was coyotes in a trap. Any Grant man I see over my rifle sights is dead! I . . ."

"And that will make it all right," interrupted Llano, softly. "You'll kill Grant men. You'll rustle Grant

137

cattle. You'll raise hell with the Grant and it will make things all right for what you did. Mat . . ."

"It'll help!" snapped McCarthy, savagely.

There was silence between the men. Over by the fire Shorty Hamarick straightened and rubbed smoke from his eyes. Virge Savoy came out of the tarpaulin tent. There was a plaint in McCarthy's voice when he spoke.

"What else can I do, Llano? I didn't know . . ."

"I don't know, Mat," comforted Llano. "I just don't know."

Again there was silence. Llano broke it, "Jack Ames was killed in Ladron," he said reflectively. "I found that out. He was killed there and buried. There wasn't anything on him that identified him. Mulligan, the barber down there, told me. Mulligan told me about burying a yellow-haired man with a wedge-shaped birth mark on his chin."

McCarthy half turned so that he faced Llano. "Mulligan?" he questioned. "Are you sure it was Jack, Llano?"

"There's no doubt," said Llano grimly. "Mulligan said that the man's left leg had been broken between the knee and the ankle. Who else but Jack could it be?"

McCarthy thought for a moment and then shook his head. "It was Jack," he said positively. "What are you goin' to do, Llano?"

"Find the man that killed him," answered Llano, grimly.

"How?"

"By tracing the horses Jack sold." Llano fumbled for the makings and began to roll a cigarette. "There's one at Ladron House and Greybull's got one. That will put me on a trail. Someone who bought a horse from Jack will know who he was friendly with and when he went

138

to Ladron and who was with him there. Then I'll go on from that."

"You don't ever let go, do you?" asked McCarthy admiringly.

Llano licked the flap of his cigarette and grimaced. "I'm not getting ahead very fast," he said ruefully. "Greybull thinks I'm a Grant man and he wouldn't talk to me. He . . ."

"Why does Greybull think that?"

"Because of Kent Null," Llano lit his smoke. "Null told him I was and it looks like it. You see, Mat, I had to go to bat for Null."

By the fire Shorty Hamarick called softly. "Come on an' get it while it's hot."

Llano and McCarthy stood up. "To bat for Kent Null?" asked McCarthy, incredulously.

"I'll tell you," said Llano. They walked toward the fire and in brief, sharp sentences Llano told McCarthy of what had happened at Gra'maw Stamps' and afterward in Marthastown.

"Well, I'll be damned," said McCarthy when the tale was finished. "An' now what, Llano?"

"I don't know," answered Llano.

McCarthy stooped and picked up a plate. "There'll be word out here soon," he said, moving around the fire. "Bill Westfall will be out from Ladron an' he'll tell us what's happenin'. You lay up with us, Llano, until we hear. Then we'll all know what to do."

Arch Savoy, spearing steak from a frying pan, looked up and grinned. "I don't give a damn what we do," he drawled, "as long as we got Shorty to cook an' there's plenty of Grant beef."

When the meal was finished the men left the fire, Hamarick and Arch going to look after the horses, Virge

139

bringing water from a spring by the bog. With the dishes washed the fire was extinguished and the men crawled into their blankets in the tarp tent and under the lean-to.

The next morning, when the dawn broke, the men got up. Breakfast was cooked and eaten and Arch Savoy, carrying a rifle, pulled out of the camp, crossed the bog and climbed the ridge. From that vantage point he could see anyone coming toward the canyon below. Thus guarded the men relaxed. The camp was improved in minor details and Hamarick found a deck of cards. He inveigled the others into joining him and on a blanket spread beneath a pine tree a game of draw pitch raged. At noon they ate a cold snack and Virge Savoy went to relieve his brother. So the day wore on and when darkness fell in the canyon Hamarick again kindled a fire and cooked.

"We'll butcher a Grant heifer tomorrow," said McCarthy as he drank hot coffee from his cup. "Bill ought to be out . . ."

McCarthy stopped in mid-sentence. There was a horse coming across the bog. Arch Savoy picked up a rifle and stepped back from the fire. McCarthy alert and hand on his six-shooter, stood in the shadows. Hamarick had disappeared and Llano Land had stepped away to join Virge Savoy in the shelter of the pines. The horse came on steadily, feet splashing on the marshy ground. Then the splashes were changed to regular, dull beats on the dry earth and a rider came into the dim light of the fire, stopped and dismounted.

Mat McCarthy stepped into the circle of firelight. "We just spoke of you, Bill," drawled McCarthy.

The others moved forward. Llano found himself examining this newcomer. He saw a boy, apple-cheeked

140

and innocent, blue-eyed and with down still upon his cheeks. A kid, thought Llano, and then as the blue eyes encountered his he revised his opinion suddenly. This Bill Westfall looked like a kid, but his eyes gave the lie to his appearance.

"This is Llano Land, Bill," said McCarthy, making introduction.

Westfall nodded. "Land," he said, and his voice was a boyish tenor. "They're kind of lookin' for you around Ladron, Land."

"Why?" demanded Mat McCarthy. "What . . ?"

"You can give me a cup of coffee," said Westfall. "I'll tell you while I eat. Mulligan sure had an earful for me when I come in."

Mulligan! Llano was startled. So the peg-legged, taciturn barber was the connection for the outlaws in Ladron! Llano would not have suspected.

"What did he have to say?" snapped McCarthy.

Westfall crunched on a sandwich of bread and meat and took coffee from the tin cup. "There's hell to pay in Ladron," he said and seemed to relish his words.

McCarthy was impatient. "Go on, tell it!" he commanded. "We know that there was hell in Ladron. We raised some of it. Capes come out to the cabin to plant an empty Wells Fargo box on us. There was a posse right behind him. Capes run into trouble an' we packed up an' pulled out before the posse got there. Was that what you figured to tell us?"

"So that's what happened to Capes," drawled Westfall. "They was wonderin' about it in Ladron. Nope, that ain't what I had to tell you. Preacher Gunther was killed yesterday, up by Segundo creek. He was brought in an' the word has gone out that you killed him, Land!"

Dead silence struck the group. Then McCarthy snapped a question. "Who says that?"

"It's just around," answered Westfall. "Nobody is sayin' it particularly, but it seems like everybody has got that idea. There was a dance hall woman named Juell stayin' with the preacher and the story is that Land an' Gunther had words over her."

"Why . . ." began Llano.

McCarthy forestalled that. "Land was with us yesterday!" he said. "He was the one that fixed Capes up with what he needed. He couldn't of killed Gunther. He . . ."

"Do you think," drawled Westfall, "that killin' Capes is goin' to make the Grant love him? Mebbe you'll ride in, Mat, an' make him an alibi. They're sayin' in Ladron that you an' Virge an' Arch an' Shorty was the ones that stopped the stage an' killed the messenger. Nobody in particular sayin' it. Just talk. Mebbe you'd like to ride in an' stand up for Land."

McCarthy swore helplessly and Llano Land, his eyes on Westfall asked a question. "What happened to Rose Juell?"

"She's still at the preacher's house," answered Westfall, drinking again from his cup. "That ain't all I got to tell you, Mat."

"Git on with it," growled McCarthy.

"The Grant has stopped Greybull an' the fellows at Marthastown from workin' their claims," Westfall relished the announcement. "The miners are bunchin' up an' they're goin' down an' take Ladron apart. Mulligan says that Cameron has sent for the soldiers from Bridger."

"What's that to us?" asked McCarthy.

Westfall grinned. "Nothin'," he answered, "only now

142

wouldn't be any too good a time for you to start takin' it out of the Grant in case you had it in mind."

"What else do you know?" rasped McCarthy.

Westfall refilled his cup. "That's about the size of it," he said. "You want me to go back to town tomorrow?"

McCarthy walked around the fire. "I'll tell you tomorrow," he answered. "I got to think this over."

McCarthy sat on a log. Llano Land squatted on a boot heel and rolled a cigarette, his eyes far away and the motions of his fingers mechanical. The others stood around Bill Westfall, their low voices asking questions, and the fire blinked red, dying away.

And while that fire blinked red, a glowing coal in the night, far down a canyon north of Ladron another fire blossomed. It grew from a spark into a licking flame that shot yellow along the side of a house. Rising, black smoke at its tips hidden by the black night, this second fire showed a broken fence and a weedy patch of plowed ground. It showed horses, heads lifted, ears pricked forward, frightened at the fire's growth. The horses were hooded, masked by crude covers, and the riders too were hooded and covered. A horse moved and an empty kerosene can clanged and then, from the house came a rising, wailing scream. A woman, a child caught in her arms, ran from the building. She set the child on the ground and, turning, one arm shielding her face, ran back into the flame framed doorway.

Across the fence a rider, a tall man, lifted a steel tipped arm, leveling a weapon at the tow-headed girl-child that cowered before the house. Another rider beside him struck up that arm and the shot spouted into the night.

"Damn you, Huerta!" raged Dick Wadell, "Damn

you! It's a kid!" Struggling, he caught the arm and wrenched the pistol from the tall man crazed by marijuana.

Again the woman appeared, carrying another child. Her night gown was on fire and the boy in her arm screamed again and again with the pain of burns.

The riders across the fence turned their horses and with the kerosene can clanging, rode down the canyon, while in the dooryard the woman beat out flames with work-calloused hands and then, with that accomplished, tried to quiet the weeping of her children.

Later, in Ladron, Dick Wadell knocked on the side door of Ladron House, the little door that gave direct egress to Cameron's office. There was a pause after the knock and then the door opened and a cautious voice spoke.

"What is it?"

"Wadell," answered the man outside. "We set that fire at Kinney's. The woman an' the kids got out all right."

Again there was a pause and then Cameron spoke. "Have you heard anything of Capes?"

"No," answered Dick Wadell, and remembering the bank account in Trinity, "we ain't goin' to neither."

"Be here early in the morning," ordered Cameron and the door closed.

And again while the fire glowed under Copper Mountain and while Llano Land lit the cigarette he had rolled, a rider came to the kitchen door of Gra'maw Stamps' tavern. Dismounting he knocked cautiously on the door and waited until he heard the heavy pad of Gra'maw Stamps' bare feet crossing the kitchen floor.

When the door was opened and light from a lamp

streamed out there was no one in sight but a voice whispered softly:

"Gra'maw! Gra'maw!"

Gra'maw Stamps blew out the light. "John Kinney," she answered, her voice as low as that of the man who called. "I thought you were in jail at Bridger!"

"I broke out. Let me in, Gra'maw! I've got to have a horse an' somethin' to eat."

"Come in," said Gra'maw Stamps, and stepped back from the door.

The door closed and it was dark in the kitchen. Then a match flamed and the lamp flickered feebly until the chimney was replaced. When the flickering had been supplanted by a warm yellow glow Gra'maw Stamps stood in the middle of the kitchen, covered by an old wrapper. Against the wall beside the door was a blond-haired, white-faced young fellow, his eyes worn and haggard.

"John Kinney," said Gra'maw Stamps again, "you set down. I'll get you somethin' to eat an' there's a horse in the corral."

John Kinney slumped into a chair. "I knew you'd help me," he said tensely. "Have you seen Margaret, Gra'maw?"

Mrs. Stamps shook her head. She was padding from cupboard to table, setting on the table such cold food as she could find. John Kinney picked up a piece of bread, laid a slab of cold meat on it and munched wolfishly.

"Margaret has been stayin' on your place," said Gra'maw Stamps. "She's been holdin' it down, John. The Grant wanted her to pay rent an' she wouldn't. When did you get out, John?"

"This afternoon," answered Kinney, gulping a morsel of food. "Pope Sanches got careless. He come into my

145

cell an' I got his gun an' hit him over the head an' took his keys. I hid out 'til it was dark. Then I stole a horse an' rode to here."

"Where are you goin' from here, John?"

"Home," said John Kinney. "I got to see Margaret an' the kids. I tell you I got to, Gra'maw."

The old woman blinked. There was something in John Kinney's voice, something in his tone, that had brought tears to her eyes. Kinney wolfed down more food, eating ravenously. "I'll take care of the horse I took," he said. "Nobody'll ever find him around here, Gra'maw. If they catch me nobody'll know I been here."

Gra'maw Stamps blew her nose violently. "I ain't a-carin' if they know or not!" she announced defiantly. "There's some things that a body just can't stand. I paid rent to the Grant but they don't own me. You eat some bread an' jelly, Johnny. I'll stir up a fire an' make you a cup of coffee."

But John Kinney came to his feet, protesting. "I got to go on," he said urgently. "I got to go on tonight while it's dark. Don't you bother Gra'maw. You been good to me the way it is. I'm goin'."

Before the old woman could speak, before she could protest, Kinney was at the door. He looked at her.

"Blow out the light," he requested. "Blow it out an' I'm gone, Gra'maw. An' . . . an' thanks."

The lamp died black. Darkness in the kitchen. The door opened and closed. After a while Gra'maw Stamps, listening heard horses moving away from the corrals, stealthy hoofbeats. Then those, too, were gone.

"Pore boy!" said Gra'maw Stamps. "Pore, pore boy!"

Up under Copper mountain the fire died to embers, its last flickering flame gone and only dull red remaining.

146

Llano Land got up from his bootheel and Mat McCarthy arose from his log.

"Tomorrow," said Llano decisively, "I'll go to Ladron."

CHAPTER 14

DALE FALLIEN SAT ON THE PORCH OF THE SAINT George Hotel and watched Ladron. Ladron was worth watching. The place was like a kettle on the fire just before it boils. Early in the morning men had begun to filter into the town by ones and twos. Hardy men, roughly dressed. Then later, when the sun was higher, a body of men had come riding down Ladron canyon. Pat Greybull had been in the lead of this group, and Greybull had gone directly to Ladron House. The others had gone on to town. They were there now. Men with time on their hands, men that were tense, men that felt that they had a just cause for wrath. They were waiting for Greybull to come out of Ladron House and while they waited they drank whisky and talked to each other. Greybull had been in Ladron House for over an hour. Fallien's light blue eyes were narrow slits as he stared at the black bulk of the house.

As he sat watching, a little body of men came from the town and moved determinedly toward the house on the hill. They passed the Saint George and Fallien could catch some of the words that they were speaking. Fragments of sentences drifted to him. "Been there an hour . . ." "Greybull's makin' a deal for himself . . ." "What's he care about us . . ?" Dale Fallien heard those things.

The men went on, reached Ladron House and paused. Apparently they were debating on the course they

147

should pursue. The debate seemed to resolve itself and an agreement was evidently reached, for two of the men left the crowd and went to the door of the house. They stood there waiting. The door of the house opened and Cameron and Donald Rae, accompanied by a short stocky man, came out. Fallien saw the short man lift his hand and as the men in front of the house grew quiet, Cameron's companion spoke. Fallien could not hear the words. He lifted himself from his chair, shook his long body and set foot on the steps that led down from the porch of the Saint George.

Up at Ladron House, Pat Greybull, with Cameron and Rae flanking him, spoke to the men assembled in the street. "I been tryin' to make a dicker, men," he said. "I been talkin' to Mr. Cameron an' to Mr. Rae. They got the law on their side. We're on the Grant. They showed me. They say that we can operate if we'll pay rent. That . . ."

The crowd was no longer still. It had moved as Greybull spoke and the men who had gone to the door of Ladron House had returned to their companions. Now there were angry words, voices raised to refute Greybull. The little man held up his hand again, striving for silence, but he could not get it.

"You made a deal!" a voice called accusingly from the crowd. "You sold us out, Greybull. You . . ."

"Wait!" pleaded Greybull. "Wait. I'm with you boys. I . . ."

Dale Fallien stood on the board sidewalk in front of the Saint George. There was the pound of a running horse from the direction of town. Fallien turned and the horse, sweating and barely able to keep its feet, went past him. The rider tumbled from the horse before Ladron House. The men in the crowd parted, moving

148

back to give the horseman room. He did not pause. The horse went on, staggering in its run but the rider, feet wide spread, threw up his arm and a shot rang out.

Beside Greybull, Donald Rae reeled back against the door casing. Cameron had a gun in his hand but Cameron did not fire. A rifle spoke from the window above the door, the second story window. The rider took two staggering steps back and went down. Greybull jerked himself away from the doorway, running toward the men in the street. Other windows of the great, black house were raised. Rifles, the barrels slim and wicked, projected from those windows. Cameron had swept up Donald Rae and gone through the door, all in one swift movement. The door was closed, black and solid. Out in the street a miner brought out a gun and fired a shot. That shot was answered from Ladron House. The rifles in the windows spoke and the men in the street, each striving for his own safety, scattered and ran like a covey of quail found by a hunter. Where, in one moment there had been a group of angry men, there were three bodies in the street and that was all.

At the first fire Fallien had moved. His long legs took him efficiently to the corner of the Saint George and around that corner. Now he stood peering out, waiting for the next move.

It came swiftly. A man ran from cover toward the limp bodies in the street. His purpose was apparent. He wanted to get to those men. One of them, perhaps more, was not dead but wounded. That running man had gone to bring a friend to shelter. Almost he reached his goal. Then again a rifle snapped in the great house and the running man sprawled out.

From his vantage point Fallien could see the house and the men about it. They had been taken by surprise, these miners, but they rallied swiftly. Men were coming from the town, running toward the hill. Armed men, these, angry, loaded with resentment and whisky.

"The damned fools!" muttered Fallien. "They've set it on fire now. Why did they start that?"

From various places about the house men began to shoot. Their fire was desultory and ineffective. A window pane shattered in the second floor. Chips of adobe flew from a corner. In the street a man, shot down in the first flurry of fire, began to crawl toward a wall, painfully dragging a leg.

Fallien shrugged his high, thin shoulders. "I suppose," he said, half aloud, "that I got to . . ." He did not finish his sentence. High and thin, carrying, the notes of a bugle came floating. Fallien settled back, his shoulders against the wall.

"So that's why they started," he murmured, as though answering some question in his mind. "They'd sent for the troops."

A dry voice at his elbow made Fallien whirl, hand shooting to an armpit holster. "Yeah," said the voice, "I reckon that's why."

"Land!" exclaimed Fallien.

Llano Land was standing, facing him, a saturnine grin on his thin lips. "You look like you weren't expecting me," drawled Llano.

The surprise died from Fallien's face. His eyes were impassive once more and his drawl matched Llano's. "I wasn't," he agreed. "Naturally I wasn't."

"An' why?" Llano's voice was thin.

"Because," said Fallien, "the word has been passed that you killed James Gunther."

"An' that's why I'm here," explained Llano. "Come on, let's look. The army's about got to town."

Fallien peered around the corner of the Saint George once more. There, where the bodies had been in Ladron's street, there were now blue clad cavalry men. As Fallien looked men swung down from their horses. He heard sharp commands and a group of soldiers trotted toward the Saint George.

"With all the trimmings," Llano commented sardonically. "Now watch 'em come out of the house."

Indeed there was activity at Ladron House. The door opened and men came out. Two of these were easily recognizable as Kent Null and Arthur Cameron. They walked across the porch and down the steps approaching a stocky figure on horseback.

"An' Metcalf, too," Llano's voice continued impassionately. "That makes him a hero, I guess."

Fallien's eyes were bright as he turned them on his companion. "I'm damned if I sabe you, Land," he said.

"There's nothing to sabe." Llano laughed briefly. "I come over here on private business. I been dragged into something else. Now I guess that's my business, too." He stepped ahead, turning the corner of the adobe hotel building. Fallien waited a moment and then followed. When Fallien cleared the corner, Llano was on the porch, pulling open the door of the hotel. In front of Ladron House Metcalf had dismounted and was walking toward the building with Cameron and Null on either side of him. Fallien stood on the front porch of the Saint George and then opened the door and went in.

Wayne Metcalf, pulling off his heavy cavalry gauntlets, walked through the doors of Ladron House. For a moment he stood in the great hall of the place, looking around him. Then, his eyes becoming accustomed to the dimness, he saw a couch across the room and a figure bending over the couch. Cameron and

Null had followed the officer through the door and were now on either side of him. Cameron had spoken but Metcalf did not catch the words. He walked across the room, spur chains clinking, and halted beside the couch. Gwynn Rae, her checks tear stained looked up.

"Gwynn!" exclaimed Metcalf.

The girl came up from her knees. For a moment it seemed that she would throw herself into Metcalf's arms. Then, with a visible effort at control she spoke: "Donald!" Instantly Metcalf was kneeling beside the couch. Donald Rae lay there, his face white. His coat and shirt had been removed and there was a cloth, blood stained, wrapped across his shoulder and under his arm.

"Silly of me," said Donald Rae, faintly. "It isn't bad, really."

Metcalf looked up at Gwynn. The girl stood at his right, her hands clasped and her eyes anxious. "I'm all right, Gwynn," said Donald Rae, answering that look.

"The ambulance and our surgeon are following down the canyon," announced Metcalf, rising from beside the couch. "If you'll call Sergeant Cassidy I'll have a man dispatched to hurry them."

Kent Null stepped away and Metcalf turned to Cameron.

"What happened?" he asked, his voice stern.

Cameron met the officer's eyes. "We sent for you yesterday," he answered. "As you know the boundary of the Grant has been confirmed. We find that the Grant includes Marthastown and the valley below it. Naturally Donald wished to protect the interests of the company and an injunction was issued forbidding the miners at Marthastown to operate until some settlement was reached with the Grant."

"Yes?" questioned Metcalf.

152

"They refused to obey the injunction," Cameron continued, his voice smooth. "The local officers attempted to enforce it and there was a concerted movement from Marthastown to Ladron.

"Greybull, who is the principal operator there, met with Donald and Kent and myself this morning. We reached an agreement. We were to receive a portion of the proceeds and Greybull was explaining it to a group of his men. Donald and Kent and I were with him on the porch. A rider came from town, burst through the crowd, leaped from his horse and fired a shot. It struck Donald here in the shoulder."

"And then?" snapped Metcalf.

"Naturally we were prepared to defend ourselves," purred Cameron. "We have been threatened time and again. The guards we had posted returned the fire. There were several men hurt."

"You sent word . . ." began Metcalf.

There came an interruption. Null, accompanied by a grizzled-faced soldier with the yellow chevrons of a sergeant on his sleeve, came through the door and across the hall. The sergeant saluted.

Metcalf spoke swiftly. "Dispatch a rider to the ambulance, Sergeant," he ordered. "Present my compliments to Doctor Von Weigand and beg him to come on with all possible speed. He is needed here."

"Yis sorr!" said the sergeant, and saluted. Nevertheless he did not turn away.

"What is it, Sergeant?" snapped Metcalf.

"There's a bunch of men, sorr," said the sergeant. "They come up from town. Will the Lieutenant step outside an' speak to 'em?"

Metcalf frowned. "Miners?" he snapped. "We'll look after them presently. I've already sent Sergeant

153

Connor and a patrol."

"Beg pardon, sorr," Cassidy took the privilege of an old soldier, and interrupted his officer, "they ain't miners. They're cowboys an' farmers by the looks of them. Will the Lieutenant please to come out an' see 'em?"

"Send a man for the ambulance!" ordered Metcalf. "I'll be out in a moment."

The grizzled sergeant saluted and turned sharply about.

Metcalf turned to where Gwynn again knelt beside her brother.

"The doctor is coming, Gwynn," he said, and the girl's name was an endearment on his lips. "I must . . ."

Gwynn Rae reached up and caught his hand. "We will be safe now that you are here," she said impulsively. "Come back, Wayne. Come back when you can."

There was a promise in the girl's eyes, a promise that Metcalf could not miss, nor did Cameron and Null standing beside the officer, miss that promise. Null glanced at Cameron. The dark man's cheeks were a dull red and his lips were tight and bloodless. Metcalf held the girl's hand a moment, the pressure of his own hand firm and reassuring. Then relinquishing his grip, he turned.

"You will excuse me, gentlemen," apologized the officer, and hurried across the hall to the door. Outside Ladron House veteran noncommissioned officers had taken charge of the troop. A mounted patrol had swung off, riding through Ladron. Troopers stood by horses, and just in front of Ladron House was a dismounted squad standing at ease, their carbines at the order. There were four men, ranchmen evidently, standing close by

154

the squad, and beyond and toward the Saint George Hotel there was a crowd, a mob of men. Some of these were miners but there were teamsters in the mob and a sprinkling of dark-skinned natives, but the men that stood in the front, the dangerous men, were ranchmen. Their clothing told that. Metcalf looked at the disposal of the troop and was pleased; he looked at the mob, and worried wrinkles creased his forehead. They were too silent, too ominously silent. As he glanced to his right he saw in the shadow of Ladron House four bodies laid prone on the ground. A blue clad man was bending over one of these. They were the wounded, men brought down in the shooting that preceded the troop's arrival.

A murmur arose from the crowd near the Saint George and looking behind him, Metcalf saw Null and Cameron with Dick Wadell beside them, come through the door of the house. His frown increased and he walked down the steps toward the men who awaited him. As he reached them he spoke crisply:

"What do you want?"

There was silence for a moment and then a lanky, red-headed man who wore chaps and chewed tobacco, answered the question. "We want a lot of things, soldier," said the redhead.

"Such as . . . ?" suggested Metcalf pointedly.

"We want John Kinney for one thing." The redhead shifted his chew.

"Kinney?" questioned Metcalf.

"He's over there." The red-headed man jerked his thumb toward Ladron House. "Kinney's place was burnt by them murderers last night. His wife an' his kids got out but I reckon he don't know it. They're in town. Kinney come ridin' in wild-eyed an' he taken a shot at that Rae feller. Got him, too. We want Kinney."

"If Kinney attacked Mr. Rae his place is in jail," said Metcalf decisively. "I'll put him there."

The red head was slowly shaken. "Nope, mister," contradicted the man. "Nope. John's got hurt. We're goin' to take him an' look after him. We want them murderers in Ladron House, too. We want Null an' Cameron an' that damned Wadell."

Metcalf looked steadily at the speaker. "I order you to disperse," he said calmly. "Martial law has been declared in Ladron. At another time and place I'll meet your leaders and we will arrive at a settlement. But mob rule is not to be tolerated. You men go to your homes!"

The officer lifted his voice with the last words so that they carried to the crowd. There was an angry murmur following the words, a ripple of unrest across the waiting men. The redhead spoke again.

"There's two hundred men there," said the redhead gently, lifting a hand toward the crowd. "They can blow you off the face of the earth, mister."

Metcalf made no answer to that. He wheeled, turning his broad back on the redhead and his companion. His voice came strong:

"As skirmishers . . . !"

The blue clad men moved. Veteran troopers these. For each four, one man remained holding horses. The others spread in a thin blue line across the street in front of Ladron House.

"Load!" Metcalf's command was clear. The breech blocks of the Springfield carbines snicked open. Long, blunt-tipped, brass shells went into the forty-five-seventies. Metcalf again wheeled.

"I have ordered you to disperse," he said calmly. "My next order will be to fire."

The red-headed man glanced back over his shoulder.

He was as calm as Metcalf. Behind him the miners, the teamsters, and the cowmen had spread out. They too were ready. Here a Colt glinted dully, here a Winchester lifted a wicked snout. The red-headed man looked at Metcalf.

"You an' me," he observed, "are right square in the middle. Kind of between a rock an' a hard spot. You shoot an' they'll shoot, an' you an' me won't be interested no more."

Metcalf eyed the speaker. There was a grim smile on the redhead's lips. From beyond the mob came the clatter of horses and the head of the patrol, one mounted squad, swung into view. In the lead big Sergeant Connors shot up an arm and the patrol halted.

Metcalf looked at the red-headed man. "The patrol," suggested Metcalf gently, "will charge. And then . . ."

The red-headed man spat. "Nope," he drawled, "there's eight or ten men on the roofs of them adobes above yore soldiers. They'll be knocked out of the saddle before they can move. I ain't overlooked a bet."

Metcalf waited. The red-headed man spoke again. "We want John Kinney," he declared. "We want them murderin' devils in Ladron House. Do we get 'em?"

Metcalf shook his head. The red-headed man turned. "I reckon we got to take what we want, boys," he called.

"Just a minute," Metcalf interjected. "You know what this means, I suppose? Perhaps you can wipe out the troop. A good many of you will be killed doing that. Then there will be other troops and still other troops if necessary. You can fight us, but can you fight the United States?"

His words carried to the men behind the redhead. Something of the tenseness in the crowd was gone. Somehow those words had gone home. Metcalf

157

wheeled, taking advantage of that momentary weakening.

"At ease!" he ordered. And then, turning back to the red-headed man, "Our surgeon will be here within a few minutes. I will see that the wounded have proper attention. You men disperse. Go to your homes. Tomorrow I'll hear your complaints. If possible I will adjust them. I . . ."

There was an interruption. Breaking through the ranks of the ranchmen and the miners, disheveled and panting, came a fat man at a run. He reached Metcalf, stopped and his panted words were plainly heard by all.

"Land!" gasped Leige Nathan. "Llano Land, the man that killed Gunther! He's at the hotel!"

Wayne Metcalf was no fool. He struck instantly while the iron was hot. Here was opportunity. Metcalf seized it. "Sergeant!" he snapped, almost before Nathan's panting words were out, "take a squad and accompany this man. Arrest Llano Land and hold him!"

Dick Wadell had come down the steps. No coward now was Dick Wadell. "I'm a deputy sheriff," he announced in Metcalf's ear. "I ought to . . ."

"Take the deputy with you, Sergeant!" ordered Metcalf.

"Yis, sorr," Cassidy acknowledged the order.

Metcalf turned to the red-headed man once more. "Now . . ." he began.

The red-headed man nodded. "Yo're the boss," he said slowly. "For now, anyhow. But, Lieutenant . . ."

"Yes?" said Metcalf.

"God help you if you don't do the right thing!" completed the redhead, and turning walked back to where the mob, together once more, was moving surlily toward the Saint George Hotel.

158

Cassidy, the squad of men at his heels, swept up Nathan and Wadell and at the double, followed the crowd, caught it, pierced through it, and entered the Saint George.

CHAPTER 15

LLANO LAND SAT ON THE BED IN HIS ROOM AT THE Saint George. Opposite him Dale Fallien occupied the single chair in the room. Llano, upon entering the hotel, had asked for and secured the room that he had first occupied. He looked curiously at Fallien. Fallien was completing the telling of a story.

". . . so," concluded Fallien, "I picked him up an' loaded him in the back of his buckboard an' brought him to Ladron to Mulligan's."

"And he was cut up," said Llano slowly. "You didn't find anything?"

Fallien shook his head. "Not a thing," he corroborated. "Land, the talk about you is plumb ugly."

Llano grunted. His gray eyes gleamed as he looked at Fallien. "Take me out and hang me, I suppose they say," he suggested. "I've heard that sort of talk before."

"Where were you?" demanded Fallien bluntly. "You weren't around here."

"Who is asking?" Llano's eyes narrowed as he stared at the man in the chair. "Who are you, Fallien?"

Dale Fallien shrugged. "You'd be surprised," he answered.

"I'm open to surprises." Llano got up from the bed. "There's things happening outside, Fallien. Suppose we go look at them."

"If you show yore head outside the door I wouldn't

answer for what would happen." Fallien also arose from his seat. "Can't I get it to you that these folks think you killed James Gunther an' that James Gunther was just a little tin god on wheels to most of 'em?"

"I've got it through my head," said Llano, moving across the room. "I still want to look. I always liked to see the soldiers."

Fallien took a step toward Llano and stopped. He was behind Land for Llano was at the door. Feet sounded loud in the corridor, thumping on the thick carpet. The sound drew near and metal rattled harshly. Llano took his hand from the door.

"This room," announced Nathan's voice.

The door was thrust open. A grizzled gray-haired square-faced sergeant of cavalry stood in the opening. Behind him was Dick Wadell, and behind Wadell was a file of impassive-faced troppers.

"Llano Land?" demanded the sergeant.

"I'm Llano Land," answered Llano.

"I got orders to arrest you." The sergeant took a step into the room. As the soldier moved Llano fell back a pace. Fallien, a little to his right could see the dangerous glint in Llano's eyes. Dale Fallien stepped back a pace also.

"Who gave the orders?" Llano's voice was dangerously quiet. "Metcalf?"

"Lieutenant Metcalf," answered the sergeant. "Come on."

"If you'd wait a minute I'd go outside where Metcalf can arrest me himself," suggested Llano. "His girl could see him do it and that would make him a hero. How about it, Sergeant?"

Fallien could tell, by the ring in Llano's voice, that there was trouble afoot. He had seen Llano Land in a reckless mood once before. Had seen Llano on the night of his arrival in Ladron, throw a dare at the Grant's two most dangerous men. Dale Fallien realized that Llano Land did not intend to be arrested.

"I've got orders," said the sergeant bluntly.

"Then enforce them!" Fallien could see Llano's muscles tense. "Come right in. Bring Wadell with you and Mulligan can take us all out on his shutter!"

The sergeant's mouth opened slightly. He had not expected this. Fallien could see Wadell behind the Sergeant. Wadell moved. Llano also noted that movement.

"Are you first, Wadell?" he queried coldly. Wadell froze. The sergeant apparently collected his wits. "Come . . ." he began and forged forward into the room. Dale Fallien acted swiftly. A gun slid out from its holster beneath Fallien's arm and the muzzle was jammed into Llano's back.

"Quiet!" commanded Fallien. "Search him, Sergeant!"

Llano froze. Cassidy's big fingers explored his body, removing a gun from the holster in his waist band. The pressure of Fallien's weapon did not relax. A thin bitter grin twisted Llano's lips.

"So that's what you are, Fallien?" he said softly. "I wondered a little."

Disarmed, with a trooper on either side and with troopers before and behind him, Llano Land was escorted from the Saint George. There were men on the street, lining it, filling the sidewalks. They stared at Llano as he emerged and a mutter arose from their ranks. But they made no movement, took no action. There were other soldiers along the street, a squad was posted at the corner below the Saint George. Llano,

161

turning his head, could see the men at Ladron House, could single out Metcalf and Cameron and Null. Gwynn Rae was not in sight. The troopers beside him urged him forward and falling into step with them, he marched along the street. At a little adobe building with iron bars over the window Wadell hurried forward. He unlocked the barred door, opened it, and the troopers thrust Llano inside, marched him along a short corridor and placed him in a cell that Wadell unlocked. The sergeant gave terse orders, posting his guard.

Wadell leered through the cell bars. "Llano Land!" jeered Wadell. "Tough guy, ain't you?"

Llano walked over to a pile of tattered bedding in a corner of the cell, kicked it with a boot toe and stepped on a roach that ran scurrying out. He looked back at Wadell and grinned.

"Come in and visit with me, friend," invited Llano Land.

"I'll visit you when they come to hang you," said Wadell.

Llano squatted, his back against the wall. Methodically he produced papers and tobacco and rolled a cigarette. Wadell jeered on and Llano did not lift his eyes. At the jail door a guard spoke abruptly.

"Come out of there, you!"

"I'm the deputy here," Wadell answered the guard. "I'm . . ."

"I don't care if you're Saint Peter!" snapped the trooper. "Come out of there. Sergeant's orders!"

"I'll see you when they string you up, Land," Wadell flung his parting at Llano. Llano lit his cigarette and gazing reflectively at it a moment, blew out the match.

Dragging slow inhalations deep into his lungs, Llano squinted his eyes and considered his predicament. He had no illusions. This was a tight spot, about as tight a spot as Llano Land was apt to see. The ominous quiet of the crowd worried him. Llano had seen yelling crowds, he had seen drunken, noisy crowds, he had seen quiet crowds. The quiet ones were the ones to fear. And he knew that this crowd was seething, that deep beneath that quiet surface was a repressed violence that must find an outlet. He grinned grimly. That outlet was very apt to be Llano's neck.

Metcalf had been smart. Llano gave the officer his due. Metcalf had chosen a good moment and had taken the play. In controlling the angry men of the crowd Metcalf had seized upon the one thing that would prevent attack. He had given the crowd another and more immediate object for their wrath. The object? Llano Land!

Out on the street now, in the saloons and along the sidewalk, men would be talking. There would be men who adhered to the Grant, unknown followers of Cameron and Null, and they would be talking, telling others of Llano Land and of how Llano Land had killed James Gunther. After a while that talk would come to a head. The mob would form and come storming down upon the jail, overpower the guards and then . . . Well, then, what would Metcalf do? Llano wondered.

In the meantime what would Llano Land do? A little glint of amusement formed in Llano's eyes. There were several things that Llano Land could do. He arose from beside the wall and walking across the narrow confines of his cell stood on tiptoe beside the window. So standing he could see out to the side of the little jail building, and by craning his neck he had a glimpse of a section of the sidewalk. Llano blew smoke through the bars. A guard, coming along the short corridor before

163

the cell, called Llano from the window.

"Stay away from there, you!" commanded the guard. Llano walked back from the window and to the door. He grinned disarmingly at the guard. "I'd like to see a fellow," he announced casually. "There's a barber here in town I'd like to see."

The guard looked incredulous. "A barber?" he asked. Llano nodded. "Mulligan," he answered, and then searching in his mind for an excuse he invented fiction. "Mulligan's got a razor of mine," he explained, running his hand over the stubble of beard that was on his jaw. "I gave it to him to sharpen. I'd like to get it."

"To cut your throat with?" The guard enjoyed his humor.

"Nope. To shave with."

The guard shrugged. "I'll call the corporal," he said. "'Mebbe he'll let you send for your barber."

Llano went back to the wall of the cell and squatted down. Presently the corporal presented his broad Irish face at the cell door.

"What's this about a razor?" he demanded.

Patiently Llano repeated his fiction. The corporal shook his head. "You get no razor," he announced.

"But I'd like to see Mulligan, anyhow," persisted Llano. "I want to tell him what to do with it."

There was some argument but persistence won. The corporal was Irish and he loved a sport. Llano was not excited, nor perturbed, apparently, although the corporal knew that Llano's case was desperate. The corporal had heard things from the men passing by the jail. Finally the soldier agreed to send for Mulligan. Llano, relieved, rolled another cigarette. This was a thin chance but it was a chance.

Time wore on. After perhaps half an hour Llano

heard a heavy voice at the jail door. He got up from where he squatted in his cell.

"Where's this jasper that says I've got his razor?" demanded Mulligan.

"Inside," answered the corporal and Llano heard Mulligan's pegleg on the hard floor of the jail. Mulligan came to the front of the cell and stopped.

"I've got no razor of yours, you damned murderer!" announced Mulligan, wrath in his voice.

Llano had counted on that anger to bring Mulligan. Now he took the chance that the anger had made.

"Then Bill Westfall didn't bring it in from the Junta?" asked Llano casually.

"Nobody brought me a razor," began Mulligan wrathfully. "Nobody . . . huh?"

"A friend of mine named Mat McCarthy recommended you mighty highly," said Llano, low-voiced. "Him an' Bill Westfall."

Mulligan dropped his tone. "Whist now!" said Mulligan, "what do you know about the Junta an' Mat McCarthy?"

"Nothing much." Llano also kept his voice lowered, "except that I came from there this morning with Westfall guiding me. McCarthy's a friend of mine. He'd like to know that I'm in jail."

Mulligan raised his voice again. "I've not got your damned razor," he announced, and then, the tone soft again: "Westfall's at my place. I'll tell him."

"He'd better hurry," breathed Llano, and then, loudly: "I thought Bill had given it to you. Well, no harm done."

"Not to me," announced Mulligan, and turning, stumped away. Llano relaxed, breathing a little easier. Maybe, just maybe, Mat McCarthy could do something.

165

And now time dragged. The window of the cell gradually grew dark and looking out Llano could see the gray of the sky. Rain, a small flurry, fell, some coming in between the bars of the window. A trooper came into the jail, a poncho rustling over his uniform. Another flurry of rain beat through the bars and then in a sudden downpour, the skies opened. Llano eased himself. Men might be angry, men might be determined to exact a vengeance, but Llano Land had never heard of a man's being lynched during a rain storm.

The Irish corporal came in, stopped before the cell, and grinned. "We're goin' to wait for a while before we feed you," he said, his brogue thick. "No use of goin' out into the rain."

Suddenly Llano realized that he was hungry. He grinned back at the corporal.

Rose Juell was not hungry. From the time she had learned of Gunther's death, she had stayed in the preacher's house. Crouched in the preacher's house, would be a better expression. She had gone out only once, and that to Mulligan's shop. There she had not found James Gunther. The barber had taken the body away and was not there to tell Rose where he had taken it. The woman felt as though the earth had been swept away from beneath her feet. Her last security was gone, her last refuge, and so she had stayed close in the square adobe house that had been the preacher's.

At noon, when Maria called to her to come and eat, Rose responded listlessly. She went to the table, toyed with the food that was there and with her own eyes red from weeping, looked at Maria's swollen eyes.

Maria wept openly. Rose repressed her grief. Still her sorrow was more real and greater than Maria's. Maria had been out and on the street. Maria knew what was going on in the town, and Rose did not. So it came as a distinct shock to Rose when Maria told her of the happenings at Ladron House during the morning of the arrival of the soldiers' and of the arrest and imprisonment of Llano Land.

Rose, hearing this last, got up from the table. She told Maria nothing of what she intended but went out of the house and along toward the little jail. Arriving there, with rain already beginning to fall, she asked permission to see Llano Land. This was refused by the corporal in charge of the guard. Rose stood for a moment before the small building, her mind in a quandary. Then, she became aware of men who still stood about the building, looking at her, and she heard some of the remarks that were made. These were not stifled. Rose heard a man say, "There's the woman they had trouble over," and realizing the conspicuous place she occupied, she hurried on up the street toward Ladron House, determined to see Metcalf and extract from him the permission to visit Llano. As she reached Ladron House the rain came on in full fury and the girl ran the last few steps, only to be stopped by a guard.

Rose Juell tried to pass the guard and was arguing with him when a window in the second story of the house was raised and Gwynn Rae looked out. Recognizing the girl she saw standing before the soldier, Gwynn sent word out for Rose to be admitted. So it was not Lieutenant Metcalf, in charge of the cavalry troop, that met Rose in the great hall, but Gwynn Rae.

The two women faced each other. Rose just inside the door, her hair, face, and clothing rain-wet. Gwynn stood further in the room, haughty, beautiful, but distraught.

The army surgeon had attended her brother, as, indeed, he had attended the other wounded men, John Kinney included. Donald Rae was in no particular danger at all, but Gwynn was exceedingly worried about her brother. She looked questioningly at Rose Juell and Rose returned that look. It was Rose who broke the silence between them.

"I want to see the officer," said Rose.

"Lieutenant Metcalf?" Gwynn questioned. "He is busy with Mr. Cameron and Mr. Null."

"It's about Llano Land," Rose Juell's voice was hoarse. "He's in jail."

Gwynn slowly nodded her red-gold head.

"Llano didn't kill James Gunther," burst forth Rose. "He didn't. There wasn't any reason for Llano to kill the preacher."

"The men say that he did," answered Gwynn. "Do you know that he had nothing to do with it?"

There was an eagerness in her voice that could not be misinterpreted. Rose looked steadily at the other woman.

"I know that he didn't," she said. "The Grant men killed Gunther, not Llano Land!"

The words were a blow to Gwynn. Rose could see her recoil under them. Impulsively the black-haired girl took a step forward.

"They'll hang Llano unless we get him out," she pleaded, making Gwynn Rae an ally in a common cause. "They'll lynch him!"

"But the soldiers . . ." began Gwynn. "Lieutenant Metcalf won't . . ."

"He can't stop them," said Rose bitterly. "There are too many."

Gwynn made a quick decision. "Come with me," she

commanded. "We'll go to Wayne."

Rose, following Gwynn, noted the use of that first name. Somehow it reassured the girl.

With Gwynn preceding, the two women went to the door of Cameron's office. Stopping there they could hear the men's deep voices beyond the door. Then Gwynn rapped sharply and the voices ceased.

Cameron opened the door and stood on the threshold. "Gwynn, my dear!" exclaimed Cameron.

"I want to speak to Wayne," announced Gwynn Rae imperiously. "I want . . ."

Metcalf came to the door and, as Cameron stood aside, walked through and joined the two women. Metcalf's face was tired and his eyes were troubled.

"Llano Land, Wayne," said Gwynn Rae. "This girl says that he is in danger. That he didn't kill Gunther and that the men here in town will take him out and hang him."

Metcalf looked at Rose Juell. "What information do you have?" he asked bluntly. "Do you wish to make an alibi for Land?"

Under the implication of that question Rose Juell paled. "I . . ." she began.

"Was he with you?" asked Metcalf.

"No . . ." the word came slowly. Then, in a torrent, "But Llano didn't kill Gunther. Llano had no reason. He . . ."

Metcalf turned. "I'm sorry," he interrupted coldly. "I will afford Mr. Land every protection. You need not worry about his being lynched." His tired eyes sought Gwynn's face. Gwynn was flushed.

"If I . . ." she commenced.

"I'm sorry, Gwynn," said Metcalf with utter finality. He nodded to the two women and stepped back through the door. Wayne Metcalf was under pressure and he had begun to suspect that he was being made a tool, a cat's paw for suave Arthur Cameron and suaver Kent Null. He had, he realized, overstepped his authority by moving from Bridger at the request of the manager of the Duro Grant. He had been better off to send a dispatch rider to San Felice and await orders from his commanding officer. But here he was and now he must make the best of it.

Gwynn hurried after the officer, but Rose Juell turned away, her head lowered. She had recognized the finality in Metcalf's voice.

Cameron stopped her. "Rose," he called softly.

Gwynn had gone into the office and Cameron and Rose Juell were alone. "Perhaps I can help," suggested Cameron, standing beside the dark-haired girl.

Rose looked up quickly. "You?" she questioned.

Cameron nodded and his smile was crooked and leering on his lips. "If you would be kind to me I hardly see how I can refuse you anything," he said softly.

Rose Juell lowered her eyes again. She was silent for perhaps a minute. Gwynn Rae's voice raised in anger, came through the office door.

"Tonight," said Rose Juell. "I will be at James Gunther's house tonight."

Cameron took a quick breath. "And Llano Land will be out of jail tonight," he promised. "Afterward, Rose . . ."

Gwynn Rae came through the door, head erect, cheeks flaming. She swept past Cameron and spoke imperiously to Rose. "Come!"

Rose followed her, head still lowered. Cameron watched them go. Then, with a jerk, he turned and went back into the office.

170

In the hall Gwynn paused. "You must come with me," she said. "It is raining and we must talk. Isn't there something that we can do?"

Rose looked at Gwynn, saw the blue eyes, the red-gold hair, the fresh firm lips and the color ebbing from the girl's cheeks.

"I've done what I can," said Rose Juell wearily. "I'll go now."

She walked toward the door, pushing aside the hand with which Gwynn tried to detain her. Tugging at the heavy door she opened it and passed through and then, unmindful of the rain, she went on down the street. Through store windows and from the sheltering porches of buildings men marked her progress and commented, but Rose Juell did not raise her head.

Mulligan, the barber, was in the Exchange Saloon when Rose Juell passed. Mulligan heard the men at the door speak, but paid no heed to what they said. Mulligan was drinking his third glass of whisky. Beside him Dick Wadell also raised a glass.

"Here's to crime," toasted Wadell and drank of the mixture, whisky, water and ice, that the glass contained He set it back on the bar.

Mulligan tossed down his straight whisky and called for another.

"When's Gunther goin' to be buried?" asked the bartender as he filled Mulligan's glass again.

Mulligan shrugged. "Don't know," he answered.

"How you keepin' him?" The bartender was curious.

Mulligan eyed Dick Wadell's glass with the lump of ice slowly melting in it. "On ice," grunted Mulligan. "Didn't you see him in the ice house when you come to get yore ice this mornin'?"

"Nope," said the bartender. "On ice, huh?"

Dick Wadell looked at his glass. He, too, saw the lump of ice. "Damn you!" he swore furiously at Mulligan. "Damn you, Mulligan! Why didn't you . . ."

"To hell with you, Wadell," answered Mulligan lifting his glass. "To hell with you an' yore kind."

The drink went down and Dick Wadell recoiled a step from the peg-legged man. There was a razor, a barber's tool, bright and sharp in Mulligan's left hand. Wadell took another step back.

Out in the street the rain beat down. Up in the hills the clouds hung low and spilled their moisture. On the trail west of Ladron, Bill Westfall rode a horse and cursed the rain. The feet of Westfall's mount slid on the treacherous trail and the horse lurched. Westfall swore again and rode steadily on, head bowed against the storm, the rain running in rivulets from his hat brim.

CHAPTER 16

DALE FALLIEN WAS NOT PARTICULARLY HAPPY. HE paced back and forth across his bedroom in the Saint George while rain splattered against the windows.

"The damned fool wanted to fight," muttered Fallien, half aloud. "He'd of been killed if . . . Well, hell!"

Ceasing his restless pacing Fallien picked up his hat from the bed and pulling it down on his head walked out of his room.

In the lobby of the hotel Nathan hovered anxiously behind the desk and booted men stood, water dripping from their hats and making little pools on the carpet. Fallien paused beside the lobby door. He had recognized one of these men. There, doing most of the talking, his hat pushed far back on his red head, was Park Frazier.

"Kinney's all right," stated Frazier. "That Army doctor fixed him up. They got him an' the others in a room at Ladron House. There's a guard over him but they let his wife come in to see him an' she's with him now."

"What are we waitin' for?" demanded a bush-whiskered man. "Why . . ?"

"We're waitin' for Pat Greybull," answered Frazier. "He's comin' here as soon as he gets done with Metcalf. Then we'll decide what there is to do."

The bushy-whiskered man spat and tobacco juice splashed on the carpet. Nathan winced. The red-headed man went on. "There's enough miners an' teamsters here along with us to take Ladron House," he commented casually. "But I got to hand it to that soldier boy. He's smart, he is."

Fallien leaned back against the wall beside the door he had just entered, and watched the red-headed man. There was a lean cleverness about the redhead's face. Nathan came around the corner of the desk and crossing the room, came to Fallien's side.

"Frazier is on the warpath," he whispered, nodding toward the redhead. "He's stirring things up."

Fallien nodded. Dale Fallien wished that Frazier was far away. Frazier was dangerous.

The lobby door opened and Pat Greybull, accompanied by two or three others, came in. Greybull went directly to Frazier and stopped.

"Well?" drawled Frazier.

Greybull shrugged. There was a beaten look about the mine operator from Marthastown. "They got us handcuffed," he said slowly. "Cameron made me a proposition: We can pay fifty percent of our gross output to the Grant. The rest belongs to us after we take

173

out operatin' expenses. A man can't come out on that!"

The red-headed Frazier laughed a little, scornfully. "But you'll take it," he jeered.

Greybull looked up from beneath bushy eyebrows. "There's nothin' else to do," he argued hopelessly.

"Mebbe not for you," said Frazier "but what about us on the Grant? If we pay rent we acknowledge that they own our places. Then the next thing they move us out."

Silence followed that, and then the redhead spoke again. "I never thought you'd knuckle under to 'em, Greybull."

"I ain't knucklin' under," Greybull's voice was hoarse. "I've got a big investment there at Marthastown an' . . ."

"An' the soldiers have got you tied up," completed Frazier. "The soldiers ain't goin' to be here always, Pat."

"What . . . ?" began Greybull.

"I mean that this Metcalf moved over here at the askin' of the Grant people," answered Frazier bluntly. "Pretty soon he'll get word from the south to go on home to Bridger an' tend to his knittin'."

"An' then what?" Greybull was eager.

"Why, then," Frazier drawled, "we can fight in the courts. You made a lot of money out of Marthastown, Pat."

"Some," agreed Greybull. "What do you plan, Park?"

Park Frazier grinned thinly. "I got no plan," he replied. "The thing is, do we let the Grant get away with this? We were all set this mornin' an' the cavalry come. They got the jump on us. They arrested this Grant killer, Land. Here he is, peaceful in jail, out of the rain an' safe as if he was in a church. We goin' to stand for that, Pat?"

174

Greybull looked around the room. He saw Fallien and Nathan against the wall. He looked at the men with Frazier and at his own companions. "Let's get out where we can talk," he said abruptly. "Come on, Park."

Frazier also glanced around the lobby. He shrugged his shoulders, nodded his agreement, and followed Greybull toward the door, the others trooping after him.

When they were gone Nathan licked his thick lips. "It looks like trouble for Llano Land," announced Nathan with unction. "Damn' preacher killer!"

Fallien looked at the hotel proprietor. "You sure like to see the other man in grief," he remarked slowly. "Damn you, Nathan! You ain't fit to associate with a hog!"

With the words Fallien moved, taking his long length across the lobby and out of the door. For a moment he stood on the porch, scanning the gray sky and the street. The rain still fell and the street was almost empty. Still, there were a few men about. A cavalry trooper in a poncho stood before the door of the jail. At Ladron House the troops had sought shelter in the stable, but a sentinel walked post. Other poncho-protected soldiers were in evidence along the street, and opposite the jail there were two or three men under the porch of a store. They were watching the jail, alert, unofficial guards.

For a moment Fallien stood on the porch of the Saint George. Then, pulling down his hat brim, he stepped out into the rain. As he walked down the street someone lit a lamp in a store. It was late afternoon. Within an hour dusk would settle.

Fallien walked steadily. He passed the jail, went by stores and houses and the Exchange Saloon. Well down the street, near the church, he stopped before a square adobe house and knocking on the door waited for an

175

answer. This was Gunther's house.

Fallien's knock was answered. Maria came to the door and peered out. In Spanish, Fallien asked to see Rose Juell. Maria stood aside and the tall man entered. The woman bustled away and, hat in hand, water dripping from its brim, Fallien waited. He stood for perhaps fifteen minutes before Rose Juell came. There was a strange softness about the dark-haired woman as she came through the door, stopped, and stood looking at her visitor. Fallien nodded to her, his face grave.

"I wanted to see you," he said.

Rose Juell examined Fallien's face. She gestured toward a chair. "Won't you sit down?" she invited.

Fallien sat down. Rose remained poised beside the door.

"I want to ask you about Gunther," announced Fallien. "You were here when Gunther left that day?"

Rose nodded.

"Did he say anything about any trouble?" asked Fallien.

The woman shook her head emphatically. "He did not."

Fallien paused. "Had he an' Llano Land had any trouble over you?" he questioned bluntly.

A slow flush spread over Rose Juell's pale cheeks. "No," she answered. "Llano Land and Gunther had never talked to each other."

"Yo're sure of that?" persisted Fallien.

"Sure."

"The talk is that they'd quarreled over you," insisted Fallien.

"They had not!" Rose's head was lifted defiantly.

Fallien mused a moment. "What did Gunther say, when he left that day?" he asked.

"He said that he was going to Marthastown and that was all," Rose placed her hand against the door casing, leaning her weight there.

Fallien looked at the damp spots on his knees. His hands fumbled in the pockets of his vest and he produced papers and a sack of tobacco. Deliberately he twisted a cigarette, lit it, and took a deep inhalation. Surprise covered his face and he took the cigarette from his lips and stared at it. Rose Juell sniffed the smoke in the air.

"What . . . ?" exclaimed Fallien.

"Marijuana!" exclaimed Rose Juell, excitement in her voice.

Fallien's hand went to his pockets again. Another sack of tobacco was produced and the tall man looked at the two small oblongs of muslin.

"I got that sack of tobacco when I found James Gunther," said Fallien. "It was on the ground beside him."

Rose Juell moved swiftly from the door. She reached Fallien's side and bent down, looking at the two sacks. "Marijuana!" she repeated. "I . . ."

Fallien let the sacks fall to the floor. His hand shot up and caught Rose Juell by the wrist. "What do you know?" he demanded savagely.

Rose's face was pallid. "Huerta," she answered low-voiced. "Huerta smokes marijuana."

"Well?" snapped Fallien.

The woman's voice raised. "Huerta and Flaco!" she said. "They killed Gunther! Huerta smokes marijuana. He mixes it with tobacco. That's his sack!" She pointed to the muslin bag on the floor.

Fallien released his hold on the girl's wrist. He scooped up the tobacco sack from the floor, and holding it, got to his feet.

"You stay here," commanded Dale Fallien. "Right here. Don't you leave the house. I'll be back."

The tall man stepped toward the door, pulling on his hat as he moved. At the door he turned. "Now stay here, mind!" he ordered, and opening the door, walked out into the rain.

Rose Juell stood beside the chair that Fallien had occupied. The room was gray, almost dark. The woman stared at the door and, slowly, a look of hope came to her face. She turned. Maria, carrying a lamp, came into the room.

"It stop rain," announced Maria. "Jus' sprinkle. I go home now."

She put the lamp on the table. There was a candle already on the table, and a saucer of matches beside it. Maria waited. Rose Juell said nothing. Maria shrugged and turning went out the way she had come.

Dale Fallien, leaving Gunther's house, walked rapidly up the street. When he reached the jail he halted and turned to enter. The guard at the door barred his way and Fallien, opening his coat, displayed a small gold badge pinned to his vest. "Deputy Marshal!" snapped Fallien. "I want to see Land."

The guard called his corporal and that worthy, after brief questions, let Fallien enter. The corporal had dealt with United States Marshals before. Fallien followed the corporal down the short corridor and waited until the uniformed man had unlocked the cell and stood back. Fallien stepped into the cell. He stood, a tall, gaunt man, his shadow long and wraithlike before him. "Hello, Land," said Fallien quietly. As he entered the cell the door clanged shut and the corporal walked back along the corridor.

Llano Land against the further wall, did not move as Fallien spoke, but his voice came from the grayness. "Hello, Fallien. Come to crow?"

"I've come to ask you some questions," grated Fallien.

"Do you think it's likely I'll answer 'em?" drawled Llano.

Fallien grunted. "You were set to make a fight," he said harshly. "If I hadn't jammed a gun in your back they'd of killed you."

"So you jammed in the gun and saved me to be lynched?" There was bitterness in Llano's voice. "Nice of you. Get on with your rat killing!"

"I've been to see Rose Juell," began Fallien. "She says that you an' Gunther never quarreled, that you'd never spoke. How about it?"

"We never did," Llano said from the shadows. "I'd seen Gunther once or twice an' that was all. But what's it to you, Fallien?"

"Plenty," answered the tall man. "I . . . What's that?"

From somewhere outside the jail a shot sounded. There was a faint, high-pitched yelling and then came a fusillade of shots, that seemingly were nearer.

"I reckon that's a start for me." There was a calm fatality in Llano's voice. "You'd better get out, Fallien."

Fallien had turned. He was looking out of the bars of the door. In the corridor the lantern burned. The corporal and the trooper had gone out, evidently to investigate the disturbance.

Fallien wheeled back. "They're goin' to make a try for you," he stated bluntly. "I heard enough to know that. Park Frazier was in the Saint George talkin' to Greybull. Frazier is tryin' to get the miners to throw in with the ranchers. If he can get Greybull an' his bunch to help lynch you they'll both be tarred with the same stick an' Greybull's bunch will have to stay with 'em. I figured that."

"That'll be pleasant for me," drawled Llano.

Outside the jail there was confusion. Men were calling, moving swiftly toward a common focal point. The calls, at first distinct, now were fainter. Again shots sounded, muffled by the drizzling rain.

"You better get goin', Fallien," suggested Llano again.

"I'm goin' to get you out of here," said Fallien strongly.

Feet sounded in the corridor. A man wearing a campaign hat and a poncho came down the passage, stopped in front of the cell door and a key grated in the lock. Fallien took a step forward as the cell door opened.

"I . . ." he commenced.

Something glittered in the hand of the man under the poncho. There was the dull sound of a blow. Fallien lurched and went down. From the corridor came Mat McCarthy's deep voice, a fat chuckle in it. "Git up an' come out of there, Llano," commanded McCarthy. "Your horses are out back. Git a-goin'."

Llano was out of the shadows. Bending down over Fallien he thrust an exploring hand under the man's coat. That blow that McCarthy had struck had been a hard one, but Fallien's heart beat strongly. Something pressed against Llano's hand and he jerked the coat back. There plain in the lantern light glowed the gold badge.

"A marshal!" exclaimed McCarthy bending over the prone Fallien.

"We got to take him with us," snapped Llano.

180

McCarthy swore. "Not by a damn' sight! We leave him right here. We . . ."

"We got to take him." The urgency in Llano's voice overrode McCarthy's protest.

"Quick then!" McCarthy growled, and bending, heaved Fallien up. Llano caught the man's other side and helped support him. Two men, the Savoys, were coming along the little corridor. They carried a third. Llano saw the broad Irish face of the corporal. The corporal was out, cold. Unceremoniously the two Savoys dumped the man into Llano's cell. One of them grinned at Llano.

"Think we'd forgot you, fella?" he asked. "Hell! We needed a guitar player at camp."

The other Savoy, wordless, thrust out a hand. There was a big Army Colt in the hand and Llano took the gun, shoving it down into his waist band. "Figured you'd need that," grunted the Savoy.

"Git them other two in here," ordered McCarthy briskly. "Come on, Llano."

The Savoys went out the door. Llano and McCarthy, carrying Fallien between them, followed. Fallien's feet dragged on the floor.

Outside, the Savoys were picking up another soldier, lugging him toward the jail door. Alert at a corner of the building stood Shorty Hamarick, a gun in his hand. "Who's that?" he demanded as Llano and McCarthy with their burden, came abreast.

"Friend of Llano's," McCarthy answered mirthlessly.

"Bill an' Mulligan are puttin' on a regular war." Hamarick was with his leader, going around the corner of the jail. "We still got a couple of more minutes."

"Throw this jasper on a horse," growled McCarthy.

There were horses behind the jail. In wonder Llano

recognized his own two horses, yellow Jigger and gray Singleshot. Singleshot was saddled and there was a pack and saddle on Jigger. McCarthy, heaving Fallien up so that he lay across the pack, answered Llano's unspoken question.

"Stole 'em out of the hotel barn," he grunted. "Raided yore room an' tied Nathan up tighter'n a bull in fly time. Put the barn boy in the loft an' locked it. Push!"

Llano pushed. Fallien came to rest across the pack. McCarthy made rapid movements with a rope. The two Savoys came around the corner of the jail, their chuckles deep in their throats.

"Throwed them yeller laigs in yore cell, Land," chuckled one of the twins. "Any objections?"

Llano climbed his saddle. "Not a one," he answered.

The Savoys mounted. Hamarick was already astride his horse. McCarthy had swung into the saddle.

"Come on," ordered McCarthy. And led the way into the darkness and the rain.

The feet of the horses splashed through puddles of water. Behind them they could hear men calling to each other. A steady pound of hoofs showed where a cavalry patrol was going to the scene of the disturbance. McCarthy turned in his saddle.

"That was a smart dodge you played," he commended Llano. "Gettin' Mulligan. Mulligan had Bill Westfall at his place. He started Bill out right away. Bill come a-runnin'. When he told us what had happened we saddled up an' started to town. Mulligan an' Bill staged a sham battle for 'em while the rest of us went to work. Pretty good, huh, Llano?"

McCarthy was well pleased with himself. His tone of voice told that. He was not so pleased as Llano Land. Llano said so. "It was better than pretty good, Mat," he answered. "I won't forget it."

"Shucks," grunted McCarthy, "You'd of done the same."

"Where are we going?" Llano peered through the darkness.

"To a shack out of town a piece." McCarthy answered. "Up north about six miles. Bill's goin' to meet us there. Then we can decide what to do. Why'd you bring this jasper along, Llano?"

"Because he's a deputy marshal," Llano explained.

"I ain't lost no marshals," McCarthy grunted.

"An' we aren't going to lose this one!" Llano's voice was firm. "He fits our hand, Mat."

"Mebbe." McCarthy was doubtful.

"Let's get on to that shack and we'll see," said Llano Land.

CHAPTER 17

ROSE JUELL WAITED ENDLESSLY. SHE WAITED UNTIL the wick of the lamp, unevenly trimmed, sent black smoke to soot the side of the chimney, until the small supply of kerosene in the bowl was gone and the lamp flickered and went out. She did not light the candle that stood beside the lamp, but sat there in the dark, listening for Dale Fallien's footsteps and his knock on the door. The first flurry of shots and the yells brought her to her feet, her hand pressed against her breast and her eyes wide. The shots died away and still she waited. And then there were footsteps and a soft knock on the door. Still with her hand against her breast Rose Juell went to the door. The knock was repeated. There was something about that knock, some quality of stealth in the soft

183

tattoo of knuckles that frightened Rose Juell. She had expected Fallien. Now, with a sudden flood of terrorizing recollection she remembered her promise to Arthur Cameron. Her voice was faint as she spoke.

"Who?" called Rose Juell.

"It's Cameron, Rose," came the soft answer.

Rose Juell's hand fluttered at her breast.

"Let me in," demanded Cameron.

Rose could almost feel his body pressing against the door. Fear filled her, suddenly. A terror of the man outside stifled her. "No!" she gasped. "No! No!" She could not go through with this.

The bolted door creaked as Cameron applied pressure. Rose turned as if to run. But there was nowhere to go. The man outside was losing his temper. Hot rage, flamed by passion, was in his voice. "Damn you, Rose! Let me in!"

The girl did not answer, could not answer, and again the door creaked as Cameron, furious, thrust against it. Then the creaking ceased. There was a long period of silence and then came steps pounding on the board walk outside the house, steps that receded, that died away.

Rose Juell collapsed beside the door. For a while she lay there, then scrambling to her knees she went to the room that Gunther had given her and there began to collect her scanty possessions, the few things that kindly Gunther had salvaged from her room when she had fled to him for shelter.

Arthur Cameron, flinging away from Gunther's house, was white with anger. He stamped his way up the street, making for Ladron House and then suddenly before him there was a commotion and a little crowd. Pushing his way into the crowd he saw that it was at the jail. There were voices, hot and angry, and a man at the

184

door, a man in uniform, was berating someone inside. Cameron caught words and sentences. His hot anger suddenly cooled. The man at the door was Sergeant Cassidy and he was speaking to a trooper.

"A fine guard you are!" roared Cassidy. "Three of you, and soldiers down the street, an' you let him get away! A nice time I'll have reportin' to the Lieutenant. This'll be a general court for you."

Cameron, moving closer, caught at Cassidy's sleeve. The sergeant turned. "What happened?" demanded Cameron. Cassidy recognized his questioner. Cameron was an important man. The sergeant answered. "Land's gone," he said. "A little bunch of men jumped the guards an' took him out. Fine soldiers they are! Fine . . ." Cassidy stopped. The man he addressed was gone. Cameron had turned and walked swiftly away.

He did not go to Ladron House. The rage of Rose Juell's refusal was still upon him but it was a cold rage now. Llano Land was gone and Rose Juell had refused him. Arthur Cameron craved revenge. He went across the rain-wet street and entered the Exchange Saloon.

"Where's Flaco?" he demanded of the bartender.

The bartender nodded his head toward a booth. "In there," he said. "Him an' Huerta are soakin' it up."

But Cameron did not wait for the bartender's observations. He walked to the booth indicated and looking in saw the men he sought. They started to rise when they saw him but Cameron, stepping into the booth slipped into a chair.

"I'm looking for you," he announced briefly.

Huerta, drunk, grunted, "*Sí.*"

Flaco's eyes widened.

"I understand," said Cameron slowly and distinctly, planting his words in whisky-soaked brains, "that Rose

185

Juell is going to talk to the officer up at Ladron House. She has some things to tell about you."

Flaco's eyes were wider than ever. Cameron smiled mirthlessly, licked his lips. Thick lips they were, curved and full and sensuous. "It would be too bad if she did," said Cameron.

"Where is she?" grunted Flaco.

"In Gunther's house," answered Cameron. "Alone."

He got up then, looked first at Flaco and then at Huerta and without another word, stepped out of the booth and was gone.

"Damn her," Flaco snarled. "Damn her! She'll tell, will she?" Reaching across the table he caught Huerta's elbow. "You know what that means?" he demanded.

Huerta, head lolling, came erect in his chair. "Huh?" he began.

"Get up!" snarled Flaco. "She'll talk, will she? She's alone, is she?" Huerta, stumbling and awkward, followed Flaco soddenly out of the booth.

At Gunther's house, Rose Juell had completed her hasty packing. She had taken the little bag of her possessions and was ready to go. There was one place and only one place where she believed she would be free from danger. That place was with Gwynn Rae. As she stood beside the door, the bolt drawn back and her hand on the knob, she heard feet on the walk, stumbling feet and feet that struck firmly. She paused there. Then the knob turned under her hand, the door was thrust against her, sending her reeling back, and the black bulk of men filled the doorway. Rose Juell screamed once and then again, and then her hands beat futilely against flesh and she went down.

In Ladron House, Gwynn Rae was restless. Wayne Metcalf, sitting beside her, both hands imprisoned in

186

his, sensed that restlessness and strove to overcome it. He tried to talk to the girl but she made no response and finally Metcalf ceased his attempts at light conversation and spoke of the thing that was uppermost in Gwynn Rae's mind.

"I could not do what you asked today, Gwynn," he said. "I could not free Llano Land. The man is arrested for murder. If I had freed him I would have brought down the mob on Ladron House. Men would have been killed."

"The girl said that Llano didn't kill Gunther," said Gwynn, referring to Rose Juell. "I don't believe he did. He saved my life. I can't let him lie there in jail."

"What is Land to you?" demanded Metcalf with a sudden flame of jealousy. "What is your interest in him, Gwynn?"

"He saved my life," Gwynn repeated. "He . . . I can't explain it, Wayne."

Metcalf bent forward. "Does he mean a great deal to you, Gwynn?" he questioned. "Does he mean . . ?" The young officer broke off his sentence helplessly.

Gwynn Rae tried to put her thoughts, her feelings into words. "You wouldn't understand, Wayne," she said. "He is so strong, so . . . so much a man. He wouldn't use a knife in the dark. He wouldn't strike a man down without warning. That girl must have some knowledge that would clear him. Surely she must know something or she wouldn't have come here."

Metcalf rose to his feet. "I'll go to see her," he announced decisively. "I'll go tonight, Gwynn, if it means that much to you. I'll find out what she knows."

Gwynn Rae also came to her feet. "I'll go with you," she announced in a tone that brooked no objection. "Wait until I get my cape, Wayne."

Leaving the officer she hurried to the stairs and, as she mounted them she looked back and smiled a little, tremulously. Wayne Metcalf's reward was in that smile but he did not see it. He stood, scuffing the thick rug with one booted foot, his head down, his eyes lowered. It seemed to Wayne Metcalf at that moment that his world had crumpled about him. He believed, truly, that Gwynn Rae loved Llano Land.

While he waited for the girl to reappear there was a knock at the door. A servant answered the knock and as the door opened the servant was thrust aside and Cassidy, his face red, anger in his eyes, came into Ladron House. The sergeant saluted his officer and blurted out words.

"The prisoner's escaped, sorr," announced Cassidy. "A little bunch of men come an' took him out of jail. They locked the guard in his cell an' he's gone."

"What?" snapped Metcalf.

"Yes, sorr," said Cassidy.

Wayne Metcalf snatched up his hat from where it lay. Gwynn Rae and his promise were forgotten. Here was a thing that demanded his immediate attention. "We'll see about this, Sergeant," he said dangerously. "We'll go to the jail first."

So it was that Gwynn Rae, her cape about her, found the hall vacant when she descended the stairs. The man that answered her pull on the bell cord was voluble. A soldier had come and spoken to the officer and they had gone out together in a hurry. He did not know where. He did not know why. Gwynn Rae's cheeks flushed with anger.

"I am going out, Carlos," she announced, and despite Carlos' expostulation, swept to the door. Carlos, still objecting, opened the door for her and

Gwynn went out into the rainy night.

She knew where Gunther's house was. Avoiding the main street where lights flashed and men moved, she turned the corner of Ladron House and chose another way. Down a dark street she went, now walking in mud, now stepping into a puddle, until, well past the main portion of the town she turned again and went back to the central street. On down it she went until she came to an adobe house. There she paused. The door of the adobe was a black cavity in the lighter blackness of the wall. Some premonition, some dreadful hint of evil seemed to come through that open doorway. Gwynn Rae steeled herself and stepped to the opening. Her voice trembled as she spoke.

"Rose! Rose!"

For a moment there was no answer and then, from within the door came a groan.

It took courage for Gwynn Rae to step through that door. It took more than courage for her extended hands to grope through the darkness and find a table. The groping hands found more. They found a lamp on the table and matches in a dish. A match flamed and touched the wick of the lamp but the wick would not light. Again, behind Gwynn Rae, came that feeble groan, urging her to desperation. A tin candlestick rattled under her hand and again a match flamed, and following it came a feeble yellow glow that grew as the candle wick ignited. Holding that candlestick Gwynn Rae turned. Rose Juell lay on the floor behind the door and a dark ugly stain spread from Rose Juell toward the center of the room.

Gwynn Rae gave a little scream. The candlestick trembled and almost fell from her hand. Then, nerving herself, she went to the girl on the floor. She knelt and,

189

placing the candlestick beside her, bent over Rose Juell.

"Rose!" she cried softly. "Rose!"

Rose Juell's eyes opened. Great dark eyes that were soft with suffering and hurt. Rose Juell's lips moved and, bending close, Gwynn caught the words that were formed.

"Llano?"

There were tears in Gwynn Rae's eyes. "Who did this, Rose? Who . . ?"

But the lips were moving again. Again Gwynn bent to catch the words. "Tell Llano . . . Flaco . . . killed . . . Ames."

"I'll tell him," promised Gwynn strongly. "I must get you out of here. I'll take you . . ."

Rose Juell's head moved. Rose Juell's voice was suddenly strong and firm and sweet. "I love you, Llano," said Rose Juell.

Then the dark head lolled limply, and Rose Juell's body relaxed. "I'll get you out of here," promised Gwynn Rae again. "I'll . . ." She stopped, realizing that Rose Juell was gone from the room where the candle flickered and almost died with the draft through the door.

For a little time Gwynn Rae knelt beside the dead girl on the floor. Oddly she was not afraid. There was nothing here of which to be afraid. All that was evil had been done and now was gone. There remained only this woman, bad perhaps, wild, fierce, but surely not evil. Gwynn Rae could feel that Rose Juell had not been evil.

Gathering herself, the girl from the big house arose. She stepped away from the body and as she moved through the door the candle guttered in its waxen cup and the wind of her passing stifled it. Gwynn Rae went out of a house, as black as when she had entered.

She hurried up the street away from Gunther's, her footsteps rapid at first and then as she added distance becoming more rapid until she was almost running. There was no effort now to avoid the lighted street with the men milling on it. The drizzle of rain was wet on her face and the lamps flickered through wet panes of glass and shone on her cheeks. She went on. The men she passed stared after her curiously, some of them recognizing the great lady from Ladron House. One or two moved as if to follow her, but refrained.

At Ladron House, Gwynn used the knocker and was admitted. The big hall was dark, and gloomy shadows hung in it but there was a fire in the fireplace at the further end of the room and it glowed cheerfully. A man arose from a chair beside that fireplace, moved forward toward Gwynn. It was Kent Null.

Gwynn, seeing the lawyer, stopped. Her voice was sharp as she asked a question. "Is Wayne here?"

Null shook his head. "Your friend the Lieutenant," he said, humor in his voice, "is out on business at present. It seems that his prisoner escaped after locking the guard in his cell. Wayne is looking for him."

"You mean Llano Land?" Gwynn's question was direct.

"I mean Llano Land." Null nodded. "He was not as friendless as he seemed." He hesitated for a moment and then went on, cheerfully. "I have a surprise for you, Gwynn. I am leaving."

Gwynn's eyes were sharp as she looked at the man. Null was nonchalant, even debonair. His dress, as always, was immaculate; his carriage jaunty.

"Why?" asked Gwynn.

Null shrugged. "For good and sufficient reasons," he said.

The girl took a quick step forward. "I have been to James Gunther's," she stated, her voice vibrant. "Rose Juell is there, Kent. She has been killed!"

Null took a step back. His face, already pale, became even more so, and the ruddy light of the fire could not give his cheeks color. "Killed?" he echoed.

A sudden flux of feeling swept Gwynn Rae. She had held herself, been brave when it was difficult to be brave. Now that bravery was gone. A long sob shook her and then another. Suddenly Kent Null's arms were about her shaking shoulders, and her head was against his chest while one of the man's long, fine hands stroked her hair. Through her sobs Gwynn Rae tried to tell Null what she had seen, what had happened. The words were disjointed, garbled. Null tried to soothe her, tried to comfort her. His words were soft and reassuring.

"Now, Gwynn. Now girl. You couldn't help it. You couldn't help her."

The sobs continued. A serving woman, Gwynn's maid, aroused by the sobs from below, showed her dark face from the banister of the stair. Null nodded to her and the woman came on down the stairs. Suddenly Null realized that he had taken the wrong tack, that this sobbing girl in his arms did not desire soothing words but rather promises of vengeance.

Null spoke sharply, "Gwynn!" The girl raised her head. She stifled a sob at its beginning and looked at Null. There was color now in Null's face, color and something else, something that Gwynn had never seen on that smooth countenance. "I'll look after things, Gwynn," promised Null grimly. "I'll do what I can. Metcalf is after Llano Land but I'll see him the moment he comes back. In the meantime . . ." Null let the threat die unfinished.

There was satisfaction to Gwynn in the man's voice, in the sudden arousing that stirred him, but she caught at the last words: Llano Land.

"Llano?" questioned Gwynn. "You say . . . ?"

"I say that he broke jail," answered Null. "I say that his friends came for him and took him out. He is somewhere safe. Metcalf won't find him."

Gwynn Rae's eyes lighted. The thing Null had told her made her heart beat wildly for an instant. Then she remembered. She remembered Rose Juell and the message Rose had given her and the last words Rose Juell had spoken. Something of that recollection must have shown in her face. Null turned away.

"You go with Eliza," he commanded. "I . . . I must look after things." His voice had lost its ring and the fire was gone from his face. Gwynn Rae turned away. Eliza, the serving woman, put her hand on the girl's arm. Gwynn allowed herself to be led toward the stairs.

In her room, as her woman removed wet garments and clucked her tongue at the condition of her mistress' hair and clothing, Gwynn was distraught. The ordeal through which she had come had unnerved her. She trembled and Eliza, wise and faithful and worried about her mistress, hurried to a little cupboard and brought a glass of wine for Gwynn to drink. Warmed by the wine and by Eliza's chafing hands, Gwynn allowed herself to be led to the great four-postered bed and tucked beneath the comforts. Gwynn lay there, wide blue eyes staring at the canopy overhead and her mind filled with but two things: Rose Juell and Llano Land. And then she remembered. Null had said that he would see Wayne Metcalf. There was the answer to it all, there was the man, the strong, gentle man to whom to turn, Wayne Metcalf. The thought of him comforted Gwynn. Null, she could not trust. Llano Land was wild and fierce as a hawk, and free. Llano Land was not here, but Metcalf, the man who loved her, the man who could give her comfort and security, would surely, surely come. Gwynn sat up in the great bed.

"Eliza," she said, and her voice was strong. "I must see Lieutenant Metcalf as soon as he comes back. I must dress. Bring me dry clothes and my black dress."

Eliza shook her head obstinately, but Gwynn Rae was already out of bed.

Down in the great hall, standing in front of the fireplace, Kent Null spread his legs wide and locked his hands behind him. His head, tipped forward, was vulture-like. His mouth was harsh and his aquiline nose was a jutting beak. For a while he stood there. Then, thoughtfully, he unlocked his hands and with the long tapering fingers of the right hand, explored a pocket in his figured vest. The fingers brought a weapon from that pocket, a short, stubby, double-barreled derringer, no less deadly because it lacked length. Null broke the gun and looked at the dully gleaming copper of the cartridges in the barrels. Then he laughed a short, harsh bark without mirth.

"And I am going away," mused Null, half aloud. "I am going to leave this ship like any other rat!" Again came that harsh, mirthless laugh. Null turned sharp on a heel.

"Arthur, my friend," said Kent Null cradling the derringer, "you've gone too far with this. Kent Null must be the next name on your list!"

As he spoke he strode across the room and through a door and then down a semi-dark passage. Before the door of Cameron's office he paused as though to nerve himself. Then he thrust the door open and, derringer lifted, stepped through. The office was empty. There was a lamp on the desk, lighted and burning steadily. A bottle and glasses were set out waiting to be used. The chair was turned away from the desk, inviting a man to slip into it. And that was all. Arthur Cameron was absent.

Null stood a moment, the derringer raised. Then again he laughed bitterly. "You make it easy for me, Arthur," said Kent Null to the absent Cameron.

He put the derringer back into his vest pocket and hesitated a moment. Then the harsh lines of his face softened. He stepped across and taking the bottle and the glass, poured himself a drink.

"I'd have killed you, Arthur," said Kent Null. "I'd have killed you if it were necessary. But it isn't necessary." He tossed down the drink.

For a moment after he stood there, eyeing the bottle. His hand went out slowly, took the bottle and again liquor gurgled into the glass. Null drank, put bottle and glass on the desk and looked at the heavy iron safe that stood in the corner of the room. The door of the safe stood open a crack. Null took two swift steps and reached the strong box. The door swung open and his hands went into the interior. He worked feverishly. Papers came out of the safe and were dropped on the floor. Then the groping hands brought out small canvas sacks, heavy with their contents. Null thrust the sacks into his pockets and stood up. His coat sagged with the burden. Null wet his lips nervously. The strength that had filled his face was gone, and only cunning cupidity remained. He stood looking at the gutted safe, then swiftly he slammed the door shut, turned, and blowing out the light on the desk, hurried out of the office.

Across the hall he went and up the stairs. A corridor

led him to his own room. There, by lamp light, he pulled a telescope grip from beneath the bed to thrust clothing into it. Kent Null had reverted to type.

CHAPTER 18

THE SHACK FOR WHICH MAT MCCARTHY HEADED WAS six miles from Ladron. It was a little adobe building, unused and dilapidated. But Bill Westfall had shown it to McCarthy, and McCarthy, canny in the submerged ways of his business, had decided that it might be a good place to have handy. Accordingly he had instructed Westfall to put a stock of jerky in the place, added coffee to that stock and left a filled lantern with the food. Mat McCarthy told Llano this as they rode through the rain.

"You never know," said McCarthy wisely, "when yo're goin' to need a cache an' a hideout, leastwise in my line of business. I just had Bill fix it up."

Llano, preoccupied with his thoughts, made no answer. McCarthy grunted and asked a question. "What you got in mind for that jasper we picked up?"

"I don't know, Mat," answered Llano frankly. "I sure don't know." A pause, then, "He's been under my feet ever since I hit Ladron. I want some talk out of him."

"You kind of like him, too," surmised McCarthy shrewdly. "Don't you?"

"Damn it, yes!" answered Llano.

They splashed across a little stream running in low ground, climbed a knoll, and McCarthy spoke to Hamarick. "About there, Shorty?"

Hamarick's voice, muffled by the rain, answered. "Just about. I'll ride ahead." His horse moved and

196

McCarthy checked the gait of his party while the scout reconnoitered.

There was no report from Hamarick and McCarthy swung right. Within five minutes the shack was a black blob in the darkness and as they halted the lantern glowed and Hamarick appeared in the doorway.

"Come on in out of the rain, you fellas," invited Hamarick grinning.

The men dismounted. McCarthy unlashed Fallien from the packhorse and the animals were tied to the post of a fence which still stood close to the shack, the wire stripped from the posts.

Inside the shack Virge Savoy lowered Fallien to the dirt floor. The tall man was beginning to regain consciousness, stirring and moaning softly.

"You slugged him quite a jolt," said Llano critically, looking at Fallien.

"It wasn't no time for love taps," answered McCarthy.

The men were wet. McCarthy still wore a poncho raided from a trooper. Virge Savoy was also covered by a rain coat, but the others were soaked to the skin. They made nothing of their wetness. McCarthy produced dry papers and tobacco and the smokes went around. There was exhilaration in the shack, a surge of good feeling. These men had done a task, a dangerous task, and had come through in good style. Llano, glancing at the faces about him, grinned a little. Here was a hardy crew.

"You look," said Llano, "like taking me out of jail was just picking daisies."

"It wasn't much harder," grinned McCarthy. "Westfall come ridin' into the Junta like I said. We caught our horses an' lit a shuck for town. When we got to Ladron we went to the hotel. Nathan showed us yore

197

room an' we took what we could find there. Shorty put Nathan's shirt tail in his mouth to keep him from talkin' too much an' we locked him in. Then we went to the barn. The barnboy climbed into the hayloft and we barred him up there with a piece of two by four. We didn't figure that you'd want to go back for yore horses an' such. Then Bill went to Mulligan's an' the rest of us sneaked around back of the jail. There were a lot of men movin' around an' we weren't noticed much."

"It was mighty fine of you to take so much trouble about my junk," Llano smiled. "I take it kindly, Mat."

McCarthy waved a fat hand airily. "Don't you mention it," he grinned. "Bill an' Mulligan staged a sham battle down at the edge of town, yellin' an' shootin'. We taken care of the soldiers as they come to hand. They sure do wear nice ponchos, them soldiers." McCarthy shook the poncho he was wearing. "Keep a man good an' dry," he concluded.

"How'd you get into the jail?" Llano was curious.

"Why"—McCarthy's grin broadened—"after we'd sort of argued with a soldier down the street an' got his coat an' hat, it wasn't no trouble to speak of. I run up to the jail an' yelled an' they come out an' I'd started around the corner. They come right along like they was halter broke, an' Virge an' Arch an' Shorty was there to greet 'em."

"Did you have to . . ." began Llano.

"Naw," McCarthy forestalled the question. "We just tapped 'em an' let 'em lay 'til you was out. Then we packed 'em in. We wouldn't of cared if somebody'd seen us then. We kind of owe Ladron a jolt or two an' that would of been a good place to hand it out."

Llano nodded. "It was slick, Mat," he praised.

"Slick enough," acknowledged McCarthy. "Everything went smooth except havin' that jasper in yore cell. Why did you bring him along, Llano?"

"Because," answered Llano, "he stuck a gun in my back when the soldiers came for me this morning and I'm curious about it."

"The dirty skunk," swore Hamarick. "Why don't you . . . ?"

"He's not a skunk yet," interrupted Llano. "He might have had a reason. He's a U. S. Marshal, you know."

There was concern written on the faces about the lantern. Llano, stooping over, opened Fallien's coat and the gold badge winked in the light. "You couldn't blame him," said Llano. "Besides when he was in my cell I got an idea he was trying to help me out."

Fallien blinked his eyes and opened them. "Has anybody got a drink?" asked Llano.

Hamarick had a flask in a saddle pocket. He went out to get it and Virge Savoy, stooping, lifted Fallien to a sitting position. Fallien's head rolled limply.

"I hit him pretty hard," said Mat McCarthy, eyeing the tall man.

Hamarick came back with the liquor and Fallien was given a drink. The raw whisky burned his throat but strengthened him. He held his head erect.

"Now what?" asked McCarthy.

"Wait a while until he feels better," answered Llano. "Then I'll talk to him. What do you plan, Mat?"

"To get to hell out of here," announced McCarthy. "We got to wait for Bill an' then we'll haul our freight. I ain't lost a thing here, not a thing."

Llano shook his head. "I've got some unfinished business," he said. "I'd like to go with you, Mat, but I'd better attend to that."

Hamarick swore, unbelief in his voice. "You goin' to

stick around here?" he demanded. "They'll hang you so high you won't never come down."

"Maybe." Llano was noncommittal.

McCarthy's blue eyes were bright as he looked at his friend.

"Me an' the boys helped a little, Llano," McCarthy reminded. "We ought to have somethin' to say."

"You helped a lot," Llano rejoined, "an' you got a lot to say. Just the same . . ."

"Just the same yo're a pig-headed fool," grated McCarthy.

"Well," Llano drawled, "maybe I am. Still I've got work to do. There's Jack Ames, and then they have tried to tack this preacher's murder on me. I don't like that."

"So you'll go back an' stick yore head into a noose an' git hung because you don't like it." McCarthy made a statement: "Me an' the boys won't be here to take you out of jail next time."

"I'm thanking you for taking me out once," answered Llano.

Fallien's hoarse voice made the men turn and look. "You came here looking for a man?" rasped Dale Fallien.

"So you can talk now!" snapped Llano. "Yeah, I came here looking for a man. A friend of mine named Ames brought seven thoroughbred horses over here and he was killed in Ladron. His mother asked me to look him up."

"I wondered," said Fallien. The man was much stronger. "I saw you come into Ladron Canyon. You came from McCarthy's hideout. I wondered if you were in the business with him."

Llano's gray eyes glinted their admiration. Here was Dale Fallien in desperate circumstances and he had the nerve to ask questions.

"Mat," explained Llano elaborately, "used to punch cows with Jack Ames and me. Mat was kind enough to help me look for Jack. Was there anything else you wanted to know?"

Fallien shrugged and Llano, taking the initiative, asked a question in turn. "Ever since I came here you have beer under my feet," he said. "Why, Fallien?"

"Yo're a trouble maker," answered Fallien bluntly. "It was part of my business to watch you an' I wondered if you were goin' to work for the Duro Grant."

"And you found out." Llano grated the words. "Now, another thing: This morning you stuck a gun in my back when Wadell and those others came for me. Why was that?"

"To save yore fool life!" Fallien snapped. "You was set to make a fight. They'd of shot you to ribbons."

"Nice of you," commented Llano ironically. "You saved me from gettin' shot up so that the anti-Grant boys would lynch me. Mighty thoughtful."

"I didn't think about that at the time," Fallien admitted.

"But you thought of it later," said Llano. "What would you do if you were me, Fallien?"

Fallien did not answer for a moment, then he grinned painfully.

"My head hurts," he drawled, "an' likely I ain't thinkin' straight, but if I was you I'd turn me loose."

"So you could stick another gun in my back?"

"So I could prove that you didn't kill Gunther."

The words almost set Llano back on his heels. There was incredulity on his face as he looked at Fallien. "I know I didn't kill Gunther," he blurted, "but how do you know it?"

201

"The man that killed Gunther smoked marijuana," drawled Dale Fallien calmly. "I just found out today."

"How?" The question came from Mat and Llano simultaneously.

Fallien seemed to enjoy the moment. "I picked up a tobacco sack when I picked up Gunther," he answered. "The tobacco had marijuana mixed with it. You don't smoke marijuana."

"I don't," agreed Llano, "but . . ."

"Let it go at that," rasped Fallien. "I'm an officer. I can do you some good. What do you say, Land?"

"I'm damned if I know," answered Llano.

"My head hurts like hell," Fallien's face was gray. "You think it over. Could I have another drink of liquor?"

Shorty Hamarick tendered the bottle and Fallien drank. Llano and Mat McCarthy drew aside. "I'd like to let him go, Llano," counseled McCarthy.

"I never meant to keep him," grunted Llano. "What will I do, Mat?"

"Damned if I know." McCarthy scratched his head. "We got some time to wait. Bill ain't come yet. Think it over. One thing sure, yo're crazy if you go back to Ladron."

Llano held out his hand. "Give me a smoke," he requested. "Damn it, Mat . . . !"

McCarthy proffered tobacco and papers.

"That fella's been around," announced McCarthy admiringly. "He knows how to play a hand."

Shorty Hamarick was moving around the shack. From a shelf, hung by wires from a beam overhead, he produced jerky and a sack of coffee. "Stir up a fire, Virge," commanded Shorty. "I'm gant. I could use a bait before we pulled out."

Virge Savoy moved to the little dilapidated fireplace. Arch Savoy stirred nervously.

"I wonder what's keepin' Bill," he said petulantly. "Mebbe I'd better go see."

McCarthy stepped away from Llano. "You'll stay here," he contradicted. "Bill will be along. Nobody is goin' to pull out an' hang us up waitin' for him when Bill gets here."

Savoy relaxed and the fire crackled in the fireplace. Hamarick set a battered lard bucket outside the door to catch water for the coffee. Fallien, back against the wall, let his head relax. His eyes were closed.

"Damn Bill!" swore Shorty Hamarick, bringing in the lard bucket. "He must be stuck in town."

"Bill will get here," said McCarthy, calmly.

"Bill lived hereabouts before he come with us," began Virge Savoy, his-voice deep. "Bill was the one that made the dicker with Cameron when we moved the Grant corner stone. He run between you an' Cameron, Mat. Do you reckon that Bill would go to Cameron now?"

"Not Bill!" snapped Arch Savoy. "Bill's all right!"

Fallien's eyes had opened swiftly as Virge Savoy spoke. He looked at the big, blond twin. His lips opened as if he were about to speak. Llano Land, against the wall, pulled his watch from the fob pocket of his sodden trousers. The watch guard caught on the butt of the big Colt and hung there. Llano freed it. The hands of the watch were together at twelve o'clock. It was midnight. Restoring the watch to its place Llano moved over and stood before Fallien.

"You can come and go, Fallien," said Llano, slowly. "That is, if it's all right with Mat and his boys."

"It's all right with me," agreed Mat. "But he's got to

stay put till we get away from here."

"Of course . . ." began Llano.

There was the sound, muffled but steady, of a horse outside the shack. The clop . . . clop . . . clop of shod feet on wet ground. McCarthy moved swiftly to the door. Hamarick, with a single movement reached the lantern and stood ready to extinguish it. Virge and Arch Savoy were alert. McCarthy opened the door. From outside came a voice carrying through the drip of the rain.

"It's me, Bill!"

McCarthy relaxed and Hamarick, stepping away from the lantern, lifted the boiling coffee bucket from the fire.

Bill Westfall came into the shack. Rain glistened on his yellow saddle slicker. Rain dripped from his hat brim, and a drop hung, suspended, on the end of his long, sharp nose. Bill spoke straight to Mat McCarthy.

"There's hell to pay in Ladron," said Bill Westfall. "Rose Juell has been killed an' they're sayin' Llano did it!"

"By God!" roared McCarthy.

Westfall went on, speaking rapidly. "I was with Mulligan," he continued. "We'd gone to the edge of town an' shot some an' yelled, and then started runnin' around like we was lookin' for the men that had started things. We got by all right. We got away before the soldiers come lookin' to see what had happened an' we went to Mulligan's place. We waited there. I wanted to make sure that there wasn't any kickbacks before I come on out here. There was a cavalry patrol around town. The sergeant found Gunther's door open an' Rose Juell dead inside. They brought her to Mulligan's an' there was a crowd with 'em. The word was already goin' around. They was hookin' it up with the jail break.

204

Somebody in the Exchange said that Llano had killed Gunther an' got loose an' killed the girl. Before I left there was half a dozen posses gettin' ready to ride. We better pull out of here."

"Rose?" exclaimed Llano. "Rose Juell?" Llano's face was dark and drawn. The men in the circle looked at him.

"Rose Juell," affirmed Westfall.

Llano stepped back a pace and Westfall, turning to McCarthy, renewed his urgent request for speed.

"I tell you we got to go," urged Westfall. "We got to get out of here an' a long ways off. If they find us, if we got Land with us, it's just Katy bar the door. We'll be done."

"To hell with that!" snapped McCarthy. "Damn 'em! They can get a belly full with us."

"Don't be a fool, Mat," Virge Savoy added his word "You know . . ."

Dale Fallien spoke from beside the wall. "Rose Juell talked to me before I went to see you, Land," he rasped.

"What did she tell you?" Land turned and looked down at the tall man.

"That you didn't kill Gunther,"—Fallien paused— "but that Flaco an' Huerta did," he finished.

Llano turned away from Fallien and to McCarthy. "I'm not goin' with you, Mat," he said. "You'll hit some of these riders. You can't hardly miss 'em. Westfall's right. If I'm with you it will be tough."

"An' I said to hell with that!" roared McCarthy. "I said . . ."

"We'll stand here an' talk like a bunch of fools an' those fellows are ridin'," Westfall interrupted McCarthy. "For Christ's sake, Mat, let's do somethin'."

McCarthy calmed. "We'll drink a cup of coffee and

eat that jerky," he said, the leader once more. "Then we'll go, all of us. Llano, you'll go with us an' it'll just be too damn' bad if we meet anybody. Pass the bucket around, Shorty, all you fellows grab a handful of jerky. The Lord knows when we'll eat again."

Shorty picked up the coffee bucket by the bail. He poured from it into a tin can, lifted the can to his lips and swore when his lips were burned. The two Savoys had reached out and thrust big hands into the sack of jerky. Hamarick put down the bucket and shifted the can from hand to hand.

"Too hot!" he protested. "I can't . . ."

"Let it go then!" snapped McCarthy. "Llano . . ."

Llano Land was gone. He had stepped away and out of the open door. As an answer to McCarthy's words there came the sound of a horse running.

"Llano!" roared McCarthy springing to the door again. "Llano!"

It was no use. McCarthy turned to face his men. "Come on," he ordered. "Llano Land has gone back to Ladron. I know it. We got to . . ."

"I'm not goin'," snarled Westfall. "I'll run my head into a loop for no man."

McCarthy turned. He looked at the Savoys. He looked at Shorty Hamarick. On their faces was written the same hard determination that showed on Westfall's countenance. McCarthy's shoulders slumped.

"We'll go," said Westfall, "but we'll go the other way."

"Wait a minute," Fallien's voice rasped. The men in the adobe shack turned to look at the tall man.

Fallien struggled up from beside the wall. He stood rocking on his feet, but despite his apparent weakness there was a recognizable force in the man.

McCarthy's men hesitated.

"You said a while ago that you moved the corner stone for the Grant," Fallien was looking at Virge Savoy.

"An' what of it?" snapped the man.

"Just this." Fallien's words were measured. "I'm a deputy United States Marshal but right now I'm borrowed from the Marshal's office by the Interior Department. I'm here to investigate fraud by the Duro Grant an' if what you say is so I've found it."

"An' what's that to us?" snarled Westfall. "We . . ."

"Do you want to help Llano Land?" asked Fallien. "Do you want a shot at the Duro Grant?"

"Hell, yes!" McCarthy's voice was eager.

"Then listen to me!" ordered Fallien. "Listen an' I'll tell you how."

CHAPTER 19

LLANO LAND RODE SOUTH. HE HAD LISTENED WHILE McCarthy and his men argued in the shack but he knew that the argument was futile. McCarthy would never be able to hold his men to him and Llano did not want Mat to try. So, while Shorty Hamarick passed his can of hot coffee from one hand to the other, and while McCarthy blustered, Llano had stepped out into the rain and found his horse.

Fallien had said that Flaco and Huerta had killed James Gunther. Llano knew that the tall man had not lied. He knew, too, that Cameron had ordered that killing. Also Llano was certain that Cameron had been the cause of Rose Juell's death. The man had done too many things. He had lived too long. Llano Land rode grimly back toward Ladron with but one idea in mind, with a fixed purpose that only death could change.

But he did not know the country he covered. An arroyo running full, checked him, Singleshot sliding to a stop at its edge. It took time to circle the arroyo, time to find the road again. Still that task was accomplished and Llano rode on. Then lights gleamed dimly in the wet night. Ladron was near. The town was sleepless, stirred and stirring. A certain cunning possessed Llano Land. Nothing must come between him and Ladron House. Llano swung his horse west toward the hills.

The sky was barely graying in the east when Llano reached Ladron House. There were lights in the great square building and men stirred about the place. Llano waited, his horse and himself hidden by a cedar, until a patrol went by, and then moved stealthily forward. At the corner of the house he dismounted and wrapping his reins about his saddle horn slapped Singleshot. The horse moved away noisily and from the darkness a voice called: "Halt!"

There was no answer to that command and the order came again: "Halt! Who's there?"

Still no answer and a man moved in the gloom. A horse moved too. Evidently the sentry had tried to catch Singleshot and the horse had avoided him. Llano, with the guard's attention distracted, slipped along the wall of the house.

There were words exchanged in the darkness ahead. Evidently the sentry's corporal had come to find the cause of the disturbance. Llano felt steps against his knees. He found them with his feet and went up, his hand encountering a door. The corporal said, "Whose horse is this?" and Llano turned the door knob softly. The door opened and Llano was out of the rain and in velvet blackness.

With hand extended, groping before him, Llano moved ahead. The hand found a chair. Llano circled it. The hand struck the corner of a desk. Thick carpet muffled his movement as he went around the desk. His outstretched fingers rested against a wall and he groped along it until he came upon a door. That door also opened noiselessly. Now he was in dim light, a corridor stretching before him. There were heavy portières at the end of the corridor. Llano went along it, reached the portières, and pushing them aside saw the great hall of Ladron House.

He waited there at the portières, letting his eyes become accustomed to the light. A fire blazed in the fireplace at the end of the room but Llano could see no occupants of the room. Now, ready, he moved forward and as he moved a woman arose from a chair beside the fire and turned toward him. Gwynn Rae.

Llano was well into the room now, facing the fireplace, his back toward the front door of the house. He stepped forward, three long paces and stopped. Gwynn Rae was moving toward him. The firelight caught the dull gleam of the polished floor, the sheen of silver in the candelabra, and winked from polished brass of andirons.

"You . . ." said Gwynn Rae, hesitantly.

"I'm Llano Land," said Llano, his voice a harsh croak. "I've come for Cameron."

The girl was before him now. She stood, looking up into his face, her own expression questioning. Then as she caught the expression of Llano's face fright supplanted the question in her eyes.

"For Cameron?" she asked. "What . . . ?"

"For Cameron and for Null," grated Llano.

"Why do you want them?"

Llano did not answer that. "You'd better go," he said hoarsely. "I'm going to see Cameron and Null."

Gwynn drew herself erect. "You tell me to go from my own house?" she demanded incredulously.

"It won't be pretty!" warned Llano. "Where are they?"

"You've come to kill them." Gwynn's voice was steady. "They aren't here."

"They need killing," Llano spoke evenly, some of the hoarseness gone.

"Why?" Gwynn was insistent. It seemed to a detached part of Llano's brain that the girl was sitting in judgment. Upon what he did not know.

"I can tell you," he answered, speaking to that judge in the girl. "They've done things no man ought to do and be let live. They've stolen. They've set murder loose. It's time they quit!"

"How do you know?" Gwynn stood before Llano, blocking his movement.

"How do I know?" bitterness in Llano's tone. "It's plain on the face of it. James Gunther was killed because he talked too much and turned men against the Grant. Will Loman was killed. He'd squatted on land that the Grant claimed. His wife died because the Grant kept her from having a place to stop and rest. And now Rose Juell . . . Why do I stand here telling you this? You know it! Where are Cameron and Null?"

Gwynn Rae turned and walked back toward the fire. Llano followed her, not of his own volition but as though he were being led at the end of some invisible chain. Before the fireplace the girl stopped, turning to face the man again.

"Rose Juell," murmured Gwynn softly. "I was with

210

her when she died."

"You?" The word was jerked from Llano.

"I was with her," Gwynn repeated. "I'd gone to the house because . . . It doesn't matter why I'd gone to the house. It was black and dark." Gwynn's voice was low and strained, the words coming with an effort. "She lay there by the door and she was dying."

Llano leaned forward as Gwynn stopped. His weariness and his wet, tired body were forgotten. For a moment he lived again with Gwynn Rae as his eyes. He could see this woman, this great lady, before the door of that dark, forbidding house. Could almost see her entering its blackness.

"She left a message for you with me," Gwynn spoke softly. "I'll give it to you. She said: 'Tell Llano Flaco killed Ames'."

"Flaco?" Llano rasped. "Flaco?"

Gwynn Rae did not heed the interruption. Her voice went on, even, expressionless, mechanical. The girl was back in Gunther's house and her eyes were wide with what she saw there.

"Then she lifted her head," said Gwynn Rae, "and she said, 'I love you, Llano,' and she died."

Flat silence in the great hall of Ladron House. The fire snapped and the gleams from the silver were cat's eyes in the dusk. Outside the rain fell in a thinning drizzle. Llano's head was lowered.

"I think she was good," added Gwynn Rae, slowly. "She was good and she loved you, Llano Land."

A latch clicked and there was a draft in the hall but neither of the two before the fire noticed. Llano stood unmoving and Gwynn Rae was watching him intently. There were soft steps and then Arthur Cameron spoke harshly.

211

"Stand still, Land! Gwynn, step away!"

That sharp command brought Llano to himself. He knew instantly that the man behind him had him covered. He knew that this was the end of things. He stood still. Gwynn Rae made a little, soft, hurt sound and moved.

Cameron spoke again. "Stand away, Gwynn!"

Llano began to turn. He moved slowly, holding his body rigid and his hands down against his sides. Gwynn Rae was against a chair beside the fireplace and the light of the fire was red on Cameron's face.

"So you came here?" purred Cameron. "You came here."

Llano faced the man. "I'm here," he said simply.

"That is fortunate." Cameron did not move. He held pistol raised and pointed squarely at Llano's chest. His hand did not shake and there was wild, vindictive triumph on his dark face. "Fortunate, Land. You'll die here!"

"Arthur . . ." began Gwynn pleadingly. "Arthur . . ."

"Be still, girl!" ordered Cameron.

Llano watched the man. He felt the big Army Colt at his waistband and held himself ready. This was the last card in the box, the last roll of the wheel. This was the pay-off! Cameron would shoot but before he did there would be a warning. There would be a contraction of muscles in that scowling face before the finger stirred on the trigger. There would be time, there had to be time, for one shot from the Army Colt. The fire caught at a pine knot and shot up, leaping toward the blackened chimney. Light came from that sudden burst of fire. There was a little movement, a sound to the right. Cameron tensed and Gwynn Rae said, her voice a tiny thing in the great room: "Kent . . ."

Cameron took a swift step to his right. His eyes flashed from Llano toward the stair. Llano, too, turned his head. Kent Null stood on the stairs. There was a weight in Null's hand and his face was ashen.

"Null," rasped Cameron. "Come here, Null!"

Very slowly Kent Null came down the stairs. As he moved Cameron backed further so that he could see both Llano and the man on the steps. At the bottom of the stairs Null stopped. He carried a telescope grip that bulged in its straps and his coat sagged. From one pocket protruded the top of a small canvas sack.

"So . . ." said Cameron harshly.

"I am leaving, Arthur," Null's voice was uncertain. "I . . ."

The gun that Cameron held so steadily on Llano shifted suddenly. "Leaving?" Cameron rasped the word. "Damn you . . . !"

Under the menace of the gun and voice Null broke. He dropped the grip he held. His hands snatched wildly at his pockets and heavy metal protected by canvas, thumped on the floor.

"Arthur!" beseeched Kent Null. "Arthur . . . !"

He seemed to shrivel as he screamed the words. Cameron's gun was leveled. Llano Land's own hand moved and the Colt came from his waistband.

The gun in Cameron's hand thudded heavily and Kent Null, his scream broken, pitched down to sprawl across the gold he had dropped. Cameron wheeled, weapon still raised, and Llano Land, stepping forward, spaced two even shots. Cameron's coat seemed to move as invisible fingers tugged at it. His raised hand lowered slowly and the weapon dropped from his relaxing fingers. Cameron stood a moment, poised and then full length, his joints rigid, pitched down upon his face.

213

Gwynn Rae, beside the chair, caught at her mouth with one hand. Her eyes, searching Llano's face, saw the triumph there, saw the blaze of light in his eyes, saw the man that had hidden behind an immobile mask. For a moment the girl stood, trembling, and then she collapsed, falling into the chair.

At that movement Llano turned, gun in hand. He saw the girl in the chair and stepped toward her. Then there was confusion at the door. It swung open. A man burst through, other men behind him: Wayne Metcalf and Cassidy and others. Llano wheeled from the girl, and running, made for the portières. They swung behind him. A door was flung open. Another door banged under his hands. Then rain beat into his face and from his right a man shouted and a rifle cracked. Mud splashing as he ran, Llano flung himself away from Ladron House.

In the hall of Ladron House Wayne Metcalf gathered Gwynn Rae into his arms and stood up. The girl was limp, lifeless. Cassidy, straightening up from beside Arthur Cameron, strode across to Null and moved the lawyer. There were men, soldiers, clustered about and on the stair the white night clothing and pallid faces of servants showed. Metcalf looked at Cassidy and Cassidy shook his head.

"They're dead, sorry," said Cassidy.

Carrying Gwynn, Metcalf moved toward the stairs. A woman detaching herself from the group there, came toward him, Eliza, Gwynn Rae's maid. Poised at the bottom of the stairs Metcalf gave orders.

"Search the town, Sergeant!" he commanded. "That was Llano Land!"

Out in the rain Llano Land moved from shadow to dark shadow. The light was growing in the east. It was

214

but a matter of time until daylight was upon him. There was yet a task. Llano knew that he had not much time. He knew that he was hunted, would be searched for. Before he was found he had a duty to perform. Beside the corner of a building he stopped and considered. Where might he find Flaco?

The Exchange Saloon offered the best opportunity. Llano knew that he must gamble on his first choice. And he must reach the Exchange without being seen. He moved forward, peered around the corner of the adobe and then, swiftly, ran across the street.

His crossing made in safety, he went on until he came to an alley, turned to his left and followed down through the mud and the refuse that was there. Again he crossed a street, flitting through the darkness. Then he went on. Presently he paused. There was a building to his left. Cautiously Llano tried the door. It was unlocked and it opened under his hand. Llano stepped in.

The odor of stale beer and of whisky assailed his nostrils. He worked his way cautiously across the room he had entered, paused, and with his ear against a door listened.

In the barroom of the Exchange a weary bartender watched behind the bar. There was a little group at one end of the bar, not drinking but waiting. Pat Greybull was in that group and red-headed Frazier and others, miners and ranchers. Further up the bar Dick Wadell stood and talked with two or three men, Grant adherents, and in a booth Flaco and Huerta sat drinking, drinking steadily.

"We'll go in the morn'n'.", said Frazier to Greybull.

"I think the Grant people let him out of jail. They wanted the boys to get out of town followin' him. He killed that girl, all right, no mistake about that, but their

215

scheme didn't work. There's still plenty here to make the Grant walk a chalk line."

"But the Cavalry," expostulated Greybull for the twentieth time. "What about . . . ?"

Frazier snorted. "The Cavalry will keep law an' order!" he snapped. "But the way we'll work it . . ."

Frazier broke off. Horses were coming along the street.

"Some of the boys got tired an' come back," said a bearded man by Frazier's elbow. "Had 'em a wild goose chase in the rain."

Frazier nodded. Flaco called from the booth: "Baldy! Bring another bottle."

"I'm comin', Flaco," answered the bartender wearily.

Beyond the booth, at the back of the room, a door opened and a man stepped through. He was hatless, wet, and his shoulders sagged. He moved steadily, as a man with a purpose. Frazier, turning, saw the man. Dick Wadell saw him and recoiled against the bar. Llano Land walked unwaveringly past two empty booths and stopping, looked into the little enclosure where sat Flaco and Huerta.

"Flaco!" said Llano Land.

Wadell was reaching for his gun. Frazier had started forward. Greybull was turning. There were steps on the walk outside the Exchange. Steps crossing the tin canopied porch. The bartender, with a yell, went down behind the bar.

Then came the shots. Three of them, roaring in the room, beating out of the booth, reverberating between the walls. A squealing followed the shots, a high-pitched, shrill sound as a stuck hog makes in a slaughter house. Llano Land, legs spread wide, braced against the blow that had struck him, peered through the smoke that

216

came from his gun. Deliberately he lifted his gun and fired again and the squealing ceased.

"It's Land!" yelled Frazier.. "It . . ." He started forward. Wadell, his gun out, lifted it to fire. Llano Land took a step and clung to the wall of the booth for support, and through the doorway of the Exchange Saloon stepped a tall, stern-faced man with a gun in his hand and his hat set over a rag that was bound about his gray head. There was a gold badge on the man's wet coat, a badge that gleamed in the light of the kerosene lamps.

"Stop!" rasped the tall man. "Stop right there!"

Behind the tall man others crowded in. A fat man who wore an Army poncho and a campaign hat that was too small and that sat rakishly upon his head; two tall blond men who were surprisingly alike, a small wiry fellow, and a man with a long sharp nose and sharp eyes. Their steady hands held weapons.

Frazier, confronting the tall man, rapped a question: "Who are you?"

Dale Fallien answered, his voice an even drawl. "I'm a deputy United States Marshal. These are my men. We'll take charge here."

CHAPTER 20

THE ARMY SURGEON SAID THAT LLANO LAND WOULD not live a day. He might, the doctor intimated, live a trifle longer than that if he, Doctor Von Weigand, operated. On the other hand operations on abdominal wounds were not as a rule successful. Frequently patients died while the surgeon worked. Dale Fallien and Mat McCarthy and the Savoys and Bill Westfall stood by and listened to the doctor. It was Bill Westfall that put a stop to Von Weigand's speculations.

"Gra'maw Stamps," said Bill, "can take a ghost an' bring him back to life. I'm goin' to get her." So Bill Westfall, who had not slept for twenty-four hours, saddled a fresh horse and hit the trail up Ladron canyon.

Dale Fallien, seeing that Llano was attended to by McCarthy and the others, left the Saint George where they had taken the wounded man, and went to Ladron House. Dale Fallien had a bandage on his head now in lieu of the rag that had been tied there. He was tired and worn, but there were many things that claimed his attention.

In Ladron House Fallien closeted himself with Metcalf. As a result of their consultation Dick Wadell was brought in and questioned. Wadell, under pressure, told all that he knew and more that he guessed.

When Wadell had been taken to the jail under guard, Fallien and Metcalf consulted further and then called upon Donald Rae. Rae, despite his shoulder wound, accompanied the two officers to Cameron's office and there they delved into the papers that were still in the safe and those that Kent Null had scattered on the floor. It was while they were so engaged that a servant announced the arrival of Mulligan, and Fallien ordered that the barber be admitted.

"What do you want done with Cameron an' Null?" demanded Mulligan, standing in the doorway. "I got Flaco an' that pardner of his ready to plant, but I don't know what you want done with the other two."

Fallien looked at Metcalf and Metcalf turned to Donald Rae. Rae, all the ruddiness drained from his face, was staring at the barber. Finally he spoke.

"Have lead coffins made," he said slowly, "and put

218

them in them. After a while we can tell you what disposal to make of the bodies."

Mulligan still hesitated and Rae spoke again. "The Grant will pay you," he said.

With that Mulligan left and the men turned back to the work at hand. While they worked they were joined by Gwynn Rae. Despite protests the girl had refused to stay in bed. Now, white and wan, she came into the office. She listened while the men talked and studied papers. Finally she spoke.

"I don't know what must be done," said Gwynn Rae, "but I do know that the Grant must repay everything that it has taken. I count on you to see to it." Her eyes encompassed them all and one by one they nodded agreement.

It was not until late in the afternoon that Greybull, a few representative miners from Marthastown and the adjoining district, Park Frazier and one or two of the men who had fought against the Grant, were called in. When they had assembled in the little office Fallien spoke to them.

"It will take time to get this straightened out, men," he concluded. "A commissioner has to come from the land office and in a good many cases there's got to be court held. Until that can be done yo're to go ahead just as you were. You won't be bothered an' your rights won't be questioned. Miss Rae and her brother asked me to tell you that the Grant wants to make everything right. How about it?"

It was Frazier that answered. Frazier looked at Fallien and at Metcalf. He glanced at Donald Rae and then turned to his companions. "That's all I want to hear," announced Frazier. "I reckon we can go out an' tell the boys to go home now."

And so they left. The town of Ladron emptied of the men who had come from Marthastown and from the canyons in the Ladrones. They went home, sure for the first time in months that they would wake up in the morning with their houses intact and their stock untouched.

At the end of that long day Dale Fallien went to the Saint George and before he went to his room walked down the corridor to the room that housed Llano Land. Gra'maw Stamps met him at the door, her finger lifted.

"Shhhhh!" warned Gra'maw. "He's sleepin'."

"What are his chances?" asked Fallien anxiously.

Gra'maw sniffed. "Good," she answered. "Doctors don't know much. He'll be up eatin' an' goin' strong in six weeks. You go on. I'll look after him."

Fallien nodded and turned. He went back down the corridor with his shoulders drooping with weariness. Before he slept he wrote a long letter to the Land Commissioner and saw that it was dispatched. Then, his work temporarily done, he stretched out on his bed and let sleep roll over him.

For ten days there was much activity in Ladron. The Bishop of the territory came and preached a funeral sermon for James Gunther and Rose Juell. The Bishop signified his willingness to officiate in behalf of the others who had died but this was declined. Mat McCarthy talked to the Bishop on that score.

"We got Cameron an' Null in lead boxes," he told the Bishop. "We're waitin' to hear from folks we wrote to an' then we'll ship 'em out. They ain't worth prayin' over, Reverend. Flaco an' Huerta we just stuck in the ground and covered over. Ladron wants to forget 'em." Mat paused a moment and then looked up at the big cleric. "But you stick around," continued Mat. "Mebbe

220

Llano'll die. If he does you can orate over a damn' good man! . . . Excuse me, Reverend!"

The Bishop was not shocked. He put his hand on Mat's fat shoulder and comforted the ex-cowthief. "Your friend won't die," said the Bishop. "He's too good a man." And Mat McCarthy was so pleased that then and there he offered to buy the Bishop a drink.

Llano and Gra'maw Stamps made the Bishop's word good. Gra'maw worked and watched and Llano kept on living, and at the end of ten days Gra'maw allowed Dale Fallien five minutes with her patient.

The tall man stalked into the room that Llano occupied, walked across and stood beside the bed. Gra'maw hovered anxiously behind him. "I wouldn't of let you come at all," she said, "but he's frettin' so I thought you could stop him."

Fallien looked at Llano. Llano was white and weak and there was a question in his eyes. Fallien answered that question. "It's cleaned up," he said. "Cameron an' Null are dead. Gwynn Rae told us what happened. Donald Rae has taken hold of the Grant an' there's a Commissioner comin' from the Land Office. The troops have gone back to Bridger. I'm in charge till the Commissioner comes. It's all right, Llano."

Llano asked a question. "Mat?"

Fallien grinned. "Fat an' rollin'," he answered. "I deputized Mat an' his boys an' they're with me. I'll take care of Mat, Llano."

There was another question that Llano wanted answered but he did not ask it. He wanted news of Gwynn Rae. Somehow Fallien knew that.

"That Rae girl is a hand," said Fallien. "She's more man than her brother is. I don't know what we'd do without her."

"You been here long enough," declared Gra'maw advancing from behind Fallien. Fallien reached down, caught Llano's lax hand with a quick, strong grip, relinquished it and went out. Llano relaxed on the bed. To Gra'maw, hovering over him, he looked weaker. She put her hand on his forehead and Llano stirred. He was asleep.

Llano's next visitor came five days later. Gra'maw ushered in Mat McCarthy and retired to the door. Her patient was out of danger as far as Gra'maw could tell. He was gaining strength every day. Mat walked across the room, got a chair and sat down beside the bed.

"Well," grinned Mat, "yo're makin' it, Llano."

Llano smiled.

Mat shifted his chair. "I reckon," he announced cheerfully, "that you want to know what's goin' on."

"Tell me," ordered Llano.

Mat took a breath. "There's a heap," he cautioned.

"Gra'maw told me some," said Llano.

"That Dale Fallien," McCarthy glanced toward the door, "he's a twister, Llano. After you'd left us in the shack he taken hold. He talked to us plenty. Some way he sold us the idea of stringin' with him. He made us all his deputies an' we rode out of there. I won't say there wasn't a hot argument," Mat grinned at the recollection.

"We hit town," he resumed, "an' things was stirrin' around. Ladron House was like a bee hive but we passed it up. Fallien took us right straight to the Exchange. He was ridin' a hunch, I guess. Anyhow we walked in there right after you'd had yore business with Flaco an' Huerta. That was a good clean job, Llano."

Again McCarthy paused and the man on the bed moved a little.

"Yes," prompted Llano.

222

"Well, sir," McCarthy went on, "there you were on the floor, gun-shot an' down. There was Wadell an' Frazier an' Greybull an' some more all ready to finish yore business an' Fallien stopped 'em. 'I'm a deputy United States Marshal' he says. 'I'll take charge here.' An' he done it. Wadell he throwed in the jail. The rest of 'em he marched out of the saloon. We took you to the Saint George an' got the doctor. Then we branched out. Seemed like Fallien knew every man that would make trouble. Some of 'em left an' some he put in jail. He's a twister, Fallien is."

"Null?" questioned Llano.

McCarthy shrugged. "Cameron killed Null," said Mat. "An' you settled Cameron. Null was runnin' away. He had some gold from the stage robbery in his pockets. Cameron must of seen that an' then I reckon he hated Null's guts anyhow. He sure give Null his needin's."

Gra'maw Stamps put her head through the doorway and eyed Mat McCarthy. "Time for you to go," ordered Gra'maw.

McCarthy got up reluctantly. "She's worse than a round-up boss," he complained, grinning at Llano. "Lays out who you can see an' how long. I'll be back. The boys all want to see you an' they said to tell you howdy for 'em."

Llano moved his head on the pillow in a nod, and Mat went on out.

So the days passed. As Llano gained strength he was allowed more visitors. Fallien came in daily, as did Mat McCarthy. The Commissioner arrived from the Land Office and held a long interview with the man on the bed. The Commissioner, a young lawyer, was green but he was keen and honest. He wanted to do the right thing. He listened to Llano and to Fallien as they talked.

He asked questions and when he left Llano had his promise and that of Fallien that Mat McCarthy and his men would go free.

Gra'maw Stamps had been a source of news to her patient. From her Llano learned of the funeral that had been given James Gunther and Rose Juell. A funeral attended by most of Marthastown and all of the families on the Grant and in its vicinity. He learned from her, too, that Cameron's body had been sent to California to his family there, and that the body of Kent Null had been shipped east to Philadelphia where it would lie in the burial lot of his family, among lawyers and judges and statesmen. The things that happened in Ladron and on the Grant came to Gra'maw Stamps' ears and she retailed them to Llano.

"John Kinney's back at his place now," Gra'maw told Llano one day. "Him an' his wife. John's feelin' pretty good. Rae wouldn't prosecute him for that shootin' an' Missus Kinney told me that the Raes had give 'em a fund to send their kids off to school. There ain't nothin' wrong with the Raes. They just had the wool pulled over their eyes by that Cameron!" And Gra'maw sniffed.

Still the visitor that Llano awaited did not come. Gwynn Rae stayed away from the Saint George. Llano heard of her and of her brother but he did not see them. He was up now, out of bed and dressed, moving around a little, sitting on the porch of the Saint George during the warmth of the day. Summer had gone and the hills were bright with frost. Sitting on the porch Llano could see the purple and the yellow and the red and green of pine and aspen and scrub oak. The colors framed the dark bulk of Ladron House when, as he did so often, he looked toward it. Before long Llano Land would leave Ladron.

224

Gra'maw Stamps went back to her hotel at the head of Ladron Canyon. Her patient was recovered. Gra'maw had enough money to build an addition to her inn, or, if she wished, to see her through many years of life. She kissed Llano before she left and called him her boy. Gra'maw Stamps, mother to half the Duro Grant.

With Mrs. Stamps' departure, Llano planned to leave Ladron. He gave yellow Jigger to Mat McCarthy and he bought presents for each of the Savoys and for Shorty Hamarick and for Bill Westfall. They were useful presents, things that could be used by men who might not always stay in one place. At the moment McCarthy and his men were working for the Grant, handling cattle, but they were restless and Llano, knowing them, realized that they would not long follow their present occupation. Not while there were unwatched herds and men who would buy cattle and not be particular as to the origin of their purchase.

To Mulligan Llano gave a razor, grinning thinly as he did so. "Here," said Llano, presenting the razor, "is that razor that Bill brought down from the Junta."

Mulligan boomed a guffaw.

To Dale Fallien Llano gave his best, the horse Singleshot.

"I'm going out on the stage," he told Fallien when he made the gift, "I can't make a long ride yet and I've got to go to Carpenter to see Mrs. Ames. I've written to her but she wants me to come and see her and tell her about Jack."

Fallien nodded gravely.

"He's a good horse, Dale," continued Llano. "He'll take you a piece and bring you back. I want you to have him."

Fallien accepted the gift. "I'll look after him," said Fallien.

225

Silence fell upon the two men and Fallien, musing, broke it.

"What will you do now, Llano?" he asked. Llano turned his head and looked toward Ladron House. From the porch of the Saint George he could see horses before the big house, and a soldier stood, talking to a servant. Wayne Metcalf had ridden over from Bridger that day.

"I don't know, Dale," said Llano hesitatingly. "I'm too old to change my ways. Remember when you told me that?"

Fallien nodded and Llano spoke again. "I'll go back to work, I guess," he said, and rising from his chair he went to the door of the hotel.

"Yo're leavin' tomorrow," stated Fallien. "I'll see you when the stage leaves." He, too, arose and watched Llano enter the Saint George.

In his room, Llano sat in a chair and stared at the wall. His possessions, packed and ready for departure, were about him. There was nothing else to do. In the morning he would take the stage and go east, riding to Carpenter. There he would see Mrs. Ames and talk with her, comforting her as best he might. The things that had happened since he had ridden from Carpenter passed in procession through his mind. His arrival at Ladron. Mat McCarthy and his men. Dale Fallien. Cameron and Null. James Gunther and Rose Juell. Rose Juell had loved him. Rose Juell was dead. There was sorrow in Llano's mind, regret for Rose Juell and for Gunther, and yet he could not help but wonder if, given a choice, Rose Juell and the preacher would not have preferred things as they were. His meditations were interrupted by a knock on the door. Turning, Llano said: "Come in."

The door opened and Gwynn Rae and Wayne Metcalf entered.

Llano looked at them. There was a brightness about the girl, a softening, and in the soldier's proud eyes was happiness. Llano needed no announcement of what had happened. He got up from his chair, bowing toward the two.

"I wanted to see you before you left," said Gwynn Rae. "You are leaving, aren't you?"

"In the morning," Llano answered.

"I'll say good-by then," said Metcalf, advancing, his hand outstretched.

Llano took the hand and gripped it. "Good-by," he said.

Metcalf released Llano's hand. He looked at the girl, smiled, and as though by prearrangement, turned and walked from the room.

Gwynn Rae stood facing Llano. "I wanted to thank you," she said when the door had closed behind the officer, "There is a great deal to thank you for."

Llano glanced toward the door. He knew of one thing that the girl included in her thanks. "You and Metcalf . . ?" began Llano brusquely.

Gwynn nodded, her eyes bright.

"I'll wish you luck," said Llano gravely. "Luck and happiness."

"Thank you." Gwynn turned her eyes from Llano's. There was silence for a moment. The girl spoke again.

"There have been things happening," she said, a little tremor in her voice. "Terrible things. I was partly to blame for some of them. I didn't know . . ."

"You didn't know," agreed Llano.

The girl looked up again. "I wanted to tell you before you left," she said bravely. "You did what you had to. I can see that now."

She paused as she said that final word and Llano

knew that she was giving him justice. Something prompted him to ask for more than justice, to attempt at least to explain to this girl the things that he had done.

"There's times," said Llano slowly, "when a man must do what's required. There are times when he pays his just debts . . . yes, and collects 'em, too!"

He was thinking, as he spoke, of Null and of Cameron, of Flaco and of the gangling Huerta. Once more Gwynn Rae saw the man that hid behind Llano's eyes, the fierce, untamed being that knew but one code and that would live and die by that code. She turned her face from him and with that movement Llano's eyes became once more blank gray walls that hid his thoughts.

And Llano was remembering. He was recalling Gwynn Rae as he had first seen her, riding wild on the bolting mare. Each meeting with the girl, few in number as they were, had brought something to Llano, a feeling, indescribable, as of something that hung between them, some tentative, hidden thing that neither could express. It was gone now.

Llano spoke again. "The right thing," said Llano Land stubbornly, justifying himself.

Gwynn nodded slowly. "You will do what you believe is right," she said. "I think you will always do that."

Silence came between them. Gwynn broke it. "I came up to tell you good-by," she said, "and to tell you that the Grant will set things to rights here. It is a promise. No one will suffer more."

"I know that," assented Llano Land.

He waited for the girl to continue. Then when she did not speak, Llano moved forward.

"Metcalf is waiting," he said, his voice hoarse. "I'll

wish you luck again."

Passing the girl he opened the door. Metcalf stood in he corridor. He glanced up as the door opened and when Gwynn had come through, took her arm in his hand.

"Good-by," said Llano Land, carefully.

The soldier and the girl walked along the corridor, shoulders touching.

In the morning Llano stood on the porch of the Saint George. The stage that was to take him from Ladron was drawn up before the porch and his saddle-bags, his saddle and his other possessions were aboard. Around Llano stood his friends, McCarthy, the Savoys, Hamarick, Bill Westfall, Mulligan and Dale Fallien. One by one he gripped their hands and bade them good-by. Then, moving forward, he climbed to the top of the stage and took his seat beside the driver.

Settled there on the seat Llano glanced down at the men he left and then turning his head looked back at the hills, Ladron House, square and solid, was set against the mountains. The driver clucked to his team and the stage moved ahead. There were clouds above the hills and shadows fell upon them, but in Ladron the sun was shining.

We hope that you enjoyed reading this
Sagebrush Large Print Western.
If you would like to read more Sagebrush titles,
ask your librarian or contact the Publishers:

United States and Canada

Thomas T. Beeler, *Publisher*
Post Office Box 659
Hampton Falls, New Hampshire 03844-0659
(800) 818-7574

United Kingdom, Eire, and
the Republic of South Africa

Isis Publishing Ltd
7 Centremead
Osney Mead
Oxford OX2 0ES England
(01865) 250333

Australia and New Zealand

Bolinda Publishing Pty. Ltd.
17 Mohr Street
Tullamarine, 3043, Victoria, Australia
(016103) 9338 0666